MAGICAL ALIENATION

A Samantha Brennan and
Annabelle Haggerty
Magical Mystery

MAGICAL ALIENATION

A Samantha Brennan and Annabelle Haggerty Magical Mystery

Kris Neri

Red Coyote Press
Phoenix, Arizona

MAGICAL ALIENATION
Copyright © 2011 by Kris Neri

All rights reserved. No part of this book may be used or reproduced in any manner whatsoever without written permission of both the copyright owner and the publisher except in the case of brief quotations embodied in critical articles and reviews.

This novel is a work of fiction. All the characters, places and events portrayed are either fictitious or are used fictitiously.

Cover by Jack Hillman/Hillman Design Group
Cover photos:
Blond girl in blue dress: ©iStockphoto.com/Дарья Петренко
Sunset in Sedona: ©iStockphoto.com/Malou Leontsinis

ISBN-13: 978-0-9766733-1-6
ISBN-10: 0-9766733-1-2

Library of Congress Control Number: 2011934909

Published by
Red Coyote Press, LLC
P.O. Box 60582
Phoenix, Arizona 85082
www.redcoyotepress.com

For Pam and the now-departed Star, wherever he may be

MAGICAL ALIENATION

Groom Lake, Nevada
Area 51

Desperate times called for daring measures.
Perfect for him! He knew others would consider his bold solution as a reckless disregard for everything his kind held sacred, but he cared not. He'd always carved his own trail, thumbing his nose at those in charge. Of course, it was precisely that attitude that had brought about his present dilemma.
Dilemma? Hah! He'd never been in such threatening straits. The being in Cellblock One gasped with surprise as an unfamiliar sensation constricted his air passage and set his blood racing. Anxiety—the first time he'd felt it in his lengthy existence. While a quest for novelty had long been his ruling passion, he could have done without this *new experience*. When had time become the enemy, instead of his plaything? How could a bit of merriment have turned so dreadfully against him?
He glanced around at the space that had housed him for decades. This place they called Area 51 wasn't where he arrived in their world. He'd appeared to them first in Roswell, New Mexico, in the year called 1947 in their calendar. Not that he'd remained there for long. They'd whisked him away fast to quell the rumors that flourished to this day, and had kept him hidden here ever since.
Though they called it a cell, it looked more like a utilitarian suite, with sitting and sleeping zones. A far cry from the luxury he'd known at times, but more than comfortable. While this installation contained many other units, the creature remained the cellblock's only occupant. His captors had expected more of his kind to come, believing they'd fill the entire wing. As if they had a clue about his kind. Was it any wonder he couldn't resist toying with them?
The creature made his way to the window. Six inches of some indestructible acrylic, surrounding titanium bars, made it hard to see through. What children they were, his jailers. If they only knew the times he'd slipped from their grasp after light's-out. It had to be beyond their comprehension to think that someone would find enjoyment from pretending to be their captive.
However much these pitiful little beings would never grasp, they understood this: They knew the balance had shifted now. When

the creature looked through the thick pane, he could see them walking out there, on the soil he had long used to hold them in a terrifying stalemate. At one time they would not have known whether setting foot on that ground would reduce them to such a state of dreamy oblivion as to render all action impossible, or if it would turn them into raving psychopaths. Oh, yes, he had really kept them guessing with that. What grand fun!

But his magic was waning fast, and his captors had caught on to that fact. It was too much to hope that they wouldn't solidify their domination over him now that they could.

The creature heard a sound at the unit's entrance. A guard paused at the clear panel in the cell's door. Acknowledging him with no more than a brusque nod, the guard moved on, confident in what he'd seen through that pane. The being actually chortled out loud. His charade still had the power to tickle him. He'd always planned to surprise them someday with a look at his true appearance. Now it was too risky. He had to keep the sham going, even if it sapped his precious strength.

With a last look out the cell window, he saw the caravan gathering in the distance. Now they would finally succeed in moving him to another facility, as they'd wished to for some time. With his failing strength and their reinforced installation—hidden on a secret Air Force base in the Arizona desert—the creature had no doubts that this time they really would contain him.

Or his own kind would come for him, and they'd imprison him in a way his present captors could never imagine, harnessing him so he'd never escape.

Yet he had one chance, a single opportunity to save himself from an existence of bondage and drudgery. There was a place that, for one night, could charge his failing strength with the power he'd need to resist everyone who wished to control him. But it would take all his weakened magic to make it there. He'd have to charm his caravan captors into altering the route—directing them not to the place of certain captivity, but to the site that promised him robust renewal. And he'd have to keep them under that spell for the entire journey, to prevent them from correcting the course. The creature simply didn't have enough power for that.

There were some who could help him, but would likely not, out of principle or fear or some such nonsense. Fortunately, there

MAGICAL ALIENATION

was one he might safely tap without her awareness. The one advantage to having lived as long as he had was that he knew all the ancient tricks and magic, forgotten by many. Given how she'd cut herself off from their ways, his benefactor might not notice. If he worked it right, he could steal enough of his unwitting accomplice's powers to keep himself going. Too bad her resources were so limited.

It might also help to drag in someone else, to further distract his unwitting helper. More power lost, he thought uneasily, dealing with limitations he'd never had to consider before, but a worthwhile investment if he pulled it off. He'd have to devise just the right trick to capture that facilitator's attention.

Now, what should it be?

CHAPTER ONE
Airborne, Near Phoenix, Arizona
Samantha

Pinch me.

Not really. Pinches bruise. What I meant was that I couldn't believe my amazing luck. Less than a year ago, I'd scraped so low, I'd dealt myself in on a crazy scam that nearly took my life. Now I was thoroughly ensconced as a solid citizen of Fat City, and my brilliant star was about to glow even brighter.

If only I could escape that creepy sensation that something bad was about to happen again.

Maybe I was just queasy—eating a pound of premium chocolate will do that. Still, who could blame me for pigging out? I mean, there I was aloft in a luxurious private jet, where they plied me with anything and everything I could possibly want, on my way to Phoenix, Arizona, where I'd co-star on the national news for weeks to come.

Sure, lots of people would loathe my boss and me, but there's no such thing as bad publicity, right? My new employer had built his career on irreverence, and they loved him for it. I was crazy to worry.

I should introduce myself. I'm Samantha Brennan, a Los Angeles-based spiritual advisor to the stars, just a year away from the big three-oh, if it's any of your business. Actually, I'm no more psychic than a tire iron. My clients believe I am because, after I tell them what they obviously want to hear, they unconsciously move mountains to make my predictions come true. Senseless from my point of view, but as long as it pays the bills, why should I argue?

At one time I considered all claims of supernatural abilities to be pure hooey, a trap for the more gullible among us. Despite my non-sensitive status, however, I'd now had two genuinely psychic experiences. One saved my life and the other allowed me to repay that debt and rescue my savior. I hadn't experienced a single supernatural sensation since, though, and I hoped I never would.

There was something else people believed about me—that I was a descendent of an ancient Celtic goddess. A hoot, huh? Since I

MAGICAL ALIENATION

always forgot the name of my supposed ancestor, I only threw that mythological crap around with people I felt sure knew less than I did. Fortunately, that was almost everyone.

Gods and goddesses—more hokum you're thinking, right? Wrong. No, I wasn't really a goddess, though I did own some really special clothes. But I swear they exist. I'd met actual ancient deities myself. Right here on Earth, if you think L.A. qualifies for that description. Not that I chose to see them anymore. Though I still ran into Angus, the ancient Celtic god of youth and love and laughter, far too often, I hadn't crossed paths with his modern descendant, Annabelle Haggerty, lately. If I ever did, I planned to run the other way. It was because of my association with Haggerty that I nearly went on to my Final Journey, as we say in spiritual advisor-speak. As for Angus, I never wanted to see him again. That rat absolutely broke my heart.

Enough with the trip down Memory Lane! I'm strictly a today-kinda girl, and today was great. If you doubt that, look at where I found myself: Aloft in the chartered Gulfstream of none other than Rand Riker, the frontman of the aging bad-boy band, Devil's Disciple, being feted by a flight attendant with such a snooty English accent, she made the Queen sound like a scrub woman.

Since the publicity generated by my past near-demise had brought me a better class of client, my financial prospects had been looking up. But this jet had introduced me to a whole new strata, one I was going to fight to hold on to.

Rand and I had met at a party the week before, and he hired me to serve as his personal psychic on the Sex, Drugs & Rock 'n' Roll tour, to be kicked off with a benefit concert in Sedona, Arizona just two days from now, although the actual tour wouldn't begin for another couple of weeks.

It did surprise me, when I showed up at the Van Nuys Airport earlier this morning, to learn Rand and I were the only passengers. I assumed the whole band would be flying with us. Apparently, the other musicians traveled by bus, while Rand flew in style, and usually alone.

People—just when you think you've got them pegged, they'll fool you every time.

Especially since the cushy Gulfstream could easily have carried many more lucky souls. I'd plopped myself down in one of four leather club chairs at the front of the plane. The empty cheap seats—two rows of standard seating—followed behind my section. Rand sat at the dining table farther back, where he had been shouting into the satellite phone to his attorney ever since we'd taken off.

His voice rose now above the roar of the engines, "So you think I've got protection on this thing, Dan?"

That sounded pretty cautious for a guy who'd built his reputation by flaunting rules. I tuned him out. Knowing too much about my clients' actual lives leeched all the artistry from my readings. Occasionally, though, his voice became too loud to ignore. And despite the billions he'd made singing, I found the sound irritating. After decades of living in the U.S., only the broad vowels and the odd expression betrayed the Down Under roots of an Aussie upstart, who'd hitched a ride on the British Band Invasion on the theory that Americans couldn't tell the difference between the accents.

Speaking of Brits, the flight attendant approached. She was a pretty gal, around my age, with finely chiseled features, artfully tousled highlighted hair and big brown eyes. She wore a body-hugging navy skirt suit that bore the charter's insignia embroidered onto the breast pocket. The only tacky touch was a plastic nametag pinned above the charter's logo, on which she'd written her name.

Given her ritzy accent, I kept thinking of her as "Princess." Now I saw that her name was Holly O'Neill. She had looped the tail of the "y" over the names on the hand-written nametag and ended it with a little heart. See what I mean about surprises? I would never have taken Princess Holly as the heart-drawing type. The surprises made my job so much fun.

Princess Holly carried a tray with a champagne flute filled with some amber-colored bubbly.

"I thought you might want to wash the chocolate down with some champagne," she said in that frosty accent. "It's Cristal."

No kidding? I'd always wondered how good champagne would taste. I refused to let her see that, though. Instead, I nodded nonchalantly, as if to say I was so used to it, I brushed my teeth with the stuff. I swilled a gulp and waited for the ecstasy to hit. To my surprise, good wine didn't taste like wine at all. It tasted like…apple juice.

Huh? I took another sip. Sure enough, apple juice. Even the

bubbles had gone flat. How could that have happened?

Apples made me think of Annabelle Haggerty, my goddess companion in that earlier caper. Celtic deities, I'd learned from Haggerty, regard apples as a sacred symbol of their divinity. Apparently, apples grow everywhere on their homeland, *Tir na N'og,* their place of immortality, which means "The Land of the Young."

Enough with the Celts! It wasn't like I'd never seen an apple before I met Haggerty and Angus. I had to be wrong about the champagne anyway. That chocolate had simply numbed my taste buds.

When Holly said we were starting our descent, I asked her to bring me my carryon bag. I'd decided to change my clothes on the plane, since it struck me as incredibly decadent to wear two outfits for a one-hour flight.

In my stiletto, open-toed pumps, I wobbled past the dining table where Rand still shouted into the phone, beyond the small galley and the jet's business center, with its fax and copy machines, to the restroom at the rear of the plane.

I was known for my really special clothes. The dress I planned to wear for our landing was a white mid-calf gown with flowing organdy layers. The clerk at the vintage store told me it had been worn by some actress chick named Adriana, for the opening of a TV show she did back in the fifties. But my grandma said, since I was probably a size…or ten…bigger than that Adriana-girl, I shouldn't pass on that story.

Hey, I liked chocolate too much, and just about everything else. But even if some would regard me as a tad pudgy, I never lacked for male attention. I had my pick of guys.

And I'd better choose one soon just to show that rotten Angus I was really over him.

Come to think of it, shouldn't I be longing for some mattress athletics? It had been months since Angus and I did the wild thing, yet I still felt adequately satisfied. Maybe god-sex just had a longer shelf life than regular-guy-sex.

After slipping on my dress, I admired myself in the mirror. Tossing the organdy layers out and letting them fall around me, I thought I looked like a really built Tinker Bell.

When I stepped from the restroom, Rand was finally off the phone. He sat there, idly drumming his black polished fingernails against the tabletop.

You know Rand Riker, of course—or as I thought of him, Thick Lips and Crater Face. He had to be the most legendary bad-boy in the rock world. When my mom was a girl, she attended the first of the concerts at which he was arrested for indecency, after he appeared on stage covered in nothing more than red paint. When nudity no longer attracted sufficient attention, he went on to something else, and something after that. Always ahead of the curve.

With that kind of reputation, you'd be surprised by what he looked like today. The hair he'd once dyed primary red had returned to its natural black with gray streaks, and it reached to his waist. He wore wide cotton pants above sandals and a loose jacket such as an Eastern monk might wear. The only sign that he was still Devil's Disciple's bad boy were the fingernails and toenails, as long as an armadillo's, which he painted black.

When I passed the table, his gaze met mine. A sparkle of recognition rose into those famous hooded eyes, as pitch as midnight in a coal mine.

Since I was on the clock, I paused beside him. "Everything okay? You seemed to be shouting a lot back here."

"Just hedging me bets," he said with a flickering grin. "You know, some might consider what we're about to do in Arizona as a fair dinkum risk." He gave his hair a toss that sent a ripple through it that made it look like the skin of a seal. "Ah, no worries. I've built my entire career by adding one dare onto another. Wouldn't have it any other way."

I slipped into the chair across from him. "Anything I can do?"

He lifted his fingertips to his forehead and seemed to be unconsciously trying to flatten its deeply etched lines. "Such as what?" he asked absently.

What he was paying me for, to act as his psychic. Okay, so maybe I had begun substituting the word *mugs* for *drugs* in the name of the Sex, Drugs & Rock 'n' Roll tour. *Mugs* because anyone who thought I could tell a psychic impression from a Fig Newton was a first class patsy. But he had hired me. Other people made the impossible happen purely on the strength of my predictions.

As if he were the one with telepathic abilities, Rand said, "Oh, I get it. You want to tell me my future. Is that it, Madame

MAGICAL ALIENATION

Samantha?"

Not precisely how I would have expressed it, but why else was I there?

He reached across the table and gently traced my jaw with fingertips callused from decades of strumming guitar strings. "Maybe, luv, I could tell you yours."

Was *that* why he hired me? Despite the sixty-plus years of hard living reflected on his face, I had to admit there was something about him. When a wicked grin caused his full lips to twist crookedly, he seemed to be saying that he knew what you wanted, how you wanted it and that he was just the guy to give it to you.

Whoa! He was old enough to be my father. If my mom had had her way, he would have been. Besides, Rand Riker had cut so many notches in the bedpost, he'd reduced hundreds of headboards to kindling. I didn't need another guy who had never heard the word *fidelity*.

Even more unsteadily on my towering shoes now, I babbled something about needing more chocolate. Rand gave me a look that pierced through my lie. I wasn't sure whether he was trying to say he knew I wanted to escape, or if it was obvious there couldn't be any chocolate left.

At the front of the plane, I sank into my chair, careful to drape my elegant gown around me. Until it occurred to me that I might be making myself too gorgeous to resist. I didn't notice the clunky approach of Princess Holly's sensible shoes until she stood before me.

"Madame Samantha, is the champagne all right?" she asked.

I wanted to say, *No, it tastes like kiddy swill*. Naturally, I told her it was fine.

Holly hovered expectantly before me. Sure, I said I wasn't any more psychic than a jelly donut, but even I could sense that she wanted a reading. At least someone respected my sham-skills. I urged her to sit across from me. She threw a quick glance to the rear of the jet, where Rand was once again yammering on the phone, before she perched on the edge of the other chair.

Her story poured out fast, and it was a familiar one. Concerned a guy, of course. A cheater, of course.

I put up my hand to stop her. "I got the picture. You're working your tail off to scrape together enough bucks for your wedding, while he's off nailing some mermaid."

She wrinkled her small, elegant nose in confusion. "A mermaid? You mean one of those sea creatures...? No, it was his assistant."

"Assistant, mermaid—what's the difference?" But it hit me, what I was saying. Okay, so maybe I wasn't as over Angus as I thought. I drew myself up and said with unaccustomed dignity, "It's a metaphor."

Holly O'Neill nodded slowly. "I see that. Like a siren, you mean."

Siren? The noise an ambulance makes? Whatever. "Exactly," I said. "Dump that loser before he hurts you again."

"But he said he'd never—"

I sighed loudly. "They always do. And they always do. Cheat, I mean. Trust me, you're meant for someone else. It's written in the stars."

That usually convinced them. I couldn't say why. If you can erase something written on paper, why should stars be exempt? Nothing in life is set, I believed. Even if it were, wouldn't most of us resist it? Holly, I felt certain, would find someone better, now that I'd sent her off in that direction. I'd really done her a favor.

She wasn't getting with the program, though. "It's hard for me to meet men. Our passengers...well, they regard me as either their servant or a flying call girl."

I felt an unexpected kinship with her, thanks to Rand's recent come on. But that gave me an idea. "The man you're supposed to be with is right here."

"The pilot? He's gay."

"Not the pilot." I tossed my curly blonde mane toward to the back of the plane.

"You mean...?" She gave her head a speculative tilt.

Good. Since Rand had chartered this jet for the entire tour, we'd be seeing more of Princess Holly. If she went after him, that would distract Rand and save me from my own self-destructive impulses.

I looked out the window when the plane banked into a curve. "Ooh! Look at that mountain."

"That's Camelback Mountain."

"It does resemble a camel," I said, gushing. "Look at that. It even has the distinct look of a camel's face."

Holly's lips twisted skeptically. "I can't say I ever saw much facial resemblance. The hump, of course, and the head, but not the face."

Was she kidding? A camel's face distinctly stared back at me. Actually, there was a cartoonish quality about it. How could a rock assume that form?

"Come on," I said. "Look out this window and tell me you don't see—"

The most incredible thing happened then. The camel stuck out its tongue at me. I swear! I sank back in my seat, shaken.

My fear didn't last long, though, as I put it all together. Cristal Champagne transformed into apple juice...a face on a mountain that nobody else could see...a tongue wag.

I didn't have to ask what was happening—this had to be the work of one of the Celtic deities. I just didn't know which one. It couldn't have been Angus. He wasn't that subtle, if you could describe putting a cartoon face on a mountain as subtle. And it sure wasn't Haggerty—she was too stingy with her powers to waste them.

Who else cared about attracting my attention? And why?

CHAPTER TWO

By the time we landed, my chocolate high's bubble had burst. I felt so wiped out, I wanted to sleep for a week. Naturally, that wasn't going to happen.

I hadn't experienced any more odd perceptions. With sheepish honesty, I admitted I must have been wrong about the earlier ones. A mountain that wagged its tongue at me? Sugar had just made me lightheaded.

The Gulfstream landed in some small airport in Scottsdale. When Princess Holly opened the hatch, two burly guys met us in a black Yukon with darkened windows. They hadn't punched those boys out of precisely the same mold, but they hadn't made a lot of modifications to the design between stampings, either. Both were muscle sausages, and both wore black leather bomber jackets that seemed too heavy for the warmish spring weather. The stockier one sported a five o'clock shadow and had a neck as thick as a tree trunk. The taller one shaved his head so closely, his scalp shined in the sunlight.

Rand greeted the pair with no more than a nod. They grunted back. Since nobody bothered to introduce me, I thought of them as No-Neck and Baldy.

They began to transfer our bags to the rear of the Yukon. The unseasonable coats no longer surprised me when No-Neck's unzipped jacket parted, and I saw he wore a shoulder holster.

Well, Rand Riker was a huge star. Even if the critics had been increasingly unkind about his advancing years, he needed more security than the average Joe. Armed guards weren't overkill.

But I began to wonder whether they were merely contract muscle men. Neither Rand nor I had traveled light. Our bags filled all the cargo space of the voluminous Yukon. While transferring a few bags, No-Neck said with a sneer, "Didn't leave much at home, huh?"

I expected Rand to remind the stupid lug who paid his salary. He'd enjoyed too many years of outrageous entitlement to take crap from a security guy. To my surprise, while he pressed his full lips together until they turned white, Rand didn't utter a peep of reproach.

Holly walked toward the terminal, pulling a roller suitcase

behind her. She waved at me and sent a doubtful look Rand's way. He didn't seem to notice. You'd think such a determined womanizer would have eyed her cute little caboose.

Baldy and No-Neck climbed into the SUV and started it up, while Rand and I piled into the backseat. As we wove our way through the city streets, I tried to pay more attention to the camel mountain, which was visible from many angles. But all I really wanted was to take a nap. If I ever think about eating that much chocolate again, somebody hit me.

Too bad that was when Rand decided to get his money's worth from me. "I haven't come a gutser, have I?"

Shouldn't this job have come with an Aussie phrasebook?

"This will work out, won't it, Madame Samantha?" Rand went on.

He wanted my advice *now?* Maybe he should have asked before he aligned himself with Normal Frankly, the most reviled man in the country.

Nobody really knew much about Normal Frankly, the man we'd gone to Arizona to help. Once the Feds looked into his history, they found it didn't hold up. Everything from his college transcripts, to his resume as a high school chemistry teacher had been faked. But even though his trial was still in its early days, while nobody knew where he'd come from, few doubted that he'd end up in prison.

The government had identified Normal, a Northern Arizona militia member, as the person who had raised the country's collective anxiety level when he mailed a series of poison gas vials to the offices of several senators who had sponsored a bill that would have curtailed militia activities.

I hardly ever watch the news, but even I became glued to the tube as the national fear level ratcheted up with each new vial that arrived.

The strange part was that most of the vials had been sent to the senators' D.C. offices. Only Kenny Campbell, the junior senator from Arizona, received one at his Phoenix office. And Senator Campbell's vial was the only one that broke. The prosecution alleged that the thickness of the glass used in the other vials guaranteed that all the Washington packages would probably arrive intact, while the one sent to Senator Campbell was so fragile, it was engineered to shatter when the package was opened.

Even more damning for Normal was the fact that the package arrived a week after Senator Campbell was shown on TV opening his own mail in his Phoenix office. Anyone with two brain cells to rub together would have regarded that as an obvious photo op. Big-time politicians do not open their own mail, except when TV cameras roll. But the government maintained Normal believed Senator Campbell would open that package himself. Even more, the prosecution contended he had been the sole target from the start, with the other packages sent to Washington merely smokescreens. Too bad an aide actually opened it; she was killed within instants, and it took two weeks for a Hazmat team to sanitize the office.

Since it was understood that Senator Campbell planned to make a run for the White House, you might have predicted that half the country would have supported him, while the other half wouldn't have been too broken up if the vial had reached its intended target. But even if Kenny Campbell was running on a simple-minded Family Values plank, he was generally regarded as more honest than the usual politician. Even his political opponents respected him. Given that, and the way that Oklahoma City and 9/11 had angered Americans, it was amazing that Normal Frankly hadn't been strung up from a Saguaro Cactus already.

And *that* was the man Rand Riker had chosen to defend.

I'd about swallowed my tongue when I heard that, well before the start date of the Sex, Drugs & Rock 'n' Roll tour, Rand decided to include a benefit concert in Sedona to help defray Normal's legal bills.

"Even a penniless man deserves a fair trial," Rand had announced at a press conference. "Bloody hell, I've been railroaded by the sanctimonious types from the start of my career. I know how it feels."

Normal didn't seem that penniless. He owned a sizeable compound outside of Sedona, built right into a mountain, which was supposedly more unassailable than Fort Knox. He wasn't exactly getting railroaded, either; the government had apparently built a tight case. It also didn't seem like Devil's Disciple would raise any money. Since ticket sales weren't great, after expenses, the benefit concert might lose bucks. So why do it?

That was what I'd asked Rand when I met him at that party.

A twinkle had risen up in his flat eyes. "I'll tell you

something, Madame Samantha—you do like people to address you as 'Madame,' right, luv?"

Not when they were laughing at me, which I figured he had been.

Rand reduced his voice to a whisper. "It's not only politics that makes for strange bedfellows, it's also self-promotion."

The promotional part I understood. When he asked me to sign on as his personal psychic, I agreed in a flash. Self-promotion was my real life's work. But when the Sedona City Council tried to secure an injunction to stop the concert, my doubts surfaced. Even after the band won the right to continue, the idea of supporting a guy so despised started looking less attractive. I've got the hide of a rhino when it comes to words, but what if people decided to string us all up? Still, I didn't bail when I could have. Yeah, I needed the money. But mostly, I needed not to be home when Angus came by begging me to take him back. I had to show him I'd moved on.

I noticed Rand was still blathering about something. "What about the harmonic convergence? How will that affect me?"

Har-what? That sounded more like a woo-woo word than an Aussie one. I threw loads of them about in the course of my job, but that was a new one by me. I prided myself on being able to shoot the bull with the best of them, but not when the chocolate bubble burst, and my brain had turned to mush.

"Madame Samantha?" he asked.

Time for a diversion. After spotting what I needed up ahead, I told No-Neck to pull over. "Coffee. I need coffee."

No-Neck parked before some country-looking coffeehouse. Wow, it had been a long time since I'd seen an independent coffee shop. Not since Soma Café had locked up all the coffee business from coast-to-coast. Actually, though I couldn't get through a day without several Soma Cafs, I couldn't explain how they came to be on every corner of every city in the country. They burned their beans and their baristas were snotty know-it-alls. I only knew I was as hopelessly devoted as everyone else.

"Not here," I snapped. "Go down the street to Soma Café."

With a sigh, he pulled back into traffic and moved the Yukon a few spaces along. "I'll get your coffee," No-Neck said, cutting the engine.

Baldy gave him the slightest of nods. "I'd better go," Baldy said. No-Neck agreed with pursed lips.

What was that all about?

"How do you take it?" Baldy asked. "Cream? Sugar?"

"Regular coffee?" I wrinkled my nose. "I'll have a Venti percent cap with easy foam and an extra shot." One shot? As tired as I was today, what was I thinking? "Make it two shots, as well as a shot of vanilla. And have them drizzle some caramel over the foam."

Baldy stared at me. "You'll need a bank loan to pay for that."

Rand pulled a twenty from his baggy monk pants. "Buy her what she wants, so we can get on with this."

Baldy nodded. "Tell me again—"

I snatched the bill. "I'll get it myself."

That was what I wanted to do anyway. Before anyone could object, I hopped out. Despite how desperately I needed coffee, I stopped the instant I was through the door and looked for someone with a computer. I didn't own one myself. I was the last dinosaur who'd never received an email. As for spam—well, that was what most people considered me. But I had learned how to do Internet searches when I could steal a few minutes on someone else's laptop.

Amazingly, I didn't see any laptops today. Just the usual loud overhead music and about a dozen people talking on their cell phones through headsets, so that it looked more like the day room of a loony bin.

I stepped up to the counter, but before I ordered, I asked the clerk, "What's a harmonica convergence? Or a hormonal one? Something like that."

The skinny twit looked down his long nose at me. "Is that something on our menu?"

See what I mean? Snotty. I ordered my coffee; no matter how I felt about the place, I needed that. But somehow I had to find out about that harmonica-thingie before Rand asked about it again.

Someone had stuffed several newspaper sections in a paper rack. While the barista made my drink, I yanked out the front section. No harmonicas, and no hormones, either. What was that word?

Before I could toss the section away, though, something did catch my eye. "Militia Denounces Frankly," the headline read. The article went on to say that the Arizona Friends of Freedom Militia had condemned Normal Frankly's attack on Senator Campbell, breaking their ties with him.

MAGICAL ALIENATION

A color photo depicted a dreary-looking man, identified as Harold Hinkley, wearing combat fatigues and sporting a graying chin-warmer beard, standing before a bank of microphones. The space behind him on a stage, placed before some crimson rocks, was filled with fellow travelers, all also wearing fatigues or flannels. Surprisingly, one of those guys was No-Neck.

The barista placed my drink on the counter. As desperate as I felt, I didn't reach for it. Instead, I glanced at the black SUV parked outside. Though the Friends of Freedom had broken with Normal Frankly, at least one of their members—and I was betting two—chauffeured around the man who intended to pay their enemy's legal bills.

What were those strange bedfellows up to?

CHAPTER THREE

The caravan had begun its journey, earlier than the being from Area 51 expected. Excellent. As long as the charm he'd placed on his captors continued to hold. Though the lead vehicle used technology to monitor its course, none of the soldiers assigned to their caravan recognized that they had veered away from their desired destination. What delightful fun!

The caravan consisted of only three vehicles. After much discussion, the higher-ups had decided a lower profile made more sense than a better equipped force, because nobody would take a cluster of only three military vehicles for anything other than a routine shipment. All the decades the creature had remained mute paid off—they'd concluded he couldn't understand their language, and they felt free to say anything in front of him.

The last vehicle in the chain was exactly what it appeared to be, a simple supply truck that stored food and held a small galley to prepare it in. The lead one was the scout. The second vehicle housed the being. From the outside, it also looked like an ordinary truck. However, the inside of that unassuming shell was lined with titanium. After he'd been placed into that metal room, the doorway had been welded shut. The only openings consisted of a small rectangle, through which his food tray was pushed, and a Plexiglas window a guard could use to monitor him.

Poor fools. Even in his weakened condition, he didn't need doors to escape.

And escape he would, when the time was right. He calculated that they would arrive at the destination early. Not only had they started out before he expected, they were making good time, even if they traveled exclusively on rural highways. He didn't minimize the difficulty he would face once he liberated himself—they'd unleash an unprecedented manhunt. But despite the challenge hiding out would present, earlier was better than later. If he missed that one sliver of time, he was finished.

Everything was working adequately well for him. His waning energy stores were holding, thanks to the power he'd begun siphoning from his unwitting benefactor.

MAGICAL ALIENATION

The only setback was the signal he had sent the facilitator he'd chosen. He knew she picked up on his message—the surge in the universe's collective energy had been too dramatic. But it died away fast. Had she discounted her perception? She should have made contact with the one who could help her interpret what she'd seen.

He'd have to send another message, one she couldn't ignore.

Now what would it be? He chuckled softly. It was good to know that even in these sorry times, there was still amusement to be had. As long as it wasn't at his *expense.*

CHAPTER FOUR

The main Phoenix Federal Courthouse wasn't far from the Soma Café coffee shop. Fortunately, I'd already chugged most of my drink when the Yukon stopped. Needing all possible juice, I swallowed the last drop. But I'd developed such a caffeine tolerance, even a Venti with extra shots didn't give me the slightest buzz.

The courthouse surprised me. I'd been expecting the typical mausoleum to justice, gray with grime, dripping with concrete grapes and whatnot. But this was a new building, all angles and curves. A glass crescent took a deep swipe through the front of the structure. And jutting out from it was a round extension that looked like a flying saucer. As if such a thing could exist.

No-Neck told Baldy to call when we were ready to be picked up, and No-Neck stayed with the car. After his kisser appeared in the newspaper with his leader denouncing Normal Frankly, I'd guess he didn't want to be seen helping the *verboten* cause. Were they defectors? Baldy yanked his gun from his holster and popped it into the glove box.

As soon as we stepped from the SUV, reporters gathered there rushed at Rand. Baldy kept them away, while Rand and I dashed toward the door. The atrium that rose many stories within that glass crescent looked equally as dramatic inside. Baldy immediately began acting as a negative tour guide, deploring the waste of tax dollars, "that shouldn't have been taken in the first place," he'd insisted, while simultaneously explaining how the place worked. The atrium wasn't air conditioned in the usual way, he told us. There were misters at the top, which released fine sprays of water that cooled it. By the time those bursts of mist hit the ground floor, they felt like puffs of cool air.

Perfect for the Adriana-dress. While Baldy steered us toward the security checkpoint, I pirouetted to send the organdy layers floating out. He frowned in annoyance. *Live with it, pal.* I noticed he kept his political views to himself when we went through security. Hypocrite.

Baldy guided us into the elevator. When it stopped at our floor, he ushered us down the hall. He left us at the courtroom door, after assuring Rand that he'd meet us again when we left. While the guys talked, I inched the door open to peek inside. It was a modern courtroom awash in some light-colored wood. Apart from the design, though, it contained all the usual courtroom components, if TV was any guide.

Court was in session, but we barged right in. People spotted Rand immediately, causing a murmur to swell through the spectator area. The judge was a wiry woman in her fifties, weathered by the desert sun. While she didn't look in our direction, grooves cut deeply between her eyebrows, as the noise built.

She banged her gavel. "Silence, or I'll clear—"

When she finally spotted Rand, her speech sputtered to a stop. He offered Her Honor one of his full-wattage grins, causing a flush to rise up through her mummified skin. Had that dignified woman been one of the girls who once threw her undies on stage at his concerts? Or did she just wish she had?

Celebrity has the craziest effect on people. Was it any wonder I wanted to be a successful celebrity psychic? The women in the spectator area, no matter what their age, looked like they'd love to toss their unmentionables right now, while the men all seemed to want to befriend him. The lone holdout to Rand's appeal was a woman seated in the first row, a petite, mid-forties fashionista, who frowned at him. Rand would have had to wrestle her if he wanted her shorts.

We took our seats without any more fuss. Only then did Normal Frankly glance into the spectator section. Though I'd seen flashes of him on TV, close up the defendant looked anything but *normal*. His head towered over that of his male attorney, making me guess the guy was tall. A better word might have been *elongated*. Everything about him looked stretched out. I wondered if, after the obstetrician squeezed his head with forceps when he was born, making it unnaturally long and thin, he went back and gave the baby's body a matching squish. Normal's hair was a wispy light brown, and he had such pale eyebrows and eyelashes, they almost disappeared. He wore an olive flannel shirt that matched his unexpressive gray-green eyes. When he spotted Rand, his benefactor, his only acknowledgment was a twitch that moved through his thin lips.

He didn't seem to notice me at all, and I had dressed so

nicely. Death penalty cases sure warp people's priorities.

Then again, he was about to face his nemesis, so maybe that distracted him. Another murmur went through the spectators when Senator Campbell stepped forward. I did wonder what Normal's reaction might be to the man he allegedly tried to kill, but he didn't really have one. He rested his chin in his hand and studied the senator with casual detachment.

Senator Campbell looked twitchy enough for both of them. He couldn't seem to get comfortable in the witness chair, changing position several times. Sure, he was facing a man he had reason to fear, but you'd think a senator, who must receive plenty of angry mail, would have handled it better.

I hadn't expected to like Kenny Campbell, since our politics didn't exactly jibe, to the extent that I had political leanings. But there was something appealing about him. He felt familiar, too, in a totally unexpected way—not as if I'd seen him on the tube, but like I actually knew him, which I didn't. While fifty-something, there was a boyish quality about his slim, energetic form. His chocolate brown eyes, behind rimless glasses, crinkled attractively when he made an amusing, often self-deprecating, remark. I wasn't the only one who felt his appeal, either. Whenever he directed his engaging grin at anyone, it always seemed to elicit a warm smile in return. He touched people.

Of course, he was a politician, and they know how to play the charisma game. People say you can't con a con, but that's not true. I was as much a mark as anyone else. The vintage clothing stores saw me coming from miles away.

But when Kenny, as he'd always encouraged his constituents to call him, began to speak, he didn't couch his answers as carefully as politicians tend to do. Was it possible? A genuine politician, who harbored no secrets?

As his testimony progressed, I discovered something about real court that I hadn't guessed from TV. They drag out every nit-picky detail. Boring! Despite my having chugged enough of a Soma Caf to sink a tanker, I might have drifted off for a while. See what I mean about my coffee tolerance? An elbow in the side from Rand rousted me.

Kenny was still on the stand when I finished resting my eyes. But he'd finally gotten to the day the package arrived. Say what you will about sensationalism, it's really the only good part of the news.

"Lindsay, the intern who opened that package, had a birthday the prior week," Kenny said. He put finger quotes around the word, *birthday*. I didn't understand why, but then, I'd never understood the point of digital quotation.

"She was only twenty-one, and now she'll never get to live out her dreams." Kenny's voice broke. He cleared his throat and gave the bridge of his glasses a push with his finger, though they didn't appear to have slipped.

But his distress seemed real. Was this Lindsay-girl just an aide? Or had he proved senators can monkey around with interns as well as presidents can?

"Kelly and I haven't had children of our own," he said. "We'd always hoped we would." Another set of finger quotes fell somewhere in there. "We even had names picked out, all beginning with the letter *K*. Cute, huh?"

Pardon me while I puke.

"So, you see, these young ones on my staff...we think of them as our kids."

He looked at the tiny woman who'd scorned Rand earlier. So that was his wife. I should have guessed—seated beside her were a couple of standard-issue Feds, obviously on their security team. Guys who wore earpieces and kept whispering into the lapels of their dark suits, which made them look even nuttier than the folks I'd seen talking to themselves at Soma Café.

I gave her a closer look. She was expensively, but oddly, dressed—and that was coming from me. She wore a camel-colored cashmere sweater; even from a distance, I could see some fine goat had given its best for it. But around her neck, she'd wrapped a thick, off-white, homespun scarf. It must have been so big that she'd had to fold it several times before wrapping it above her narrow shoulders. It made her small head look like it was floating over some puffy neck brace. And people think *I'm* a fashion dunce.

The scorn she'd directed at Rand made sense now. Naturally, she wouldn't have any love for the man helping the goon who tried to off her old man. If Normal actually had tried to kill the senator, that is. I'd considered him as guilty as anyone before today. Really weird people are capable of really weird things—trust me, I had firsthand knowledge of that. But if Normal Frankly felt any personal animosity toward Senator Campbell, he did a good job of hiding it beneath his absolute lack of interest in these proceedings.

Kelly Campbell, on the other hand, looked overly engaged. It was as if she wanted to climb over the railing and sit in the witness box with her husband, where she'd do his testifying for him. She leaned forward as he spoke, occasionally moving her lips along with him, and frowning when he said something she obviously didn't like. She was an attractive woman, if a tad severe. The contrast between her black hair and fair skin alone could have had that effect, but the rigidity of her tense little face sealed it.

Kenny continued to yammer on about his aides. "No, we weren't blessed with our own offspring. But since so many good young people have passed through our lives, in a way, we've been blessed many times over."

At the back of the courtroom, someone grunted. I was pretty sick of hearing about his non-blessings myself, so I turned to see who had made that noise. The sound effect came from a woman, whose face was largely obscured, apart from coral lips pinched tightly together. Though a few red tendrils fell over her forehead, covering the rest of her hair was a Native American-style shawl that not only sheltered her head, but also wrapped across her forehead and chin. Large dark glasses covered her eyes. Even though she'd hid as much of her appearance as possible, she looked familiar to me, too. Funny, I'd never been in Phoenix before, yet I kept spotting faces that looked like other faces I knew, even if I couldn't remember which ones they were.

The trial wore on. At one point, the judge addressed the question of whether to take the jury, along with the defense and prosecution teams, to Normal's Sedona compound, where he supposedly cultivated the biological weapon that had killed Kenny's intern. The judge made the decision to go on Friday morning, two days from now, to allow time for security to be put into place.

To my surprise, Rand stood and asked to be included.

The prosecutor nearly choked. "Your honor, I object—"

The judge waved a hand in his direction to silence him. But Her Honor was oddly respectful of Rand. "I'm sorry, Mr. Riker," she said, not pretending she didn't recognize him. "But you're not a part of these proceedings." She really did sound sorry.

See, celebrity.

Since the next witness was tied up in traffic, the judge called a fifteen-minute recess. A cute bailiff led Normal off, while everyone else started shuffling out. Kenny went to his wife and held her in the most touching way. He wasn't a tall man, but since she was so tiny, he towered above her. While holding her close, he glanced across her head to the rear of the courtroom. There his gaze locked on something. I followed the direction of his widened eyes to the woman in the shawl. She stared back at him.

His face suddenly produced the oddest reaction. The kind of mottled blanching you might create if you threw cranberry juice into milk and didn't mix it. He paled and flushed at the same time.

The woman held his gaze for a moment more. Then she turned and slipped through the crowd. Still clutching his wife, who now struggled to free herself from that relentless embrace, Kenny stared after the mystery women.

The senator, it seemed, had a few secrets after all.

CHAPTER FIVE

The taste of freedom the short recess had given me made it harder to endure the trial once it began again. Instead of soaking up the warm Phoenix sun, as I could have been doing if I'd escaped outside when I had the chance, I had to suffer through the kind of chemistry recitation that used to put me to sleep in school. When I feared my head would explode, I whispered to Rand that I needed to leave. Modestly lowering my eyes, I tried to convey the idea that I had something girly to do. True, actually, if you regard it as girly to want to stuff your face with junk food.

At the courtroom door, a cat waited to be let out. Who would bring a cat into a courtroom? How did he get it through security? But there this kitty was. His green-gold eyes issued a plea to be released, which he followed with a silent meow. What the hell, I wasn't Animal Control. I could scarcely handle Samantha Control. I eased the door open and allowed my furry friend to leave first.

Once in the hall, I had no idea where to find a cafeteria. I stood there, head whipping around in fruitless directions. Unlike me, the cat turned left and took a few quick steps.

He was a big cat with brown tabby markings, along with hairy ears, a puffy tail and longish fur. He also had big furry feet, larger than some dogs. And he loped along with prancing steps, lacking the usual feline grace. After he'd covered a few yards, he turned back to me and issued a cry.

For a big guy, he had a high squeaky voice. When those green-gold eyes settled on mine, I almost thought he looked exasperated with me. Was he trying to say he could show me the way? How could a cat know what I'd been thinking? Most of the time, *I* scarcely knew.

His way seemed as good as any to start. We walked along, turning occasionally when corridors bent. The cat's purposeful canter stayed a step or two ahead of mine. He did turn my way now and then, mewing pointedly. He sounded like he wanted me to understand something. Those cat cries couldn't actually mean anything, right?

Considering how crowded the courthouse had been when we arrived, there weren't many people in the halls now. Some did pass occasionally, and I kept worrying that they'd throw the cat out. But nobody ever looked at him. Of course, he remained silent whenever anyone else went by. You'd almost think he knew enough to keep a low profile. Sure.

At a staircase, the cat led me down. Along the way, I asked, "I wish I knew your name, fella. It's a shame you can't tell me."

From out of nowhere, an Austin Mellencamp song floated into my head. You know, that troubadour who sings the Celtic ballads. Where had that come from? I felt disloyal to Rand. I ought to be hearing Devil's Disciple tunes exclusively now. But, hey, Rand didn't buy my mind. For that matter, he didn't buy my body. When you get down to it, he really didn't get much for his bucks.

The Austin Mellencamp medley continued. "Mellencamp!" I said with a sudden gasp. "I'll call you Mellencamp." I'm nothing if not creative.

I swear I saw a flash of approval in those enigmatic eyes, and perhaps a touch of pity. Just my own head playing games with me—the cat certainly wasn't judging me.

When I began to think I'd wasted time following him, the scent of grease made my nose twitch. A sign on the wall announced the location of the cafeteria.

The cat actually led me there? Had to be a coincidence.

My steps quickened, moving in the direction of the grub. Until something happened that caused me to sputter to a stop.

I spotted a woman some distance ahead of me whose presence there sent a jolt of dread through me. That might seem an extreme reaction to a conventionally dressed woman, but I swear it was justified. You can't imagine the stuff that happened to me the last time our paths crossed. Though I saw her from the rear, I recognized her in an instant. I knew her slender erect form, covered by a steely gray suit, as well as that wavy auburn hair pulled back so tightly into a knot, its natural wave scarcely showed. Mostly I recognized the purposeful walk, the determined way those low, sensible heels struck the tile floor.

While she marched on, my own steps, in my ultra high heels, hesitated. The big cat lifted his face toward mine. I looked back at him in panic. While some part of me wanted to shout out happily to her, the strongest debate warring in my mind was not *whether* to run in the other direction, but if I could run faster if I removed my shoes.

An irrational idea occurred to me. Had Mellencamp delivered me there? Had he known I would meet up with her? Nutty, huh? All the experiences we'd shared came flooding back in vivid detail. The dangers, the fears, the challenges to the way I viewed the world. And then, inexplicably, other thoughts came to me, such as the apple juice that morning, the cartoonish mountain that flapped its tongue at me.

By hesitating, I lost the one chance I had to escape, if escape was even possible. Before I could turn away, the woman whirled toward me. Not in a surprised way, but as if she knew she'd find me there. Her full lips curved into a knowing grin. "Sex, *Mugs*, and Rock 'n' Roll, Samantha?" she asked, toying with me. "I don't know that I'd call Devil Boy an all-out mug, but maybe I can see where you're coming from."

My heart thudded to a stop. I hadn't told *anyone* my secret name for the Devil's Disciple tour. I used that phrase to amuse myself within the privacy of my own mind. Privacy? Hah! I could never keep a secret from Annabelle Haggerty, the woman in the gray suit, who was so much more than she appeared to be. While an FBI agent right at home in a federal courthouse, Haggerty was also a genuine Celtic goddess. Given that the Bureau was Skepticism Central, she kept her real nature a secret. I was one of the few mortals who knew the truth about her, an honor I could have done without.

She took a few steps toward me. "I hadn't thought about you in months, but yesterday your voice floated into my head." She paused. "We're connected again, Samantha."

Noooo. I refused to believe that. Our meeting there was just a coincidence, and a fleeting one at that. I rejected my own earlier panic.

Faking a carefree attitude, I said, "Haggerty, I'd like you to meet a friend of mine." Let her try to shake hands with a cat. I looked down.

Mellencamp had disappeared.

CHAPTER SIX
Haggerty

In Samantha's presence, Annabelle Haggerty felt lighter, brighter...freer. It made no sense. Samantha was the flakiest person to ever cross her path. But Samantha also had the strongest *joie de vivre* of anyone Haggerty had ever known, including her own carefree ancestors, the gods whose antics filled the mythology books. She stopped trying to fight it—Samantha's joy was contagious.

It did surprise her that she felt this connection to Samantha so strongly. Sure, their link went deep. Samantha had actually saved Haggerty's life once. It wasn't often a goddess could say that about a mortal. That had forged an inexplicable bond with the last mortal Haggerty would have ever chosen for that relationship.

Yet what really surprised Haggerty was that she felt *anything* so strongly. The powers that were her birthright, the underlying awareness of life's spiritual side, which she monitored constantly through a different set of senses, had recently become muted. Dimmed from the level that she'd always known.

If she didn't know better, she'd say she was sick. Mortals often felt their energies decline when they came down with some infection. But deities rarely succumbed to anything until their time on this plane was winding down.

Besides, this was different. She felt as she did when she had overused the vast reserve of energies available to her, when her powers were temporarily unavailable until she recharged them. That had happened at times, when she'd performed great magic. But she'd done nothing lately. There was no reason for this dwindling of her special strengths.

Even now, Haggerty didn't acknowledge that her secret desire had always been to be an ordinary mortal. She still refused to put it into words. How could she, a goddess, who'd been blessed with so many advantages, wish for a lesser life? But the awareness of that longing swelled within her nonetheless. Maybe this was her chance to see what it might be like to live without the powers her kind took for granted, but which she'd always regarded as somewhat of a burden. Besides, it wasn't as if she used her powers much anyway.

She decided to let this dimming go on for now, and not to say anything to anyone with the capacity to reverse things. Not her mother, nor their ancestors. She'd experience what it would have been like if she'd been born to Samantha's path, instead of her own.

How could that hurt?

CHAPTER SEVEN
Samantha

Haggerty and I went through the cafeteria line without speaking, but the choices we made screamed volumes about our differences. I asked for a double order of curly fries covered with chili; she took a green salad with the low-fat dressing on the side. I also grabbed a mug of coffee. Not a Soma Caf, but I wasn't going to survive this lunch without caffeine. I selected a table in a quiet corner and waited for her there, as I might anticipate the dropping of the guillotine.

While watching her approach, I thought about the first time I'd seen her, in the reception room of the Los Angeles field office of the FBI. I'd been so quick to write her off as just another Bureau drone, a woman who couldn't possibly have any unusual inner life. Considering that I made my living peddling knowledge about another plane of existence, that was proof that I didn't know diddly about this one. I hadn't seen beyond the exterior she used to protect herself from those who would deny or exploit her unique skills.

She was about my age, with impossibly big blue eyes, fanned by thick rows of dark lashes, and the high cheekbones and full lips that make models world famous. It was only the way those lips often pursed that gave an inkling to how stubborn she could be.

Haggerty and I were nothing alike. She was earnest to an annoying degree, while I took nothing seriously. She was the real thing, and I, the fake. Even with all that I knew about her, I still regarded her as something of a drone, while she considered me a P.I.T.A.—that's "pain in the ass" to the more refined among you.

Something had brought us together once before. Haggerty had been there for me when I needed her most. And she was the first person in my life that I refused to give up on, even though I knew saving her life might take mine. I'd even risked what had been my new relationship with Angus for her. We were connected in a way I couldn't understand or explain. In a way I couldn't fight.

But that didn't mean I wouldn't keep trying.

At the table, I threw my tray down and ate directly from it. Haggerty removed her salad and iced tea and gracefully set her place, placing the tray to the side. But then, neither of us dug in. I stared at the mountainous mess before me and felt queasy. And it takes a lot to put me off my feed. Haggerty lifted her own fork, only to have it fall from her fingers, hitting the thick white plate with a clang. When she took her head in her hands, her smooth forehead corrugated into lines.

"Headache?" I asked, my voice shrill.

Haggerty nodded.

"How do you mean that? A regular old headache, or one of…your kind?"

I wasn't being silly. Debilitating headaches often preceded her visions. Unlike her mother, who had descended from two deities, Haggerty was half-mortal. Her father might have decamped in her infancy, never to appear again, but his DNA had diluted hers. She had powers beyond anything I'd ever imagined when I believed I was making up that Celtic goddess-stuff. But using them often hurt and weakened her.

"How strange that I feel it at all," she muttered.

Why strange? She'd had headaches for as long as I'd known her.

Haggerty shrugged. "I haven't eaten anything today. Let's hope it's a regular headache."

Like I believed that. Like she did. But it demonstrated another difference between us. If I had to go an hour without caffeine or grease, I'd pack it in. She'd put any number of things before eating. That's why she was thin, and I was…not. Angus had admired my figure, which he'd described as "fetching," a term he said so few women in this century warranted. Yeah? If he liked it so much, why he had sought another body, one covered in scales?

I sipped my coffee in silence. Compared to the Soma Caf I'd had earlier, it tasted like bath water, but the caffeine accumulation finally hit. My hands shook. Or maybe that was just the memory of what could happen with Haggerty around. Last time I had butted into her life, to her great annoyance. This time she was crashing into mine. I didn't like it any better.

Still, I was curious enough to ask what brought her to Arizona.

"I've been part of the Normal Frankly investigation from the start, but back in L.A. One of the senators who received a vial at his D.C. office was from Southern California. I first hit on the idea that

MAGICAL ALIENATION

Senator Campbell might be the real target. When they offered me this spot on the Campbell security detail, my mom begged me to accept it so we could spend more time together." An uneasy frown gripped her face.

The last I'd heard, Haggerty's mom lived in Las Vegas, where she used her powers to create more winners than the casinos there wanted. I'd never met Fiona Haggerty, but I'd always wished I had hooked up with the goddess-mother, instead of the goddess-daughter.

Haggerty said her mom had left Vegas. "She's staying at the home of a Hopi shaman on the reservation in Northern Arizona."

Despite my unsettled tummy, the chili called out to me. I scooped up a mound of it in the coils of a few curly fries and stuffed it all into my kisser. Haggerty absently tossed lettuce leaves aside with her fork, as if she were searching for something beneath them. Something edible?

"Why's she seeing a shaman? That's like a medicine man, right? She's not sick, is she?"

"Unlikely."

Gulping down another wad of chili, I said, "Maybe the shaman is offering, you know, psychic healing."

"Possible," she said with apparent skepticism. "He should know something about the journey—he has been dead for two hundred years."

That comment rendered the chili instantly rancid in my stomach. That was what I hated about her. Not that she could say stuff like that—hell, I could *say* it. But she *meant* it.

She speared a lettuce leaf, dipping a tiny part of it into the tub of salad dressing beside her plate. "She's been so secretive lately, but she promised me she'd open up about everything. I took a personal day and drove to Hopi. Didn't even stop for lunch. But when I arrived, the shaman's great-granddaughter told me that Mom had left yesterday, without explaining where she was going."

Stood up by your own mother. I wouldn't question it if my mom did that, but I was betting Haggerty's family didn't need to elude the cops as often as mine did.

"And I had to miss Senator Campbell's testimony for that runaround."

I filled her in on what I remembered about it. I also shared my impression of him.

Haggerty tilted her sleek red head. "I like him, too. Things have been so tense in his camp, but Senator Campbell always makes me laugh. Everyone else runs around as if the sky is falling, while he and I continue to share our little jokes."

"You and Kenny aren't..." I wiggled my eyebrows in one of the thousands of gestures that represent sex.

"No!" Haggerty snapped. "He treats me in more of a fatherly way."

Ah, she was another of his non-blessings.

She cleared her throat. "I'm not sure Mrs. Campbell appreciates that. She's perfectly nice, you understand. But I can feel her tension spike when I'm around."

Then it must have shot into the stratosphere, because Mrs. Campbell struck me as a real uptight-kinda gal.

Haggerty eyed me over the top of her iced tea glass. "You and I, Samantha—we're on opposite sides this time."

I squirmed in the green plastic chair that cupped my round butt. "Not really." I was always only on my own side. "Rand is just a publicity hound."

"He's raising money for the man who tried to kill Senator Campbell. Make sure you're not the mug in the Sex, Mugs and 'n' Roll tour." She offered me a superior smirk. "We both know there's no sex between you and Mr. Riker."

That was what I wanted people to believe—well, Angus. I started to argue, but Haggerty shook her head. "You forget how easily I can read your aura, Samantha. You not only wear your heart on your sleeve, you wear your satisfaction in your energy field."

With a sigh, I nodded. Haggerty was a whiz at reading auras, and she even heard melodies coming off people, something I'd never known anyone else to do. The first time Angus and I had been together, she'd read that in my aura. I wondered how it looked now. There was no question I had lost the inner glow I'd felt when Angus and I were newly in love, but like I said, I didn't exactly feel sex-starved, either, even if I didn't get why not.

"I'm sorry I didn't call you back," I said. "You know when Angus…"

She'd left a message on my voicemail, saying, "He's a god, Samantha, not a mere man. Call me if you want to talk."

I hadn't wanted to talk. Not with her, anyway. I'd bitched to strangers at the bus stop about the guy who cheated on me. Yet I couldn't bear any contact with her family. She had warned me it would never work.

"So he's not a mere man, huh?" I asked now.

She shook her head. "If you'd ever read mythology, you'd know gods have always regarded mortals as their playthings. They're known for their mischief, and sometimes, far worse."

Pushing a pile of chili around my plate with a broken fry, I said, "Yeah? There oughta be some control over them."

Haggerty insisted there was some control. "The Governing Council oversees us all, but especially the *Danaans*." Those were the original gods like Angus, not their descendants, such as Haggerty and her mom. "But the amount of control they exercise is in direct proportion to the majority faction that makes up the Council. If the prankster element seizes control, the mischief-makers have wide latitude. If those that believe, as I do, that gods should behave with more responsibility take control, rules are put in place and punishments meted out. The ratio changes all the time, automatically, in direct proportion to the thinking of the *Danaans*." She chewed some salad, before touching the corner of her mouth with a wrinkled paper napkin. "I didn't see you complaining when you shared in the mischief. You're not very consistent, Samantha."

I preferred *in*consistency—it was easier to maintain. But she was right about my enjoying the mischief when I took part in it. Once when Angus was at the guesthouse I rent in Santa Monica, a pair of his god-pals showed up, Lugh and Taliesin. It was early afternoon in California then, which made it night in Scotland. A perfect time for leaving crop circles, a hobby they were obsessed with at the time.

Even as I wondered how we would travel there, we were instantly transported to a Scottish farm. One second I was home, modeling a new dress for Angus; the next, I was in that field. Still wearing the dress.

I figured they'd zap the crop circle into place, but Lugh had insisted they liked doing things the hard way. The only things they created magically were the boards we would use to press the crops to the ground. And wine, of course. Lots of the wine that gods favor, which didn't threaten Napa's finest when it came to taste, but created the most delightful of buzzes.

We drank and stomped for some time. And laughed uproariously. But after a while, Taliesin finished the job by magic. One thing I'd noticed about gods—they always believe they want to do things the hard way, but they never really do. Was it any wonder I loved being part of their world? I was all about shirking effort—it just wasn't as easy for me to pull off.

All the gods I knew took the easy way, except Haggerty. This chick seemed to feel there was merit in struggle. I knew her faith was true, because I'd witnessed her rituals at her home altar. She worshipped her ancestors, but she didn't always respect them. Sometimes I even believed she'd trade places with me if she could. Crazy, huh?

"Yeah, that was fun," I said with a sigh. I sipped my coffee, but after remembering that wine, it tasted worse than ever. If Haggerty hadn't been there, I'd have spit it out.

"See, you don't want them drawing any hard lines when it might interfere with your amusement."

"Not hard ones, no. I think lines should be more…" I waved my fingers before me.

"Blurred?" She shook her head. "That's a slippery slope, Samantha."

The only kind I liked. With my life, who needed to ski? "Who did that crop circle hurt? Sure, the farmer lost a few bucks on those crops. But we watched when he called a press conference the next morning. You should have seen how he preened for the cameras. It was the high point of his life."

"So your nonsense did him a favor? Isn't his life a letdown now?" Haggerty shook her head. "Anyway, it's not merely a matter of pranks. Some gods really don't wish the beings on this plane well."

"You mean Earth," I said.

"Earth and the other worlds on this plane."

"There isn't any life on—"

Haggerty smiled. "Samantha, surely you don't believe you Earthlings are the only beings on this plane? The universe is infinite. There are so many…"

She went on, but I tuned her out. That was another thing I hated about the gods. I loved going out to play with them, but why couldn't they stop before they forced me to change my view of existence?

I felt a little green, but it must not have shown. Or she didn't care. Haggerty kept rambling on. "I remember one goddess once...what was her name? Something-de?" Haggerty searched her memory. "Rele-de," she said, pronouncing it, Ray-lay-day. "She was sacrificing young mortal females to keep her eternal youth."

Gods were immortal, but they did go through an aging process, although it took thousands and thousands of years. The stages of a goddess's life were maiden, mother and crone. Haggerty once shared a vision with me, and I actually saw one of her ancestors go through those stages in my own mind's eye.

"This goddess refused to move past the maiden stage and was sucking out the youth from those women to do it. The Governing Council condemned her to live life-after-life as an ordinary mortal, who must age and die over-and-over." Haggerty ate the last of her rabbit food. "You wouldn't want her showing up at your door, would you?"

Not only was Haggerty unnecessarily righteous, she had a mania for overstating the obvious. I was starting to remember why I wasn't always crazy about her.

She put her dish back on her tray. "You don't mind if we go back to the courtroom, do you, Samantha? After all that chili you can't possibly want dessert."

Normally, I would have, since I hadn't had any yet today; the chocolate was breakfast. But she'd made me feel uneasy. I'd always thrown those woo-woo words in the course of my job, but I never believed any of them. Now I couldn't maintain that ignorance anymore. I rejected the idea of fate—this baby chartered her own destiny, I felt sure, one minute at a time, an ongoing surprise, even to me. But that our paths had crossed again made me wonder.

On the way back to the courtroom, I thought of something I had to ask her. "What's a...harmonica conveyance?"

She threw her head back and laughed. A happy, tinkling sound that all the gods make, which she didn't utter nearly enough. "Do you mean, *harmonic convergence?* Shouldn't you know, Samantha, considering how you make your living?"

"I keep myself on a need-to-know basis. When I need something, I find a way to know it."

"It has to do with the alignment of the planets and the stars.

We're nearing a day when they'll be in the most favorable position we've seen for centuries, especially because it coincides with a full lunar eclipse. Anything will be possible at that time."

Sure it would. More hooey. I'd already forgotten the words.

At the courtroom door, Haggerty brought the conversation back to her ancestors. "Do you understand what I mean about the need for governing the gods? You can see what havoc a mortal terrorist can wreak." When she gestured toward the courtroom door, I understood that she meant the defendant beyond. "An evil god with unlimited power—there's no end to the pain he could cause."

"And Normal's normal?" I asked. "An ordinary mortal?"

Haggerty frowned. "He's not a god," she said cryptically.

What did that mean? "Is he guilty?"

She nodded emphatically. "Without a doubt. Not the least repentant, either. And it's strange, since he doesn't seem to feel any personal animosity for Senator Campbell."

"You can tell all that?" I asked, screwing up my face.

"Just barely," Haggerty muttered, then shrugged. "He erects no barriers. He's even more open than you are."

I'd heard enough. I didn't want to widen my window on her world, I wanted to shut it forever. I thought again about the events on the jet that morning. Someone from her world was reaching out to me. Well, her world or some other world. I could ask her about it, but I knew if she didn't want to answer, she wouldn't.

Maybe I'd let it go on, until whichever Celt was causing it showed his cards. What harm could come from waiting?

CHAPTER EIGHT

The trial finally recessed for the day. Though I hadn't noticed him hanging around when I escaped earlier, our friend, Baldy, appeared again and ushered us through the crowds filling the corridors. Downstairs, we pressed through the front door. But once outside on the plaza, Rand stopped and stared. The media had been cordoned off in an area not far away. On the raised podium before them stood a bank of microphones.

He marched off in that direction. Baldy frowned at me, but for once he looked more confused than angry. I hadn't known a press conference had been scheduled, either, but I didn't waste time worrying about it. I ran as fast as I could in those shoes, so I could stand at Rand's side when the cameras began snapping, wishing, not for the first time, that I could wear low heels without looking dorky.

Reporters clamored for his attention. Rand waved a royal finger in the direction of one of them.

"Mr. Riker," a woman in an ugly polyester dress asked in clipped tones of disapproval, "how does it feel to be on the side of the most unpopular man in the world?"

Rand laughed softly. "I'm not on any bloke's side…"

Exactly as I thought.

"…except the side of Justice."

Ooh! Good answer.

"What happened to the presumption of innocence?" Rand asked. "Are we lynching people now in the press?"

Duh! Where had he been for decades? I started to get the idea that this could be a one-question press conference, since he kept talking.

"I've been condemned throughout me career purely for the way I've dressed."

Strictly speaking, it was for the way he *un*dressed.

"When are we going to get past the superficialities?"

Never, I hoped. Where would I be if looks didn't count?

Rand finally let another reporter speak. I focused on giving each photographer a beguiling smile. You never know when the personal touch will pay off.

Then something happened to tilt my world. I'd made eye contact with every individual in that press corral. But while I stared off, to give the photographers a chance to capture my best side, a familiar—and unexpected—voice threw out a question.

"Yo, bro. What's with you and the bird?"

That voice belonged to Angus! If the Scottish burr alone didn't tell me that, the choice of vocabulary did. My head whirled around fast enough to give myself whiplash. Sure enough, there he was, in a spot that had been empty only a moment before. Apart from the Flower Power clothes he wore—Angus had an unfortunate fascination with the sixties—he looked great.

Imagine Michelangelo's statue of David, with the life force of all the ages breathed into it. Imagine the glitter of gold spun into silky, shoulder-length hair. Or skin with the radiant glints of bronze. Or eyes as blue as the most perfect sky, with the sparkle of pure silver in them. Imagine all of that, and you might have a weak approximation of Angus.

My knees began to tremble, and they drew in my racing heart and melting loins.

Rand's craggy face broke into a wide grin. He threw an arm across my shoulders and drew me close. "We're together," he announced to the world.

Decisions, decisions. On one hand, I didn't want Rand to get the wrong idea. But that was Angus out there asking the question. He needed to know I'd found someone else. On the other hand—there was no other hand. I tried to beam like the lovesick fool I'd been only months before, only this time with the guy holding me, not the one in the audience. I pressed my face against Rand's chest. Camera flashes went off. For once, I didn't care.

Rand and I came apart, and he went on answering questions. I stared across the plaza, trying to avoid those silver-flecked eyes. That was when the senator and his entourage emerged from the courthouse. Kenny and his wife, along with Haggerty and the two male security types I'd seen inside, and a guy in a suit, who directed the whole crew our way. An aide, I'd guess.

Suddenly, the world came to a stop. Well, Phoenix. Well, as much of Phoenix as I could see. Everything froze: People walking, birds in flight, leaves blowing in the breeze. Everything and everyone became absolutely still. Everyone, that is, apart from Angus,

MAGICAL ALIENATION

Haggerty and me.

Angus's handsome face registered stunned surprise. Did that mean he hadn't created the freeze? He dismissed his astonishment with a flex of his well-built shoulder. He had so many relatives capable of far greater stunts. He broke into a big grin and seemed to regard the fact that we were both free of it, as proof that we were Meant to Be. Angus was always saying we were Meant to Be. I distinctly heard the caps. Right—us, and the mermaid.

Haggerty didn't dismiss it as lightly. She frowned.

Everyone else remained as still as statues. Rand stood with his mouth open, a finger frozen mid-stab. The senator had been stilled with his lips in a funny-looking twist. Mrs. Kenny had been caught with her eyes narrowing at Haggerty.

One moment later, it ended. Rand's voice once again filled the great outdoors. The reporters made rustling sounds. And Kenny's little woman now directed her disapproval at Rand.

Who the hell was doing this?

My panic got brushed aside when I saw Senator Campbell striding our way.

"Mr. Riker!" Kenny called.

Rand turned his aristocratic stare the peasant's way. How dare a mere senator interrupt a rock star?

"Thanks for holding the fort on my press conference," Kenny said, as he slipped between Rand and me.

So it was Kenny's press conference. Rand didn't even have the grace to look chastened when he said, "They insisted."

Kenny gave his hand a "no matter" toss. "Honestly, I'm happy to share." He put finger quotes around *share*.

When the senator turned his head, I found myself staring through his glasses. No magnification there, at all. If his vision wasn't bad, why did he wear glasses? Judging by the way he was always pushing them up, they seemed to bother him.

With the loyalty of whores, the reporters shouted for Kenny, dropping Rand like a sandwich made from moldy bread. I felt sorry for Rand, when Kenny eased him aside at the microphones. But there was a reason why Devil Boy remained on top, even if he was two days older than T-Rex. He moved himself back into the center spot, albeit with less grace than Kenny.

"I'm happy to share, too, Senator Campbell. That's why I'd

like to invite you to join me for my interview on *The Maverick Report* this Friday."

The Maverick Report, hosted by TV journalist Deni Maverick, was the hottest program on cable news. The show prided itself on presenting today's most irreverent newsmakers. Rand fit the profile; Kenny, unless he took to streaking nude through the senate chamber, did not. Though Kenny's little woman kept giving her head negative shakes, he apparently decided to seize the one chance he had to get before the *Maverick* cameras.

After that, it seemed understood that they'd share the spotlight. But two was plenty for that little stage. I slipped away and joined Haggerty.

Angus hopped over one of the sawhorses corralling the media like a world-class hurdler.

"Sammy-girl—" he started to say.

Haggerty held her hand in a stop position. "Not now, Angus." Though Haggerty's mom had always shown a great fondness for him, Angus wasn't among the ancestors Haggerty admired. She turned to me. "Can you talk Devil Boy out of this joint-appearance?"

"Rand doesn't place a high value on my advice," I whispered, hoping Angus wouldn't hear.

She pinched her lips together. "Nothing good can come of this."

She worried too much. It was a TV show—what could possibly happen?

CHAPTER NINE

I couldn't suffer through another session in that courtroom. The next day I convinced Rand that I needed to buy some of the tools of my trade, since after I packed my clothes, there wasn't room in the plane for anything else. I called up a metaphysical store and ordered some essential oils, sage wands, crystals and tarot cards, along with candles and other stuff.

The clerk told me they were having a sale on spell kits and asked if I wanted any. I adore spell kits—with a kit, you don't have to remember what herbs and oils to combine with which colored candles; nor do you have to remember the lines of mumbo-jumbo to recite. Not that I'd ever had a spell work out the way it was supposed to, but some of my clients expected me to go through the motions. I ordered kits for prosperity, attraction and banishing spells. She also asked me if I wanted a love spell. Not likely.

I charged it all to Rand's credit card and asked them deliver the whole shebang to our hotel. I spent the rest of the day at the pool, sucking down margaritas. A spiritual advisor needs to commune with nature.

We were booked into some five star resort in Scottsdale, in the Presidential Suite, no less. Though we had separate bedrooms within the suite, I'd expected another come on from Rand before we turned in. But he disappeared into his own room, without so much as a "good night." Still, even if it made me feel like someone's old maid aunt, I locked my door, though I never even heard him try the knob.

Over our room service breakfast, we were both too taken with our photos in the newspaper to say much of anything.

Very early on Friday morning, we returned to the courthouse, where *The Maverick Report* would be taped. Immediately after the taping, Rand and I would head to Sedona, for the dreaded benefit concert to support Normal Frankly, which was scheduled for that night. Unsure when I'd get a chance to change, I dressed that morning the way I wanted to be seen at the concert.

Baldy and No-Neck didn't show up with the Yukon to pick us up as promised. Word must have filtered down from their leader that they weren't to do anything in support of Normal. So? They couldn't even call? Since the sun had scarcely risen, I shivered in my gown, while waiting outside the hotel. Phoenix gets pretty warm during the day even in spring, but the temperatures drop when the sun goes down. Fortunately, the hotel produced a limo for us.

At the courthouse, the *Maverick* crew filled the receiving entrance behind the courthouse, while setting up shots inside in the courtroom. They'd provided trailer dressing rooms for both Rand and Kenny. Since nobody seemed to give a thought to me, I just hung around, getting in everyone's way.

At one point, a guy taping cable to the floor, said, "Can you get off that cable, sweetheart? You're cutting off—" He stopped speaking when he caught sight of my outfit.

The dress I wore today was a medieval gown I'd bought from some touring attraction that had shut down. The floor-length gray silk dress had looked too simple for me, so I covered it with red and black graffiti; snotty jibes written in Middle English. I'd also placed my wimple properly on my head, but my long, curly blonde hair was so wild, it kept knocking that pointy hat askew. Now I probably looked more like some crazed lunatic who'd been mugged by the Middle Ages.

When he looked at me, the guy's mouth twitched. I wasn't sure whether he was holding back laughter or tears.

Though the hour was early, there was more activity at the rear of the courthouse than merely the prep for *The Maverick Report* taping. This was also the day when the judge and jury would visit Normal's Sedona-area complex, to see where he cooked up his deadly brew. The judge and jury, and the legal teams, assembled in a couple of vans, along with bailiffs and some extra security guys. Only after everyone else was loaded, and the security contingent ready, did the centerpiece of the whole shebang emerge. A shackled Normal Frankly stepped from a jail bus.

As he shuffled along, Normal's flat gaze floated over the crowd gathered there He projected a detached attitude, like a scientist studying a bug. His tongue wet his rubbery lips. For a moment, his eyes connected with mine. A shiver went through me that raised goose bumps on my arms. That bozo scared the crap outta me.

Haggerty had said he wasn't a god—did that mean he was a man? What else was there?

CHAPTER TEN

The creature from Area 51 felt so weak. He hadn't been able to pull as much magical power from his benefactor as he'd hoped. Not without alerting her anyway. Why wasn't the facilitator distracting her? Not that she had much power to spare. She clearly didn't understand that it was only by using her energies regularly that their strength could be built up. He needed that force now more than ever. There were so many strands to keep in play, such coordination, that it sapped him. And he was so close. How tragic would it be if he managed to hold it all together this long, only to lose it on the brink?

Perhaps his benefactor wouldn't notice if he bled off a bit more from her.

There were other forces entering the fray now. Conflicting forces, that, in his present state, he could no longer identify. Would he have the power to fight them all? Or any of them?

CHAPTER ELEVEN

They'd set the interview up in an actual courtroom, with Rand seated behind the defense table and Kenny and his wife at the prosecutor's. The host, Deni Maverick, microphone in hand, strolled up the center aisle, as if she were hosting a talk show before an audience. I'd argued that it would look more balanced if I took the seat next to Rand, or even one in the empty spectator area. Since I now stood *behind* the cameras, you can guess how well that went.

Deni paused between those tables. The hotshot reporter wore a suit today that fit her only slightly more loosely than Rand's red paint had often covered him. When she moved, her oversized breasts strained at her jacket like a pair of cats fighting to break out of a sack.

I couldn't say how far we were into what would be an hour-long interview when it aired. This gig was so excruciatingly dull, life ceased to move forward. Granted, I had a low boredom threshold, but I wasn't the only one who thought so. Though her fortyish face had been pulled tighter than Scarlet O'Hara's corset, Deni found this interview disturbing enough to allow a frown to form between her brows.

Who could blame her? The love-fest Rand and Kenny were conducting was sweet enough to cause a cavity epidemic. If it weren't for Kenny's ridiculously inappropriate finger quotes, there wouldn't even have been anything to laugh about.

"Come on, guys," she said. "Do you expect anyone to believe that before today you two were sworn enemies?"

"I'm gobsmaked that you think that, Deni," Rand said.

Enough with the Aussie lingo, dude. They hadn't lit Rand well. His wrinkles stood out like a relief map of the Grand Canyon. Given the heat he took about his age, I always wondered why he hadn't gone the knife-route as Deni had. But I read a magazine interview with him in which he'd said, "There's no point in *looking* young. The trick is *being* young, eternally."

Despite his wealth and fame, not even Rand Riker could pull that off.

"I bet there are more areas than you think where the senator and I agree." Rand glanced at Kenny. "Such as the rule of law."

Though Kenny wasn't that much younger than Rand, his eagerness to please made him seem like a kid allowed to sit at the grownups' table.

"You're right there, Mr. Riker. We're both proponents of the First Amendment," Kenny said with a twinkle in the eyes behind his glasses. Rand's attorneys had always argued his near-nudity on First Amendment grounds. "You didn't think we'd share so much, did you, Deni?"

Gag me. The only person who seemed to feel the anger the show had counted on was Mrs. Kenny. She did the weirdest thing. She kept stroking Kenny's arm, while glaring at Rand, as if to say that Kenny had what Rand never would. What? The love of a good woman, if that was how that uptight babe would describe herself. As if Rand Riker would give her a second look. What could Kelly Campbell possibly have to offer him?

When Kenny extended an on-air invitation to Rand for drinks at their Sedona home before this evening's benefit concert, I had to get out of there. I like sugar as much as the next gal—unless the next gal mainlines it—but those two made my glands hurt. I slipped out the courtroom door.

With sugar in mind, I thought I'd find some of the real stuff. Though the crew had set up a craft table with goodies outside the courtroom, the courthouse employees had picked it clean. I headed instead to the cafeteria.

Despite halls that were crowded today, I spotted that cat I'd seen the other day. He had wedged himself into a little spot where the corridor bent, sitting with his big furry feet placed neatly before him. I swear he tilted his head my way.

"Mellencamp!" I cried.

He blinked his green-gold eyes in response.

Some hefty woman plowed into me. "Feel free to stop anywhere," she snapped.

"I will." Sarcasm just beads off me.

When I looked back to that corner, the cat was gone.

Did he live in the courthouse? Like a mascot. Or mas-cat? I abandoned the cafeteria and prowled the floor, hoping to catch sight of him, but I never did.

With my gaze focused on the distance, I almost stepped in a mess at one point. Some rusty water leaked out from under a utility closet door and spread across the floor. That stuff would have ruined the sparkly ruby red shoes I wore today. Fortunately, at the last second I stopped myself from stepping in it.

I finally headed for the cafeteria. Today I had apple pie a la mode. It was breakfast, after all; I needed my fruit and dairy. I hopped over the rusty lake in the hall on the way back, with a little regret that I never found the cat.

I did find Haggerty outside the courtroom. Considering she'd once told me she never got sick, she sure didn't look like someone in peak health today. The dark circles under her eyes stretched to her knees. Did she get any sleep last night?

"Find your mom yet, Haggerty?"

"She's still blocking me." She yawned.

I noticed a cell phone peeking from the pocket of her suit jacket. "Have you considered using…you know…regular means to try to reach her?" I pointed to the phone.

Always afraid of someone catching on to what she really was, she threw an anxious glance over her shoulder. "I've called the shaman's relatives, but they still haven't seen her."

At least she hadn't phoned the departed shaman himself. If she could do that, I didn't want to know.

"She's a great mother, really, but she can be so exasperating," Haggerty said. "I swear, sometimes she reminds me of—" With a sharp look at me, she stopped abruptly.

Whoa! Was her mom really like me?

Haggerty gave her head a swift shake, as if to dispel that thought. "Her shenanigans are distracting me, when I should be concentrating on security."

"You worry too much." I flipped my hand toward the courtroom door. "The senator is safe in there." From everything except expressing his undying love for Rand.

She shook her head. "No, there are forces out there… But I'm unable to tap into them." She amended that. "Too distracted, that is."

I noticed the vultures that had stripped the craft table had missed the last donut. I couldn't leave it there—it would feel rejected. I grabbed it before anyone beat me to it.

The glaze cracked when I took a bite, and bits of it stuck to my face. While I tried to capture the flaky sugar with my tongue, someone clutched my waist and spun me around. Angus.

His classically handsome features pinched together unattractively. "Sammy, I can't stand the thought of you and that bloke together. If you don't give him up, I'll turn him into something. A frog, or a flea." His silver-flecked eyes brightened with inspiration. "Or—"

"Angus—stop!" I shouted, before he could carry out his threat. Let Rand write my check first.

Angus pulled me close. My resolve melted along with my smoldering libido. If Haggerty could see that Rand meant nothing to me, why couldn't Angus? His powers were infinitely stronger than hers. Was it possible that love actually blinded him?

"Stop blaming Rand, Angus. Us breaking up, that was your fault. You and that…that—"

He gave his golden hair a toss. "Ah, my girl, I'm crazy about you. But you can't expect a god to give up all his bits of fun."

There it was—the one compromise I couldn't make. If the idea of Rand and me incensed him, why couldn't he see that I found it equally impossible to share him? Just seeing him now hurt my poor battered heart.

I pushed him away. "Angus, if you care for me, you'll leave me alone."

"Sammy, you know you don't mean that." His grin took on a lecherous quality. "You *really* know it."

Was that supposed to mean something? "Haggerty, tell him I do, willya?" I looked to her for help, but she just stood with her shoulder pressed against the wall, staring out as if in a trance.

"See, Annie knows," Angus said.

With a gaze that vacant, I wasn't sure what she knew.

A janitor ambled past, pushing one of those buckets on wheels. "Sir, there's some spilled water on the floor outside a closet," I said, describing where I'd seen it.

The man assured me he'd clean it up when he could.

Pointedly avoiding Angus, I said to Haggerty, "Fortunately, it was red like my shoes, but that water would have wrecked them."

At last she stirred. "You saw reddish fluid on the floor?" With a gasp, she became alert. "Show me where."

Before we could take a step, she slumped again. Her breathing became ragged, and her face pinched with pain. I remembered what she said about the forces out there. Was she tapping into them? My dismissal of her concerns suddenly seemed stupid.

"Angus, help me." Haggerty's voice sounded shallow. It took a lot for her to ask for his help.

Angus wrapped his large mitts around her fragile shoulders. "Steady now, Annie." He closed his eyes.

In an instant, she took one deep breath, clearly having been released from the pain. I stole a glance at Angus. He frowned, staring off as Haggerty had, as if he now saw whatever she'd briefly seen.

Haggerty gave my arm a tug. "Show me this water, Samantha."

Though I was the one who had seen it, she stayed in the lead. Yanking me forward, making me run faster than I should in those shoes, while I shouted directions. From behind, I heard the sound of Angus's feet, dressed in old-fashioned Desert Boots, keeping pace with us.

We made it to the closet before the janitor. Haggerty looked at the liquid draining from under the door. She rattled the doorknob, but the door was locked. If people hadn't been around, she'd have found a different way to open that door, one not available to us mortals. But once the janitor appeared, she simply ordered him to unlock it.

After removing a ring of keys from his belt loop, he sorted through them at a sluggish pace. When he finally unlocked the door, an impatient Haggerty eased him aside and yanked the door open.

I gasped. Three men I thought I recognized as guards had been stripped to their underwear and crushed tightly together in there, like some grisly pretzel. I only saw a bullet hole on one forehead, but since they were all bloody, I assumed they had all been shot. Their combined weight had knocked over a bucket of water at the bottom of the closet when their bodies pressed down on it.

Shock stuns some people into silence. It makes me ask ditzy questions. "Why are they in their underwear?"

"Because someone needed their uniforms to blend into the courthouse caravan heading north. They took out the legitimate guards to substitute fake ones." Haggerty had already yanked out her cell phone and placed a call. "Agent Gerard?" she asked after a moment. "François? Is everything all right up there?"

I watched as horror grew in her eyes.

"How many?" she asked. Then, "Who...?"

When she disconnected, she said in a ragged tone, "You're really on the wrong side this time, Samantha. Normal Frankly's militia friends stormed the court's caravan. They killed some of the people and took the rest hostage. They're holed up now in Normal's Sedona compound."

Before I could react, her phone rang. "Yes," she demanded. She raised one well-arched brow, the way she did when she was surprised. After ending her call, she said, "More innocent by-standers—in the confusion, they also took hostage an army convoy that was headed in the opposite direction."

"Why?"

She shrugged. "Probably because they could, because the idea of a bunch of toy soldiers flaunting their power over legitimate military personnel was too delicious a coincidence for them to pass up."

"Poor slobs," I said. "What lousy timing those soldier boys had."

Haggerty shared an uneasy look with her ancestor. "The militia doubtless hadn't intended to attack a military caravan, but whether it was just bad timing...I wonder about that. Everything happens for a reason."

CHAPTER TWELVE

Shock also makes me babble. "This doesn't make any sense. How could anyone take those court people hostage? You didn't see the firepower they brought along with them."

Haggerty's pretty face knotted in concentration. "Some of their guards were working for the other side—militia members must have been wearing the uniforms of those men we found in the closet. And the army caravan was probably taken even before they understood why traffic had slowed." She shrugged. "Besides, sometimes guns are no match for gas."

"Gasoline?"

She rolled her eyes. "A gaseous substance. The Resident Agent in Sedona thinks they were knocked out by some kind of gas."

She marched up the hall, with that determined stride of hers, while placing another call.

"No, I won't hold!" Haggerty said. "I'm an agent with—" She shook the phone in anger. "He put me on hold," she said to the universe more than to me.

"Are they dead?" I asked.

She re-dialed. "The gas just knocked them out. The victims weren't killed until the militia members shot them. They left the dead all over the road."

The shock finally rendered me mute.

Haggerty continued up the hall. "Don't you dare put me on hold again," she warned someone at the other end of her call.

I remembered watching those people pile into the vans a few hours earlier: The judge, the jury, and various court employees. Some had been joking, while others were serious. But they'd all been alive.

I also thought about Baldy and No-Neck. That was some good joke they played on everyone. Obviously, the militia's denunciation of Normal had been a smokescreen. I should have realized that, since those two clearly couldn't stand Rand and me. Well, me. My steps sputtered to a halt with an awful thought: What about Rand? Had he been in on this attack?

I finally noticed Angus hovering at my side. His silver-glinted eyes showed sympathy. "Some funky stuff going down here, huh, Sammy-girl?" he said. "How should we help Annie?"

His next girlfriend really should do something about his slang. Maybe the mermaid could teach him to talk Fish. Angus didn't care about Haggerty's troubles. Like most of the *Danaans*, our world's petty concerns didn't faze him. He was just trying to get on my good side.

"Not now, Angus."

The gods invented mood swings. Even during a roaring PMS siege, my feelings had never shifted as fast. His magnificent face darkened now, and those silver flecks flashed like lightning bolts. I left him to deal with it alone.

Haggerty stood at a conference room door, which the janitor was unlocking for her. I wandered back to the courtroom, to check on the interview. Someone had refreshed the craft table. I sucked down a donut, but for once, I didn't enjoy it.

I eased the courtroom door open. The interview was still progressing. A cameraman with a thick brown unibrow put his finger to his lips to remind me to be quiet. Angus came up beside me and draped his arm across my shoulder. I wanted to shake it off, only I didn't think I could do it without making noise. Honestly, that was the only reason why I didn't.

I couldn't focus on the interview now. I kept staring at Rand, and wondering.

As I did, the strangest thing happened. Rand's image began to flicker. One second he was the Rand Riker the whole world knew; the next, a frog. A frog! An honest-to-heavens amphibian. One moment, his thick lips moved, and words came out. Then, the frog's tongue shot forward and caught a fly. Even stranger, nobody else reacted, even though the frog kept flashing.

As I reeled, my wimple thumped against the doorframe. The cameraman sent me a frown that caused his unibrow to wiggle like a caterpillar with the D.T.s. Any other time that would have cracked me up. Now, I scarcely noticed. Finally, though, I made a connection I would have made earlier, if my brain weren't already in meltdown. I looked at Angus. His happy nod acknowledged that he'd created that little show for my benefit. A preview of what he could do to Rand if he chose to.

I shut the courtroom door. "Leave Rand alone, Angus," I hissed. "Trust me, he's in Haggerty's sights now. She'll take care of him."

I went to join her. When I turned back to make sure Angus wasn't following, I saw he was gone. Good. That was what I wanted. Really, it was.

I found Haggerty seated at the conference room table, now on a landline phone, making notes on a yellow pad. "Good," she said, after listening for a moment. "Keep them there." She pressed the hold key and glanced at me. "Samantha, they stopped the buses transporting the Devil's Disciple band and crew at the I-10 roadblock. Weren't they afraid they'd miss the concert?"

"That's why Rand travels alone. He says his band-mates often roll in just as they're about to go on stage, higher than the clouds. Amazingly, it doesn't affect their performance."

"I've heard their music. If the audience wasn't even more inebriated, it would never work." Haggerty's finger released the hold key. "Have someone question them," she said into the phone. "Then send them back to L. A."

"No!" I shouted. "What about tonight's concert?"

It was good to know I could still shock her. "Tonight's concert is history, Samantha. You want to hold a fundraiser for the man who orchestrated the murders of a federal courthouse staff and a U.S. Army contingent?" She gave her head an incredulous shake.

I hadn't considered Normal, but it made sense. He must have been behind the carnage.

"Normal's back in his compound?" I asked.

She shrugged. "That's a likely guess. He wasn't among the dead."

Haggerty asked where we were scheduled to stay in Sedona. I told her the name of the swanky inn that Devil's Disciple had reserved exclusively for the band.

She made a note on her pad. After a moment, she placed the pen down and flexed her fingers. Any other god would have let the pen go on, writing unassisted. Not Haggerty. I headed for the door.

"Where do you think you're going?" she asked.

I shrugged. "I thought maybe I'd just head home." If tonight's concert was kaput, would Rand still pay me for the days I'd worked for him?

She directed as nasty a look my way as I ever remember getting, and most people consider me a fraud. "Nice try, Samantha, but you're not going anywhere. I need you to act for me...as you did last time."

To do the psychic tap dance, she meant, so she could give her superiors the benefit of her special skills, without them knowing the information had come from her. She didn't like the arrangement. It wasn't even that effective. Some people doubt the value of supernatural insights when they come from me. Go figure.

But the Bureau hadn't paid me last time, unless you count "the appreciation of a grateful nation," and I didn't. "What if I won't?"

"You don't have a choice. When this interview ends, we'll all take a helicopter to Sedona, where you should consider yourself under house arrest in your hotel as a material witness."

"A witness to what?" I shrieked.

"That remains to be seen."

CHAPTER THIRTEEN

Haggerty mobilized fast. While the TV crew packed up, she drew Rand and Kenny off to the side of the courtroom. I wasn't close enough to hear what anyone said, but I guessed from their reactions that she told them what the militia had done. When Kenny covered his head with his hands, his grief and anger looked overwhelming.

Rand never lost control. His ruddy complexion did take on a greenish tinge, but maybe that was because, even after the image stopped flickering, I couldn't look at him without seeing that frog. Even if I couldn't hear their conversation, I felt sure I'd know the moment when Haggerty told Rand that, while his band wasn't coming, he'd have to accompany her to Sedona and consider himself in custody. I figured he'd pull a lawyer right from his pocket. Surprisingly, he seemed to acquiesce. Too bad he nodded so deeply that his hair fell forward, and I couldn't read his expression.

Had he given in too easily? As Haggerty turned away, Rand directed such a withering sneer at her, it shook me to the core. When you consider that I protect my core with more than a few pounds of cynicism, it takes a lot to reach it. Did he just dislike her, or was he finding it hard to hide that he knew about the assault on the court caravan even before she told him? Was self-promotion really at the root of his association with Normal Frankly? What else could be involved?

Moments after the TV crew departed, we were whisked to a small airport, where Rand, Kenny, Kelly and me, along with Haggerty and a couple of others on the Campbell security detail, boarded a large helicopter. I balked at leaving my stuff behind, until Haggerty assured me the Scottsdale resort had already packed our luggage and was forwarding it to Rand's hotel in Sedona. Somehow in the shuffle to find seats, Kelly ended up next to Rand. She crossed her arms over her chest, rather than share the armrest, like some spiteful kid. It didn't help, though. Rand's well-built arms often connected with her stick-like ones. It must have pissed her off.

I didn't realize we were ready to take off until the helicopter levitated. Whoa! What a rush, like a burst of air up your skirt. Way more fun than a plane, even if nobody served pricey chocolates and apple champagne.

I didn't pay much attention to the stretches of desert that passed below us, except to notice that we flew overland, not following the route a car might travel. So I was unprepared for what suddenly rose up before us.

Sedona.

Man, was this a day of surprises. They came at me in every way possible.

Visually, the Sedona landscape, with its craggy red rock formations, was a staggering sight. I knew the rocks would be red, but I didn't know *how* vivid they would look, nor that their color would pop against a sky bluer than anything my smog-trained eyes had ever seen. Nor the way all the shades of green, everything from sage to forest, in low bushes and small trees, would stand out in stark contrast against the shocking red dirt.

I felt as if I'd been transported to Mars, only a better Mars than the one in the pictures that crappy little Tonka truck had sent back to Earth.

I'd seen photos, and I thought I knew what to expect, but those shots didn't begin to capture Sedona's awesome scope. I'd even planned to move there if I could ever save the bucks, but only because I considered it a place where people appreciated a good fake psychic like me. I never thought that rugged country locale would take hold of a city girl like me.

What really hit me with a wallop was the way it made me feel emotionally. Someone once described Sedona to me as "the place of the gods." Naturally, I'd dismissed that as romantic tripe. "The place of the woo-woo marks" had seemed more like it. Yet it floored me now to find myself feeling so awestruck by a place I had still only seen through the helicopter window.

Never would I have expected this to happen to a hardened cynic like me.

The true nature of the woman seated beside me suddenly struck me. I didn't think reverentially about the gods when I was with them. They had been merely my lover, my playmates and the woman determined to mess with my life. But in this strangely sacred place, I felt a fleeting awe of Haggerty. I hoped she hadn't sensed it. Especially not after she made a crack about my wimple, which I had to stuff between my knees for the flight.

And yet, I also felt a shiver of dread pass through me. The fear that if I ever set foot on that red dirt out there, I'd regret it, that my whole life would be changed, and not for the better.

What kind of bunkum was that? Haggerty was the one who got the intuitive impressions, not me. I tripped over the present, one moment at a time. Besides, millions of tourists came here every year, and they had fun. Why should it be any different for me?

I caught Haggerty's questioning gaze, and I realized she had arranged this little detour for me. None of our fellow passengers even glanced out the windows. I gave her a big goofy grin of thanks, and this time I meant it.

After giving me that view of Sedona, the helicopter swung south of town, assuming my sense of direction still worked, giving us a flash of Normal's compound, which wasn't far outside the city. I couldn't judge the size of the place, but I'd heard in court that the property stretched to over thirty acres. The towering red rock wall that slashed across the land and the several large, windowless buildings that had been built right into that rocky cliff just made it look more compact.

A heavy metal fence, topped with barbed wire, surrounded the property; courtroom testimony had established that fence as electrically charged. There was also supposed to be a monster generator on the grounds, so the Feds couldn't even neutralize that fence by cutting the power. Automated rifles and rocket launchers had been mounted on all the structures, which were aimed in every direction. The place was said to be impregnable.

After a quick eyeballing of the compound, we traveled a short distance to a four-lane country highway with a wide median running through it, which we hovered over. That must have been where the assault on the two caravans took place. The dead were gone now, but dark patches stained the pavement. The road was also marred with blackened tire streaks where various vehicles had been brought to sudden halts.

The Feds had enclosed a large section of the road by ringing it with crime scene tape. Only one of the four lanes was open now. Cops directed traffic, alternating between north and southbound cars, allowing only a few of the vehicles that stretched endlessly in both directions through at a time. Hundreds of lookie-loos had gathered on both sides of that barrier.

MAGICAL ALIENATION

After Haggerty had seen enough, she spoke to the pilot through the headset she wore, directing him back to Normal's compound. The helicopter followed a car's route this time, flying above one dirt road after another, until he finally set us down on a dusty patch outside the compound gate. The instant we touched down, Haggerty was on her feet, ready to open the door. She dragged me out with her. I struggled to put my wimple back on, as she pulled me across the open field, while the helicopter's blades kicked up so much red dirt, one of Rand's famous red capes might have flopped over my eyes.

Haggerty stopped at a parked truck. Apart from the satellite dish on the roof, it looked like an ordinary delivery truck. She pulled the rear door open. Electronic monitoring stations lined both sides of the interior. Two wilted-looking guys slouched before consoles on either side, while a short, wiry man positively bristled with energy in the center aisle.

I lumbered in after Haggerty. It got a little crowded with the three of us there, but I couldn't budge once my wimple became wedged against the ceiling.

"Special Agent Gerard?" Haggerty asked. "I'm Agent Annabelle Haggerty."

Gerard, huh? She'd already told me François Gerard was the Flagstaff Resident Agent. She explained that smaller cities don't have field offices like Los Angeles and Phoenix and other large urban centers. They have lone Resident Agents. When small towns like Sedona need a Bureau presence, the closest Resident Agent is often assigned.

The bristling guy, the palest person I had ever seen, turned my way. I had no prejudices, I swear. For a fake psychic, marks came in all races, shapes and sizes. But albinos like François just weirded me out. Give 'em a transfusion, I say, rush them to a tanning booth. Something.

The albino curled his prissy lip and said, "Agent Haggerty, can you tell me why you thought bringing along Guinevere on acid would add anything to this explosive situation?"

I might have taken offense from that, if it weren't such a good description of my outfit. I searched for some humor in his icy blue eyes, but he must have been too droll to let it show.

"She'll grow on you, Agent Gerard," Haggerty said

dismissively. "Any progress here?"

"Nothing from them, nothing from us," one of the guys at a console said. "Washington is sending an expert to negotiate."

Haggerty grimaced. "That was to be expected, but it's our baby until the expert arrives, right?"

"Wrong," François said. "Our orders are to have no contact with the militia."

"What is Washington thinking? Hostages' lives are at stake," she said.

"There's something else going on here, beyond the obvious," François said in a soft, pensive tone. "Militia units typically buy guns, sell meth and practice war games. These guys create gases nobody has ever seen. As to why we're being kept in the dark…I wish I knew."

Haggerty shrugged. "So we'll take the investigation in a different direction. Starting with Mr. Riker."

François confirmed that he'd set up a local office, having recruited additional agents and staff from the Phoenix field office. Speaking into a radio clipped to his collar, he ordered someone to escort Rand to the Bureau office, where he and Haggerty would join him, while instructing someone else to take the Campbells to their Sedona weekend home.

"Let's go, Samantha," Haggerty said.

After freeing my wimple, I started for the door.

"Guinevere's included?" François asked.

"Samantha is quite a gifted psychic," Haggerty said with a straight face. "She's played a role in a number of cases the L.A. field office has taken on."

His pale eyes narrowed to slits. "You do things differently in California."

Considering some of the beings that worked there, he didn't know the half of it.

François, Haggerty and I climbed into an open Jeep. Rather than get in line with all the civilian traffic, a cop waved François onto the bumpy, uncultivated medium, which allowed him to weave around crowds of people and other cars. I just hoped I didn't fall out during the five or six mile drive back to Sedona.

MAGICAL ALIENATION

Why did Haggerty want me along? She didn't seem to be getting any psychic impressions that I could pass off as my own. Now that I'd seen the aftermath of the violence, I wondered about her meager visions. She had known Normal was guilty of trying to kill Kenny. She'd also sensed something about dark forces. But she hadn't suspected the way Normal's militia friends would come to his aid. She was starting to seem even less sensitive than me.

The Bureau had set up operations in a small structure on 89A, the main highway into Sedona. The single-story wooden structure looked like it might have been a home at one time, but had since been converted for commercial use. I didn't know what kind of business had rented that space before the FBI, but the rose carpeting and pink flowered walls made me think it must have been something frilly. The Bureau's utilitarian furnishings and their electronic gear gave it a real yin-yang feel.

Haggerty deposited her things in a small office. With a crick of her finger, she directed me to follow her down a hall. At least her powers were working well enough to find her way around that joint without having to ask. She opened a closed door, painted in magenta enamel, and we both went in. Security monitors on a counter along the far wall displayed video of both the highway and the entrance to Normal's compound. A wooden table filled the rest of the space. Rand sat on one side of it, and François had taken a chair on the other side where he could monitor the video, while also scrutinizing Rand.

I found it curious that Rand still hadn't called for a lawyer. Or even me, his spiritual advisor. While his relaxed posture seemed unconcerned, I saw even greater strain in the aging lines of his face than he'd shown on the plane.

Haggerty took the seat next to François. Unsure of where I belonged, I slipped into one beside Rand.

François slapped his hands against the table. They were unexpectedly large for such a small man, with strong ropey muscles. He obviously used hand lotion on them—small flecks of the white goo remained between his fingers. Did that pasty faced-guy just want to feel pretty?

"Why did you agree to help Normal Frankly?" François demanded. "I don't buy the promotional angle you've been selling."

Rand shrugged. "Can't see why not. I give people the controversy they expect from me."

"So you're merely self-serving, huh, Riker? Too bad that after you announced your support for Normal Frankly, the ticket sales went *down*." An angry flush brought a welcome bit of color to François's waxy face.

Rand glanced at Haggerty. "Yo, luv. Can you rustle me up a coldie?"

Both agents stared at him.

"You know, amber fluid," Rand snapped. When they still didn't react, he said, "A beer. Can't you Yanks understand English out here beyond the black stump?"

I thought he was laying on the Aussie bit kinda thick, considering he'd lived more of his life here than in his homeland. Was that the extent of his act?

"Special Agent Haggerty is not your waitress," François said. But then he added with a sigh, "Maybe we could all use a break." Through his collar radio, he ordered someone to bring coffee, not beer, for everyone.

When François turned back to Rand, he seemed unsure of how to proceed, so he directed his irritation at me. "Annabelle, do we really need Guinevere here?"

That "Guinevere" was getting old. What's the point of dressing creatively if people refuse to appreciate it?

Haggerty laughed, but she insisted I stay.

A male staffer eventually arrived with a tray of coffee containers from some coffeehouse. Not Soma Café, of course—I'd heard Sedona didn't have one. Generally, I supported independence, but not when it came to Soma Café. I took a gulp of the black coffee. Within minutes, the jolt of caffeine hit me like a shot of electricity, which never happened from Soma Cafs, yet somehow regular coffee didn't make me feel as good.

François started in on Rand again. Finally, eons after he'd begun to show strain, Rand snapped, "Look, the sight of Normal Frankly makes me skin crawl." And that was from a guy who sometimes used snakes in his act. "I didn't *want* to help him, I was ordered to."

"By whom?" François demanded in a voice as frosty as his complexion.

"No idea. But I received a mighty convincing threat."

"How was the threat delivered?" Haggerty asked, her voice

anxious and low.

A smirk flickered across Rand's thick lips. "You'd never believe me."

"Try us," François said.

Haggerty stiffened. I had a feeling she feared it hadn't come through the US Post Office.

CHAPTER FOURTEEN

The carnage appalled him. The creature from Area 51 had seen so much in his long existence, but the depths to which these pitiful beings could sink never failed to astonish him.

There hadn't been much warning to the assault. Gas had been released around the caravan headed the other way, as well as his own convoy. It hadn't affected him, of course, though he felt so weak, it scarcely mattered. To save some power, he took a risk he'd never taken before, to marshal what little energy he had left.

Though the militia hadn't intentionally targeted the military vehicles transporting him, he gathered, neither did they let them pass. The doppelgangers would denounce regulation soldiers as their enemies, when they probably actually feared the soldiers' superiority.

After the gaseous cloud's release, the militia began firing random shots. Killing this one and sparing that one, simply because they could. While the being from Area 51 had always believed life should be all about enjoyment, he also considered it too important to be shed lightly.

They had moved his cage beyond a gate that clanged heavily and put it into a room where they gathered the other hostages. He heard their voices beyond his cage. The hostages from the other group surmised that they were being kept at what had been their destination. His own escorts sounded lost—his charm was still keeping them confused.

The creature wasn't much clearer, but even in his weakened state, he felt the presence of rocks quite strongly. He had to hope that they'd arrived at his destination. Just to be sure, perhaps he could siphon off a bit more strength from his benefactor.

A door rattled. He felt a spike in fear from the other hostages—someone had entered their prison. Cries went up instantly, with some demanding their freedom, while others begged for their lives.

The newcomer shouted, "Shuddup, alla youse. No one's going anywhere." The words were crude, the accent brusque and anything but local.

MAGICAL ALIENATION

Someone tapped the creature's cage. "Who's in here?" Brusque Voice asked.

"What do you care?" someone else said. That voice belonged to Private Hanover, one of his regular guards. The other soldiers called him Handy Hanover, because that slick young man could steal anything anyone wanted from the base's supplies and sell it at a premium.

"The enemy of our enemy is our friend," Brusque Voice said. He sounded as if he were quoting something he may not have fully understood. *"Open it up."*

"Can't. The prisoner is welded in there." The creature heard a smirk in Hanover's tone. *"You probably killed the only person who could easily open it."*

Irony had always been one of the being's favorite pleasures. He allowed himself to drift off for a moment, savoring his amusement. He failed to notice that someone—Brusque Voice, most likely—looked through the window in his titanium shell. It was only when he saw dark, unfamiliar eyes staring back at him that fear shot through him.

The eyes went away. The creature held his breath, as the scenario he most feared played out. Why hadn't he been more careful? Why had he taken the risk of appearing in his genuine form?

"Wait," Hanover said. *"You didn't see anything strange in there?"*

Brusque Voice hesitated. *"I'm not explaining myself to you, soldier boy."* After a moment, he asked, *"Whattaya mean by 'strange'?"*

Hanover laughed. *"I'll tell the guy in charge. Take me to him—I've got something to deal."*

"You're not going nowhere," Brusque Voice said.

The creature heard a grunt, as air whooshed out of someone. A moment later a door opened and closed.

Brusque Voice's unwillingness to deal with Hanover had bought the creature some time. But he feared he had just made the worst mistake of his long life.

CHAPTER FIFTEEN

Rand's questioning went on. Even after his admission that someone forced him to support Normal, he still refused to divulge how the warning had come, insisting that nobody would believe him. If he only knew the stuff Haggerty and I were used to believing.

François lost it. "Enough with your games. Tell me now, Riker, or you'll find yourself in federal lock-up, wrapped in so many charges, it'll take your lawyer a month to sort through them."

Rand's world famous tongue flickered out and licked his chapped lips. "Could I have some water?" His tone sounded remarkably humble.

Haggerty left, returning with a Styrofoam cup of water. Though Rand accepted it, he didn't take a sip, he just wrapped his hands around it. The water level rose depending on how tightly he squeezed it.

"One of me cats went missing a few weeks ago," Rand said at last.

He didn't mean ordinary kitties, like that sweet guy I met at the courthouse. Rand was known for keeping a pride of bobcats in his Beverly Hills mansion.

"Normally that wouldn't worry me. They wander," he went on.

Weren't his neighbors lucky?

"One night I was chatting on the phone with my roadie—when the cat just popped into the room. Instantly." Shaky hands lifted the cup to his lips. After a greedy drink, he blurted, "Bandit, me cat—he was encased in a block of ice!"

Ooh, no. We'd seen that before. Haggerty's narrowed eyes briefly met mine. François alone seemed unfazed by it. He reacted with a sardonic twist of his lips, as if to say that Rand should be capable of a smarter lie.

"Uh-huh. Let's review this: The cat returned in a block of ice that popped into the room." Despite François's droll tone, his hand slipped from the table, hovering instead, where his sidearm was hooked to his belt. "So, where was the extortion message? Stuck to the ice?"

Rand released a shaky breath. "It was written in fire that rose out of the ice and hovered above it."

Fire letters? That was a new one. My heart thudded erratically in my chest.

François continued to lace ordinary speech with sarcasm. "Fire writing? You were able to read it okay?"

A bit of Rand's spirit returned. "It helps that the walls of me home are all black."

I cleared my throat. "What happened to the cat? Is he still frozen?" The last person I'd seen encased in ice had never melted.

"Good question, Guinevere." François didn't hold back on the sarcasm with me, either, but for once I didn't care.

"I was pretty shaken by that ice, you know?" Rand said. "So I had a few drinks...did some...stuff. I guess I passed out. In the morning, the cat was fine. No ice. Not even any water where it thawed."

Haggerty offered Rand a warm smile. "Mr. Riker...Rand."

Was she flirting, or just being nice? I found both possibilities equally shocking.

She kept the smile in her eyes. "What did this message say?"

Rand leaned forward. He seemed desperate for someone to believe him. "It warned that if I didn't announce my support of Normal, I would be burned alive." His Adam's apple bobbed. "It also ordered me to hire Samantha."

"Me?" I asked in a squeak.

He nodded. "I didn't run into you at that party by chance, *Madame* Samantha." He didn't inject a trace of respect into that. "I went there to meet you."

So fire-writers were getting me gigs now.

Spite flickered in the bottomless pitch of his eyes. "By the way, luv—you're fired. Once we get sprung from here, I want you to hit the road."

CHAPTER SIXTEEN

François's disgusted demeanor suggested that he considered the interrogation a waste of time. He and Haggerty kicked around the idea of putting Rand in an ankle-monitoring device, but in the end, they allowed him to leave unencumbered.

Rand rose slowly from his chair, like a broken old man. He'd retained his spite, though. "Samantha. I'll have me business manager send you a check. But considering how little you've done, you should make up for it now by telling me what the future holds."

"You want a reading?" I spat. "Fine. You're screwed."

I whirled around in a "you can't fire me, I quit" mode. Pretty lame. But short of sticking my tongue out, it was all I had.

I followed Haggerty to the office she'd claimed earlier. We didn't talk along the way. She'd grown inward since news of the ice-cube cat and the fire writing surfaced, while I mourned the loss of the luxurious digs Rand had promised me. I didn't worry about finding another berth—if Haggerty wanted me there, she'd come up with something. I always land on my feet, though rarely with a Jacuzzi and a mini-bar.

Once Haggerty and I slipped into the office, I whispered, "It had to be Angus who sent that cat." He had been responsible for the last guy I'd seen encased in ice.

"Angus hates the idea of you and Devil Boy together. Why would he have arranged it?"

No question, she thought things through better than I did.

"Besides, Celtic gods often use ice. Didn't you and your friends pull some ice caper?"

Man, she didn't miss a thing. Once when Angus was away, I popped over to Tahiti with Lugh and Taliesin, where they made an iceberg wash up on the beach.

"The weather guys loved it," I said. "Loads of them got a week in Tahiti out of it."

"You're just the little man's benefactor." She sighed. "Don't you see what this means? We're not merely fighting a freak with a chemistry lab and some toy soldiers. What we're up against here sounds more like a rogue god."

I sank into a funk. I'd seen how cavalierly gods who weren't rogues wielded their powers. Haggerty seemed no match for whatever we were up against.

Suddenly, her face brightened. So dramatically, it was as if someone had thrown a switch within her and a light went on. Only then did I realize how lacking in vitality she'd been lately.

"You look like you just fell in love," I said. "Don't tell me tight-assed albinos push your buttons."

She choked out a startled little laugh. "Samantha, you're so funny."

What did I say?

She beamed even brighter. "It's my mother—she surfaced."

And Haggerty knew it? Icebergs on the beach hadn't bothered me, but that she knew where her mother was, without a phone call or anything, gave me the creeps.

"Come on, Samantha. I'm going be staying in the Campbells' guest cottage, even when I'm off duty. Now I know where I'm going to stash you."

She told me she needed to let François know she was leaving. She slipped down the hall for a moment, before returning to grab her purse. "They haven't arranged a car for me yet, but we can walk."

Easy for her to say in her sensible shoes.

We walked along 89A toward a traffic light. People still stood around everywhere in clusters, many pointing in the direction of Normal's compound, even though you couldn't see it from here. Once again, the staggering sight of Sedona's crimson rock formations floored me. I also felt an overpowering sense of optimism, well beyond my usual blithe hope. Such a contrast to the fear that took hold of me earlier.

When I told Haggerty, she nodded. "It's the vortices. Their powers are growing this close to the harmonic convergence."

Right. I still didn't get that harmonica-thingie. But I'd come across the subject of vortexes before, or "vortices," as the Grammar Police, like Haggerty, say. Some people believe there are magnetic, mystical spots around the globe, with several being located in Sedona. Hah! Like a rock can make you feel anything.

"How is it that vortexes work?" I asked, humoring her, even if not to the extent of mimicking her correct grammar.

She shrugged. "They amplify the energies already inside of you. The frequencies."

If I had frequencies inside of me, how come I had to turn on the radio for the traffic report?

Haggerty clicked her tongue. "Such cynicism, Samantha."

I stumbled. "You...*heard* that?" I hadn't said it aloud.

"Not your exact thoughts, but I felt your derision."

"So it's true—we are connected. More than last time."

Haggerty agreed with an irritated nod. "And what am I missing while I'm monitoring you against my will? Especially since I can barely..." She let her voice trail off.

We crossed the street and began walking down a winding road without sidewalks. The crowds were thinner there, but lots of folks still stood around.

"You know where you're going?" My toes had begun to throb.

"No, but I'll find it."

"Just zeroing in on your mom, huh? Like a psychic homing device?"

Haggerty laughed. "Something like that." She told me a cousin of theirs had "gone home," and now Haggerty's mother was staying in the cousin's house.

"You mean this cousin died, right?" I asked.

"She went home to *Tir na N'og.*" Haggerty absently kicked a small red rock lying in the road. "It's not so different for you mortals, Samantha. We only spend one lifetime here, before returning forever to our homeland. Mortals continue to return here until they've learned whatever this place has to teach them. Then you move on to another plane of existence."

Reincarnation was real? I tried not to snort. "You mean, I'll be going somewhere else someday?"

Haggerty struggled with a superior grin. "Oh, I think you'll be coming back here for a long time."

There was an insult there, but I refused to let it stick. "So what's the deal with your mom? She knew the house was empty and decided to crash there?"

"Certainly not. Lucinda left it to Mom in her will."

Now that was what I hated about them, these gods and goddesses. First, I was supposed to believe that they can tap into each

MAGICAL ALIENATION

other like some divine homing beacon, and then they go all mundane with stuff like probate.

After too long a walk, Haggerty stopped before a house suffering from a serious case of schizophrenia, but in a good way. It was a small pueblo-style house in warm taffy, with a crimson path that led from the street to the door. I'd already noticed lots of pueblos there, just as I had further south in Arizona, though this one looked more modest than most of the Southwestern McMansions I'd seen. As with many desert dwellings, amber gravel covered the red dirt in place of a lawn. In contrast to the usual succulents and cactus, however, lush, vibrant flowers grew in wild patches. Flowers better suited to the tropics than the desert. Latticed pergolas, covered with roses in coral and ruby, draped over the path. And hollyhocks and bougainvillea grew wildly everywhere.

Haggerty flushed. "My mother likes flowers." She seemed embarrassed by the excess. She obviously forgot that *excess* is my middle name.

The path seemed to be made of some hardened substance formed with tiny red stones. And oddly, a pair of those lions you sometimes see before big city libraries guarded the path, only these had been carved from red rock, rather than poured from cement. Being worn out from that five-minute walk, I leaned heavily on the head of one of those lions.

"Samantha!" Haggerty snapped. "How would you like it if someone pressed on your head?"

"It's a rock, Haggerty. It doesn't feel a thing."

When a man and woman passed, she lowered her voice to a hush. "It's a rock *person* who took that form to guard my mother."

I leaped away from it. "Rocks have people in them?"

"Rock people are beings with minor shape-shifting abilities. They've taken this form as a warning."

Gingerly extending my finger, I gave the lion a poke. Felt hard like a rock was supposed to. "Why does your mom need protection?" She was a powerful goddess, after all. "It's not because of the militia, right?" All the folks gawking clearly didn't feel like they were in any danger.

"I doubt she sought their help. Loads of beings are simply devoted to her." Haggerty offered them respectful nods. "Most rock people hate topsiders. They deplore our pollution and overdevelopment and everything we've done to spoil the upper realm."

Topsiders? That sounded like some kind of sports shoe.

"They're more likely to side with our villains, just to shake things up for us. But these two are royals among their people. That they chose to support Mom is an honor."

For an FBI drone, Haggerty had quite an imagination. "Yeah? If their shape-shifting abilities are so weak, what could they do if a bad guy came?"

"Oh...maybe turn the path to quicksand, then harden it to stone, so the assailant would be stuck in it. Or they might use an earthquake to hamper him." She shrugged. "Come on, Samantha. Let's quit stalling."

Was that what we were doing? Following behind her, I hopped up the path with big, careful steps, just in case she wasn't making that stuff up, while simultaneously dodging the thorns of low-hanging roses.

Haggerty rapped on the carved pine door, before turning the knob and entering.

The goddess Fiona waited beyond the small entry. I'd heard so much about her, I wasn't sure she could live up to my expectations, but she sure did. On one hand, she just looked like a pretty middle-aged woman, an older, slightly softer, slightly fuller, version of Haggerty, in a long, loose dress. There were differences, of course. Her hair was a truer red than her daughter's auburn, but it also curled naturally. And while her full mouth resembled Haggerty's in repose, their smiles were different. Annabelle must have inherited hers from her departed sperm donor.

And yet, Fiona was so much more than just another middle-aged woman. Her tanned skin positively pulsed with a vibrant glow. Like Angus, her rich blue eyes contained tiny metallic flecks, but hers were gold, not silver. The most amazing thing about her was the color displayed all around her. I could actually see her aura! Despite the aura readings I did for some of my clients, I had never seen the supposed energy surrounding anyone. The transparent field radiating out from Fiona glowed in vivid coral.

"I'm glad you had no trouble finding the place, Annie." Fiona turned her twinkling blue-and-gold eyes on me. "And I see you brought Samantha. It's past time we met."

How did she do that?

MAGICAL ALIENATION

I was struck by another difference between mother and daughter. While Haggerty had brightened when she connected with her mother, Fiona's luminous quality beamed many times greater. The woman contained enough vitality to power a whole state.

She had obviously been busy making this house her own before we arrived. Among the Southwestern furnishings the prior owner might have left were other pieces that had clearly recently been deposited there, and piles of things waiting to be put away. Fiona seemed quite the Anglophile. She added enough pieces of antique furniture, covered in flowered chintz, to fill an Agatha Christie manor house.

Also stacked in corners were Fiona's own canvases. She was a great painter, with a breathtaking style. The subject matter in those paintings actually moved, if you can believe it. Some of them depicted strangely colored mists, and beyond those mists was the place that Haggerty called their homeland, *Tir na N'og*. I could stare at them for hours, trying to get a glimpse of what lay beyond the mist.

Like her daughter, Fiona had already scattered about bowls of apples. The apple is sacred to Celtic gods. When cut crosswise, it forms a pentacle, their symbol of immortality. There were loads more flowers in here, both cut in vases, and as well as flowering plants in colorful ceramic pots. I hadn't focused on the flowers outside, as taken as I had been with the red rock lions, but here I could see that the coloration of the petals of the various flowers trembled ever so slightly. The first time I went to Haggerty's house, I'd learned that flower fairies adorn the petals of all the flowers on earth and are actually responsible for their coloration. Pure hooey—you're probably thinking. But I had a particular dramatic experience with flower fairies in the course of our first caper, so I could swear with certainty that they do exist. Most mortals can't see them, or if they do, they believe their eyesight to be blurring. My exchange with them was so etched in my memory, that I was incapable of *not* seeing their characteristic shivering now.

An off-white muslin shawl, trimmed with Native American-style embroidery in turquoise and gold, had been thrown across a sofa. I moved it aside and sat. Bees and other bugs drifted by. The bees transported the flower fairies, according to Haggerty. Her house was always filled with flying things, too. My encounter there with a dragonfly had left me scarred for life.

When something buzzed too close to my ear, I swatted it away.

"No violence against the flying creatures, please, Samantha," Fiona said. "These are just short-term lives for them, but we don't want to cut them off before they've learned these life lessons."

Reincarnation again? Could it possibly be true? "What...?"

"Let's say a horse passed on. He might come back briefly as a gnat, so he learns to better live in the moment, before moving on to a lifetime as a dog, to learn generosity."

I closed my eyes briefly, to shut it all out, wishing I could also close off my ears. When I reopened them, I saw a teapot had appeared on the pine coffee table.

"Tea, Samantha, dear?" Fiona asked.

"Uh...sure." While she poured me a cup, a murmuring sound distracted me. It sounded like voices, speaking softly, though I couldn't figure out where it was coming from.

My gaze returned to the shawl. I'd seen something like that somewhere recently. "This shawl is beautiful, Fiona. Did you get it on the Hopi reservation?"

She laughed. "A department store in Phoenix. They're all the rage there. It's not as authentic as it looks."

Perfect for me—I wasn't particularly authentic, either. Maybe I'd get one before I headed home.

"Can Samantha bunk with you for a little while?" Haggerty asked.

"Of course, darling. We'll get along famously," she assured me with a sunny smile.

Haggerty perched on the edge of the sofa cushion. "Mom, we need to talk."

"And we will, darling. The time is right for so many things," Fiona said. "But it can't be now, Annabelle. They want you back at the Bureau office."

Almost instantly, the cell phone in Haggerty's suit pocket jingled. Sure enough, François asked her to return.

While Fiona showed Haggerty to the door, I stared absently at the warmly painted walls, still trying to trace the source of that strange murmur. My thoughts were interrupted by a more distinctive voice.

"Myrrh," said someone on the sofa arm beside me. I saw the cat from the courthouse. Impossible, but I'd swear he looked exactly the same.

"I see you've met Mellencamp," Fiona said.

My heart stopped dead. How could I have known his name?

"He told me he met you," Fiona went on.

"Cats don't talk, Fiona." They don't!

"But they do communicate. How else could you have known his name, dear?" she asked kindly.

I remembered the way that Austin Mellencamp song had floated into my mind. The cat blinked at me, like he was confirming it. Was I the only one who was not psychic? I gulped some tea, sorry it wasn't tequila.

"Fiona, why was Mellencamp at the courthouse?"

She hesitated, before continuing with, "He was there for you, Samantha. I knew you'd be bored, so I sent him to amuse you."

Candid eyes met mine over the top of her teacup. Sure. I was no more psychic than earwax, but I felt as certain as zits on a teenager that Haggerty's mom had just lied to me.

CHAPTER SEVENTEEN
Haggerty

Annabelle Haggerty stood within the claustrophobic confines of that government truck. To her side, François ranted about something, but she didn't pay attention. She stared instead at a computer screen, pretending to be absorbed in its content, but really unseeing.

Fear radiated through her. Her powers had fallen to an even lower level. How could she have maintained that she didn't need these abilities? She used them all the time. Oh, rarely to perform the kind of big magical feats others in her family did. No icebergs on Tahitian beaches for her. Yet she used them constantly to monitor the world around her.

She felt virtually blind. How could she hope to function well in a crisis? She'd never learned to operate as an ordinary mortal because she'd never had to. Now it was too late.

With a shaky sigh, she wrestled down the fears and forced herself to turn to her strong sense of logic. No, she hadn't been completely reduced to the level of an ordinary mortal. She could still tap into her connection with Samantha. She could even pick up emotional impressions from within the militia complex, although they were slight and erratic. But how long had it been since she'd noticed someone's aura, or heard a melody coming off anyone? Her magical abilities had been stripped to the bare-bones level.

Had she brought this about herself with the strength of her intent? Or had one of her ancestors sensed her unspoken wish and fulfilled it?

She would have to ask her mother to reverse this awful curse. Only…how would her mother feel when she learned that her precious child had scorned her birthright? Could Haggerty bear to see the look that would likely come over Fiona's face?

She'd have to struggle with this on her own for a while longer, and she'd just have to hope it didn't get any worse. But how was that possible?

CHAPTER EIGHTEEN
Samantha

Immediately after Haggerty left, Fiona announced that she had to go out. Since Haggerty had told us that my luggage had arrived at Rand's hotel, Fiona said she'd take me there when she returned, but right now she couldn't delay leaving. She grabbed her shawl and hurried to the door. She didn't even say where she was going. Not that I'd know. I'd only been in Sedona for a couple of hours, and I hadn't yet progressed beyond the fringe of it.

"If you get tired of waiting, dear, call a taxi," Fiona said over her shoulder. "I established an account with a cab company. You'll find the number near the kitchen phone."

Though I loved to charge things to other people's accounts, I planned to wait for Fiona. But I didn't know what to do with myself. I dragged a string across the floor for Mellencamp, only he let me know precisely how boring he found it. Once you realize that cats communicate, it's pretty clear how insulting they can be.

Mostly, though, the murmuring sound in that house drove me batty. Too loud to ignore, too soft to understand. I found the number for a cab company where Fiona said it would be. The Alien Cab Company, the business card read.

A taxi pulled up in front of Fiona's house, driven by a Pakistani teenager, who greeted me in a strong accent, wearing Mr. Spock ears. It struck me funny that the driver was an actual alien, in the sense that he was a foreigner—so he didn't need plastic ears for the cab company's name to work. I'd never lived any place where cabbies pretend to be extraterrestrials. I had wondered whether Sedona would be ready for me, but now I wasn't sure if I was ready for it.

"Where do you wish to go?" the kid asked in his crisp accent.

Good question. As much as I wanted my stuff, I still felt so mad at Rand, if I saw him, I'd probably knock him on his fanny. I told the driver to take me to Normal's compound.

"I will get you as close as I can. They've opened another lane, so it will not take as long as it did before. But I am afraid you won't get through the perimeter the federal authorities have set up."

I responded to his challenge with a smug, "Just watch me."

Why was I showing off for this kid? Now I might have to get arrested to prove I could do it. Sometimes I wondered how I could possibly make predictions about other people's lives when I was so clueless about my own.

In the short time since Haggerty and I had left the crime scene, the numbers of people gathered there had swelled many times. When the driver pulled to a stop practically a quarter mile away, he said, "This is as close as I can get, ma'am."

Ma'am? Was I really old enough to be called *ma'am*? I compressed a whole hissy fit into one line when I told him to wait for me.

What I saw in that crowd further bummed me. As I expected, there were plenty of mugs in need of psychic readings, but far too many competitors were already working the crowd. There was actually so much reading going on there, it might have been a library. None of the other spiritual advisors were dressed as nice as me, of course, but who would notice in that ten-ring-circus?

I shouldn't have doubted my uniqueness. Over the roar of that crowd, I heard someone call, "Madame Samantha? Samantha, over here."

Where? I stared into the crowd, but the faces blurred together. I heard my name again. This time my caller sounded closer and more distinctive, so I was able to say with certainty that the person was a woman, and maybe even the Queen of England.

Someone tapped my shoulder. My greeter wasn't the Queen, but Holly O'Neill, the flight attendant from Rand's chartered jet. What an appearance transformation she'd undergone. To her prim blonde hairdo she'd added a sparkly tiara. Instead of her uniform jacket, she wore a peasant blouse that slipped off one of her slim shoulders. And wrapped around her waist, in lieu of a skirt, she'd tied one of those embroidered shawls that Fiona said were so popular. Where the ends met, it formed a slit over a thigh that was thinner than mine had been in infancy. But the most dramatic transformation was the pretty pink glow that bathed her face.

Princess Holly threw her arms around me. "Samantha, it's wonderful to see you."

I thought the English were so reserved.

"I didn't believe it when you predicted my true love was at

hand," she said. "But you were right."

Had my flinging her at Rand actually worked? Was that why he stopped putting the moves on me and got nasty?

"You were wrong about his identity, though." She waved her index finger in my face. "I left something on the plane when I departed, and when I went back for it, after you and Mr. Riker left, the man working on the engine was—" She flashed me a shy grin. "Let me introduce you to Nicky."

Ah, the reason for her transformation.

She drew a large hunk of prime male flesh to her side. Nicky was a big guy who filled out his flannel shirt and well-washed jeans to a degree that made the region south of my own belly button do an unexpected little tap dance. His chiseled chin was square enough to make him capable of carrying the starring role in any movie studio's action flick. His straight, white teeth belonged in a toothpaste ad. About the only place he appeared to be lacking might be in the breezeway between his ears. The pale light shining out from his gray-brown eyes couldn't have been more than fifteen watt. But if Holly cared, her radiance denied it.

She wrapped her arms around Nicky's broad chest, causing me to remember an even better chest I'd once draped myself across. I felt a sharp pang of envy.

"We both knew, we just knew, from the moment we looked at each other," Holly blathered on.

The dumb ox beamed at her with the most besotted expression.

"I owe it all to you, Samantha."

A warm flush of satisfaction filled me. People don't realize how rewarding it is to be a good fake psychic. The world would be a sadder place without me.

I congratulated them both and asked what they were doing there. "Just rubber necking like everyone else?"

"Not...exactly." A little frown appeared between Holly's pale brows. "Naturally, I give you complete credit for advising me to dump my former fiancé," she rushed on. "But you were wrong about Mr. Riker. I knew that as soon as you said it. I also felt just as certain that it was Nicky who was right for me. And I thought, you know, that maybe I have psychic abilities, too. I'm out here giving it a try." She murmured in a confidential whisper, "You won't believe how much money I've made already. I'm ever so grateful to you for showing me how."

The nerve of her. Sure, I was a fake, but I'd been perfecting my craft since I was a little scam artist at my con-mother's knee. How dare this upstart think she could copy my act.

I'd have told her so, too, only someone dragged her off to give a reading. I wandered toward the Feds' perimeter and looked toward the FBI's truck. To my surprise, the door opened and Haggerty stepped from it. When she spotted me, she motioned me to her. Funny, she seemed equally surprised to see me. Perhaps we weren't as connected as she wanted me to think. Good to know. I liked to slip the harness more than she typically allowed.

"My mother let you leave the house alone?" she demanded.

I covered for Fiona, insisting she told me to stay. "I'm only taking a detour on my way to collect my things from Rand's hotel."

That seemed to satisfy her. She turned back to the truck.

But I stopped her. "Uh, Haggerty, that business before with Rand firing me—if you see Angus, you won't...?"

She smiled kindly. "Our little secret."

François popped his head out the truck. "Annabelle?" he asked, his face brightening at the sight of her. Then it soured when he spotted me. "So you're back, Guinevere. When Annabelle said you were as slippery as an eel, I thought that meant you slipped away. I didn't think we were going to have to deal with how often you'd turn up."

I'm nothing if not a unique surprise.

Haggerty's skin tightened across her cheekbones. Our association was starting to embarrass her. As much as it chafed me to be tied to her, I took comfort from knowing she disliked it more than I did.

"Did you want something, François?" she asked.

"Just got off the horn from Washington. The negotiator is on his way. Maybe an hour out from Phoenix as we speak." He sent the compound an ominous look.

"How high up in the Bureau is he?"

He rubbed his hair with his oversized hand. "That's the funny part. He isn't in the Bureau at all. He's military intelligence."

Haggerty gasped. "To negotiate with a militia for some federal courthouse employees? Someone from military intelligence will make them more recalcitrant. What are they thinking?"

"This has nothing to do with the court personnel. Apparently, they're sending an MI negotiator because of some captive seized from the *other* caravan. The army convoy that was swept up in the assault," François said. "I wish I knew who they had in there, and what makes him that important."

Haggerty looked toward the compound. When a shadow of thought seemed to cross her face, it scared the crap out of me.

CHAPTER NINETEEN

When the cabbie and I left, fortunately, the line of cars moving back to town was lighter than that headed toward the compound. I gave the driver the name of Rand's inn and asked him to take me there.

While we inched along, my thoughts drifted back to Rand's interrogation. I didn't doubt that he had told the truth, as crazy as the idea of fire letters rising from ice sounded. Why would someone powerful enough to send that kind of message drag me into it? Why me? Why not Haggerty? I'd ask her about it, only I hated to give her the satisfaction of thinking I believed half of what she told me.

I remained so lost in thought that I didn't notice, until the cabbie cut the engine, that we'd stopped before the inn's lobby. The posh hotel was made up of a number of buildings in that familiar pueblo design. Did anyone there see any irony in using that humble plan to house great luxury?

I told Spock Ears to wait and yanked open the lobby door, which caused an iron bell to clang. Posh southwestern furnishings filled the voluminous space.

A woman with hot pink curly hair pushed through a swinging door on the far side. Unseeing initially, when she finally took in my Guinevere-on-Acid presence, with all that snotty graffiti painted across my dress, she came to a halt. "My, that's quite an outfit you have there, honey."

Someone with pink hair found my dress eccentric—I felt a surge of pride. Maybe I was ready for Sedona, after all.

"I'm sorry, but we don't have any rooms available," she said. "We've let them all to a private party."

So Rand kept the whole place, even though his band wasn't coming now. And he was too mean-spirited to let me have a room.

I told her I wasn't looking for a room and explained who I was.

"Oh, sure. Mr. Riker said you'd be coming by for your bags." She led me to a closet in the corner, filled with my luggage. "I'm afraid I let my bellman leave, so I don't have anyone to help you with them."

Since I'd already told the teenaged cabbie he'd have to tote my stuff, I assured her it was okay. With a flickering smile, the woman started to leave, but stopped and turned back to me. "I just remembered—there were also a couple of boxes with your name on them, which Mr. Riker asked to have placed in his suite. Probably for safe-keeping."

Right. Because Mr. Riker was so concerned with my welfare. I couldn't imagine what those boxes might contain, but after losing out on a chance to stay there, I refused to allow Rand to rob me of anything else. Small victories count for a lot with me.

"I'm not sure if Mr. Riker is in his suite," the woman said. "I can give him a call."

He'd better be there, or I'd tattle to Haggerty. "That's okay. Why don't you tell me where to find it, and I'll check myself."

She gave her pink curls a shake. "We don't give out guests' room numbers without their permission."

Determined to seize another of those tiny victories, I said, "No problem. I'll just call him later and come back for them." I gave her a big grin to show her how honest I was. It amazed me how many people bought that.

With a nod, the woman left. I went outside and started the cabdriver transferring my luggage to his trunk. Then I paused in the cobblestone driveway and looked around. Most of the other buildings looked like they each contained several rooms, judging by the number of doors in them. But there was one building that only contained a single entry point.

I was guessing that building housed the best accommodation, which Rand would doubtless claim for himself.

"These bags are quite heavy, ma'am," the kid griped in his semi-polite way. "What do you have in them?"

The best-looking clothes you'll never see, my boy. I left him to grumble in his own language, while I ambled over to the door that might lead to Rand's suite. I was about to knock, but I wondered if someone would lock a door in a hotel where there were no other guests. Sure enough, the wrought iron knob turned in my hand.

I only intended to peek, but when I saw what decadence lay beyond that door, I stumbled in. Fortunately, it was empty, which gave me the chance to study the place without having to tangle with Rand. Besides, I was struck dumb by the sight of that room.

Room? Did I say *room?* The Palace of Versailles could

easily have fit in it. The sitting area must have been around forty feet by fifty, and that didn't include an L-shaped alcove that jutted off to one side. A baby grand piano had been tucked into one corner, and it didn't dwarf that space one bit. The rest of the place contained a few intimate sitting areas for a hundred or so of the suite occupant's closest friends. The floor was peg-and-groove pine with such a shiny varnish I couldn't believe anyone had ever walked on it. The plush area rugs were so thick you could sink in them up to your knees. I walked to the other side to take a gander at that L-shaped section. It contained a dining table for twenty.

Closed doors led off here and there. One of them probably housed the Jacuzzi I had lost by not staying there, if not a whole swimming pool. There wasn't a mini-bar, but a *maxi*-one. Covering a rustic sideboard along one wall were full-sized bottles of every variety of liquor. And unlike the little over-priced jars of macadamia nuts generally found in mini-bars, from what I'd heard, centered among these bottles was a huge crystal bowl filled with the pricey nuts. Fortunately, I don't need to be hungry to eat, so I grabbed a huge handful of them and began to nibble. After a moment, I filled the pockets of my Guinevere-dress with more of them. I might not be hungry again later.

No sign of Rand, though. But there must have been lots of places beyond those doors to get lost.

I plopped on a couch and noticed two cardboard boxes on the coffee table. They were addressed to me, in care of our Scottsdale resort. Detaching the pieces of tape that held the boxes closed, I peered inside one of them. I understood immediately why they were in Rand's room, rather than with my luggage. They contained the stuff I'd ordered from the metaphysical store in Scottsdale: Crystals, candles, sage wands, essential oils, oil warmers, a deck of tarot cards and all those spells kits. Had I really bought that much? I bet Rand figured that because he had paid for those things, that made them his. *Think again, Devil Boy.* Those boxes had my name on them.

Some people say you can't read your own tarot, but since I put no more stock in it than any other woo-woo shtick, I never let that bother me. It was sheer chance what cards came up, but sometimes they gave me ideas. I broke the seal on the deck and laid out a spread before me.

I turned over the Lovers card. Who did that represent? Was it taunting me with what once had existed between Angus and me? Was it Princess Holly and her dopey mechanic?

Nobody, I reminded myself. It didn't represent anyone. They were just cards. But when the Devil and the High Priestess cards appeared, I started to feel creepy, even if I wasn't sure why. Why was I reading tarot and munching high-priced nuts in someone else's room? I packed up the cards, grabbed the pair of boxes and started for the door.

Then I heard a muffled sound from somewhere within the suite. A giggle, I thought, higher-pitched than Rand's voice.

I crept to each of those closed doors, listening. No sounds from beyond them, until I made my way to the dining area. Even before I pressed my ear to the door there, I could hear that the room beyond it was the one that had produced that sound. As I listened now, I heard Rand's deep laugh, and again, that same melodic giggle.

Rand sure knew how to work this house arrest-business. He was in there with some chick, engaging in a little post-nooky levity.

I started to snicker. I'm not kinky or anything—the sex part didn't interest me. I just find it fun to spy on people. I caught myself mid-snort, before I gave away that I was there.

I noticed another one of those embroidered shawls tossed on the dining table. If they were that popular, they probably weren't for me—I liked to stand out. Beside the shawl was a silver clasp lightly etched with the letter "R," though the worn engraving looked faint. Was "R" the woman's initial? Or was the clasp something of Rand's? It looked like a piece of jewelry a woman might use with a scarf. The shawl was embroidered in the same colors as Fiona's.

Whoa! Was that *Fiona* in there with Rand? How would they know each other? She had left the house as soon as she sent her daughter packing, and she took her shawl. Yet it really did seem like everyone owned them.

It occurred to me that was my chance to check out that shawl. I put my boxes down and wrapped it around my waist as Holly O'Neill had. Nope, it wasn't going to work as a skirt for me. Angus might have said my plumpish form was the perfect female body, but there wasn't a woman's magazine in the last century that agreed.

A rosewood-trimmed mirror hung on the wall behind the dining table. I inched over to it and wrapped the shawl over my hair.

With a dashing flare, I threw one end over my shoulder. In my haste, it crossed over the lower half of my face. I started to move it, but the sight of that shawl, wrapped around my hair and over my face, triggered a thought. With the reddish glow thrown off by the mirror's rosewood trim, the ringlets of my blonde hair, escaping from the shawl, took on a reddish cast.

I tried to imagine how I would look if my eyes had been covered by sunglasses. The thoughts creeping into my head floored me. Good thing I had nobody there to talk to because I was struck dumb. I glanced at the closed bedroom door again. I couldn't say whether or not Fiona was the woman in that room with Rand.

One thing was certain, though: She had been the woman in the rear of that Phoenix courtroom, who, with her silent disdain, had scorned Senator Campbell.

CHAPTER TWENTY

Time was running out for the being from Area 51. His disastrous error was about to come home to roost. Two men from the militia had dragged Private Hanover away. By now Handy Hanover had doubtless revealed what had been the most closely guarded secret of the last six decades.

Why hadn't help arrived yet? Maybe his appeal had been rejected. Or maybe it hadn't been strong enough. Then again, it was possible he hadn't left his benefactor enough power to receive it. Neither his target, nor the one he'd chosen to help facilitate things, apparently understood what he wanted them to know.

The creature could still fix his mistake. He had enough power left to disprove Hanover's story, making the smarmy private a laughing stock. But why should he? Others would come for him soon, and they would enslave him for eons.

It had been such delightful fun keeping his charade going all these years. But if this would be his last stand, he should make it a good one. A circus that would change the way these pitiful creatures functioned forever. His stunt would never be forgotten.

And if, in the midst of the chaos, he managed to steal away at the most advantageous time, he might still scrap through. Fun and survival—an unbeatable combination.

CHAPTER TWENTY-ONE

After unpacking my suitcases back at Fiona's house, I flopped on the guestroom bed. The room had been furnished with a feather-top bed, covered with a Native American throw. A pile of down pillows tossed against the headboard made it, if not the cushiest spot in existence, the best I'd ever found outside of Rand's swanky inn.

Even the house's strange murmur had ceased to bother me now that I understood it. I'd asked Fiona about it when she came back earlier.

"They're voices, right?" I'd asked. "What are they saying?"

She tossed her embroidered shawl across the sofa. I checked again—a match to the one I'd seen in Rand's suite.

"No, not voices. What you hear are the residual energy and emotions of the people who've lived in this house. Every home retains traces of its occupants."

"Get out! I've never heard them before," I said.

"Of course not. You don't have that capacity. I've allowed you to hear them, Samantha."

Maybe that was why I didn't see her aura now—she'd allowed me to see it just that first time. I felt so honored.

Fiona sent me a vague smile. "After all, you're practically a member of the family."

I shook my head. "Angus and I are quits."

"I wouldn't be too sure of that, darling, but I didn't necessarily mean through our dear boy."

Fiona cupped my chin with her hand. Warmth spread through me, like a toasty liquid. But whether that came from her touch, or from embarrassment over Angus's infidelity, I couldn't say.

After that, though, I began to find comfort in the house's sounds.

Sinking deeper into the pillow pile, I gazed happily around the guestroom. The walls were a creamy ivory. Fiona had offered to change it if I didn't like it. *Change* it, not *paint* it, but I found it quite nice.

I stared at the artwork she had hung over the dresser. The unframed canvas was another of her paintings. It depicted a girl strolling along a path in a rustic park with her cat. The cat was clearly Mellencamp. He'd jumped on the dresser earlier and struck the same pose as if to show me that he'd modeled for it. At least I thought that was what he'd meant. Maybe I was reading too much into this cat communication business.

The little girl wore a print dress and geeky brown oxford shoes. I'd had shoes like that when I was a kid. Once, when we were really strapped, I'd had to wear hand-me-downs from my flat-footed cousin. My *boy* cousin. Though I'd hated them then, I felt some fondness for those shoes now. They made me feel as if I could be that girl.

Like all of Fiona's works this painting showed action. The girl and the cat began in the foreground, strolled up the winding path and finally disappeared behind a large boulder. The last action, after the girl and the cat vanished, was a puff of dust her geeky shoes kicked up. After a moment, the journey began anew.

Yet I never actually saw them change position, I only saw them farther on after they moved.

The changing images mesmerized me. I wanted to reach into that canvas and grasp the bit of dust she kicked up. Would it feel like dirt or paint? If those pillows had been less cushy, I might have tried it.

It wasn't just the coziness of those pillows that kept me in that room, however. Fiona's secrets were eating a hole through my brain, and I was afraid I wouldn't be able to keep what I was thinking from her. Still, I couldn't ask. A woman's got the right to snarl at senators, and maybe even sleep with rock stars, without everyone snooping into her business.

A tall bookcase stood in the corner, with books jammed into every possible space. Their relative, Lucinda, had been quite the reader. The fiction shelves contained everything from romances to literary novels, from mysteries to science fiction. There were also a few shelves of metaphysical titles. I had some of those same books in my own library. I hadn't read many of them, but having them around impressed my clients.

I slipped off the bed and pulled out a book on spells. Lucinda had been one of those people who jotted notes in the margins, as if she knew I'd be standing here reading them someday. "Get a load of this!" she'd written alongside one spell's ingredients. "To think they believe this will work," another caption read.

It didn't surprise me that she didn't follow the formulas. Why would a goddess need to resort to such low level spells? If they performed ritual magic at all, I felt sure theirs was of a much higher order. That reminded me of the kits I'd ordered in Scottsdale. I yanked the boxes I'd brought back from Rand's suite from the closet shelf where I stowed them. One box knocked to the floor a stack of stationery pages bound together with a blue ribbon.

The girlish handwriting on the sheets of paper looked vaguely familiar. They proved to be letters Haggerty had written to Lucinda years ago. In the few I read, Haggerty had shared her ambivalence about the magical powers that were growing stronger in her, as well as griping about the frivolous nature of their ancestors. Not much had changed there.

Lacking any interest in Haggerty's girlhood angst, I tossed the letters onto the bed and reached into the boxes for the stuff to perform a banishing spell. If I kept hanging around with his descendents, Angus would continue appearing. Maybe if I followed the directions exactly, I could finally make a spell work, banning him from my life forever.

I'd need something to work in. Fiona had placed a ceramic jar filled with cut flowers on the dresser. Removing the flowers carefully, so as not to irritate the flower fairies, I spilled the water into the adjoining bathroom sink and placed the jar on the vanity counter. I went back to the bedroom for the banishing spell kit. I took a black candle from the box and covered it thoroughly with the banishing oil contained in a small vial. The oil, according to the label, was a precise blend of pepper, peppermint, rosemary and pine. I loved that someone else measured the exact drops needed of everything, since I invariably lost count. Maybe that was why my spells never worked. Then I lit the candle with a book of matches also contained in the box.

Following the directions on the accompanying card, I chanted, "Old one, wise one, slow but sure one. Guide my spell and be it done." My voice echoed so ominously against the tiled walls. I'd never performed a spell in a bathroom before. This was sure to work.

I checked for the next step in the directions. Oops! That was why it was probably a good idea to read ahead. I needed a lock of hair or the signature on a piece of paper of the one I wanted to banish. How could I possibly get Angus to cooperate with that? Even if gods didn't perform spells, if I asked for a lock of his hair, he was sure to know how I intended to make use of it.

Wait a minute! I rushed back to the guestroom for Haggerty's letters. Sure enough, she'd written about Angus, among others, in her bitching about their ancestors. His name written by a goddess had to be as good as his own signature, right? To make extra certain that I'd nailed it, I took several of her letters. Back in the bathroom, I lit the letters with the candle.

While holding the burning sheets of paper, I performed the next direction, saying, "I name thee Angus's power." To be certain the transfer would work, since I was using Haggerty's writing, I added another line I created myself. "I name thee Annabelle's power."

I tossed the sheets into the ceramic jar to burn, while chanting the next line. "This spell shall burn your power down."

The final direction was to scatter the ashes in a stream. Where was I going to find a stream? I glanced at the porcelain throne to my right. Good enough. I looked into the jar. The letters hadn't fully burned—I should have dried it first. But there was some ash in there.

I put aside the unburned portions and flushed the rest down the toilet, reciting the final line, "Out of the ashes, I name thee gone."

I felt a little strange afterwards. My chest trembled, and my hands shook. Had to be my imagination. I was letting this hokum weird me out.

I took the unburned portion of the letters back to the bedroom and tossed them onto the dresser. My trembling finally began to fade. I hopped onto the bed and settled back into the pillows for some well-deserved rest. What a workout! If someone hadn't slammed the front door, I might never have left that room, considering how much I needed a nap. But nosiness overcame me.

I found Haggerty in the living room, gesturing wildly before her mother.

"Mom, you *really* haven't picked up on anything?" Haggerty demanded. "Even I felt something, but…I discounted it." She looked away.

Fiona, on the other hand, went to rearrange the china pieces she'd put on a wooden shelf. "I sense things all the time, Annie. Especially here in this magical space."

What was with all the evasions? To think I was a better liar than both of them.

Haggerty looked at her wide chrome watch. "François thinks I've gone to the ATM, so I don't have much time." Her gaze swept the room. "Is there a TV here somewhere?"

"I've never owned one, but Lucinda might have."

Duh! Why did they think she'd kept an armoire across from the sofa? I opened it for them.

"Look, Annie, darling, a TV," Fiona said.

And these two were goddesses? How did they get along without me?

Haggerty asked me to tune it to a national news show, on which a popular gray-haired anchor said, "Still monitoring that tense stalemate in Arizona, we want to rerun the tape that arrived at our sister station in Phoenix just moments ago."

The screen switched to a tape, shot with a hand-held video camera, of a man, dressed in fatigues, standing rigidly before a red rock wall. There was something familiar about his chin warmer beard and the angry lines of his fleshy face. After a moment it hit me—he was Harold Hinkley, the head of the Arizona Friends of Freedom Militia. I'd seen his picture in the newspaper in a Soma Café when I first arrived in Phoenix.

He announced in a booming voice, "Your government has been lying to you for decades."

Big deal. That's what governments do.

"It has kept a prisoner against his will for more than sixty years," Hinkley said. "The Arizona Friends of Freedom Militia has liberated him."

Liberated? Was that how they described attacking innocent passers-by?

"In 1947, a spaceship crashed outside of Roswell, New Mexico. Contrary to rumors that have circulated ever since, there weren't four or five aliens in that craft, there was only one. Also contrary to folklore, the being in that aircraft didn't die."

Fiona's hand drifted to her lips, but not before I saw the barest sketch of a smile.

"Despite the government's denials, the Roswell alien exists, and he's in our possession." The speaker promised to deliver demands soon. With that, the tape ended. When the anchor returned, Haggerty switched it off.

"Was that a hoax?" I asked. "I mean, isn't alien-talk strictly for folks a few acres shy of a farm?"

Fiona cleared her throat. "Maybe, Samantha, those people seem a little odd to you because they've seen something outside the usual frame of reference."

Spaceships that land on their lawns? Yeah, that was outside of it.

Haggerty fixed her sights on her mother. "This is a disaster."

Idly raking her fingers through her wavy red hair, Fiona said, "Maybe so, Annie, but it was inevitable."

Wait. They were taking this seriously? My heart began to pound erratically. Aliens! I couldn't bear it. I was only just getting used to the fact that I was interacting with an albino.

Haggerty paced before the sofa. "An absolute disaster," she repeated. "Mom, how is it possible you didn't know—" Her cell phone rang. She checked the caller ID. "François. Got to go." She stormed from the house.

Fiona stared at the blank TV screen. "Samantha, why do we struggle so hard against our destinies?"

Were we still talking about the alien? Should I be terrified or not?

"Why can't we just accept what's meant for us?" she asked.

I had no idea what she was talking about. But as sweat poured from my scalp and my hands began to shake, I was starting to get the idea that the little green guy was the least of our troubles.

CHAPTER TWENTY-TWO

Once the militia made its announcement, a thousand circuses came to town. Ten thousand. Hotels and campgrounds all over Arizona filled up. But the mugs kept coming. They slept in public parks and private yards and refused to leave. Over the next couple of days, the insanity kept building. It went beyond the local police department's ability to handle it. The National Guard was called out, but neither could they stop the flow. The Governor had declared Marshall Law, and no one cared. It didn't make one tiny dent in the chaos.

Much of the turmoil proved to be surprisingly benign, but the chaos wasn't kind to everyone. Some people stood around, sobbing uncontrollably. Or sat slumped on curbs, in such a deep funk they failed to recognize familiar voices anymore. Others kept making feverish, dire predictions. And while violent crimes were rare, when they did occur, the violence was always severe and gratuitous.

Haggerty said it all had to do with the amplification of that harmonica-thingie, which made it sound more than ever like a band to me. Apparently, it elevated whatever a person happened to be feeling all the way to the stratosphere.

Although cheerfulness is my normal state, I couldn't seem to tap into that collective liveliness, though neither did I feel depressed. Instead, it was like I'd swallowed a swarm of butterflies, whose wings kept flapping frantically within my tummy. Fiona diagnosed it as anxiety. Me? I didn't *get* anxiety, I *gave* it.

Today, I also felt a raging headache. I suspected that had more to do with withdrawal from all the Soma Cafs I was used to sucking down. I asked Fiona to heal it, but she mumbled she wasn't sure she could. Right. Even Haggerty could have done that, and Fiona was a more powerful goddess. What was the point of having friends like them if I couldn't ask for little favors?

The headache kept me away from the compound, which reportedly had swelled to a few hundred thousand now. Instead, I slumped before the TV, watching nonstop news coverage. The militia's latest video staggered me. No matter how many times I'd watched it over the last couple of days, it never failed to rile up the butterflies within me. Shot against the same rock, this time, joining

MAGICAL ALIENATION

Harold Hinkley were a few of his militia cronies, including No-Neck and Baldy. Then, into the shot came a real soldier, a man in regulation U.S. Army garb. And that soldier led—the alien.

Hinkley rambled on with their demands. He called for the dismantling of the U.S. government and all branches of the military. And for the military's weapons to be passed out among the citizens. There might have been something about distributing the contents of the treasury and a few other demands. I couldn't say. No matter how many times I watched that clip, I could never pay attention to what Hinkley called for, once *he* entered the shot.

The alien, that is.

Yet he disappointed me. Not a Steven Spielberg-alien, but one that you might see in some old black-and-white flick you watched for a hoot on a rainy Sunday afternoon. He was small, with arms and legs like ours, with only four long fingers on each hand. His hairless head looked a couple of times the size of ours, with oversized almond eyes, covered by something that resembled sunglass lenses. While lacking a nose, there was a small hole in his face where his mouth might be. But the part of him I found the most attractive was his skin. It shimmered, changing hues, depending on how it caught the light, from a ghostly white to an iridescent green.

While I didn't keep up on the lunatic fringe, unless they happened to be clients, he did look like the drawings I'd seen of the supposed-Roswell alien.

"I don't believe this," I muttered for the millionth time. "I don't freakin' believe it."

"We know, Samantha. We *really* know that by now," Haggerty said through clenched teeth. "When do you think you might start believing it?"

"Annabelle..." Fiona said, in a cautionary tone.

The Bureau had been removed from the operation, replaced by some secret military intelligence squad. While Annabelle still usually stayed at the Campbells' place, we saw her too often now.

"What're the odds?" I muttered. "Who would have thought the truck that alien traveled in would have been right on that spot at the worst possible time?"

A tea tray appeared on the coffee table. "Did you happen to notice there were no other vehicles on the highway at the time? No other hostages to take, but those in the two convoys?" Fiona asked.

"There are no accidents, Samantha. Haven't you discovered that by now?"

"You mean fate? Fiona, are you trying to tell me we don't have free will?" I accepted the chamomile tea she kept serving me. It tamed my butterflies, but did nothing to reduce my headache. How could I have landed in the only town in the country without a Soma Café? How long would this withdrawal last? And if Fiona could make tea just appear, why couldn't she cure one measly headache? Screw fate—*those* were the real unanswerable questions.

"Of course you have free will," Fiona said, taking a sip. "But your fate is your fate. No matter how much you resist, it will keep rising up to meet you until you accept it."

"Mom," Haggerty warned.

Now their evasions didn't seem to be directed at each other, but me. What were they hiding?

I heard a rustling sound from the patio outside the dining room. The people who'd camped out there earlier had knocked on the French doors when they needed to use the bathroom. But they'd left hours ago. I looked there now in time to see Angus simply move through the closed doors.

Tension cut uncharacteristic grooves between his full blond brows. I'd never seen Angus looking worried before. His features softened when he looked at me. Shouldn't that banishing spell I'd performed start working soon?

"Sammy-girl," he said. Then the TV screen caught his attention, and the lines returned. "Gwydion. How could he let them parade him like that? This isn't a joke anymore." With a groan, Angus sank beside me on the sofa. His proximity made a heat wave swell through me, starting with my southern regions.

Then his words seeped through my hormonal haze. I jumped to my feet, finally grasping what nobody would tell me. "Gwydion?" I stabbed a finger toward the alien on the tube. "*That's* Gwydion? The Celtic god of enchantment and illusion?" I'd heard his name mentioned occasionally, when Angus and Taliesin and Lugh got together. But they never told me the nature of the joke he was putting over on the mortals.

Nobody responded to me now, either. None of them even looked at me.

"He's one of yours?" I shouted. "Why would he do this?"

MAGICAL ALIENATION

Angus directed his blue-and-silver eyes my way. "For a lark, of course."

"A lark doesn't last sixty years."

Angus shrugged. "When you live forever, that's the blink of an eye."

There it was again—his immortality. If the mermaid hadn't broken us up, that would have.

His eyes surveyed the room. "Are Lugh and Taliesin here?"

"We haven't seen them, dear boy," Fiona said. Angus had always been one of her favorites among their ancestors.

"They said they'd see me in Sedona. Is there anyone else of ours here?"

Fiona shrugged. "Since Lucinda was called home, I can't think of who would be here," Fiona said. "Tea, Angus?"

He absently shook his head no. "They didn't say so exactly, but I got the impression they planned to visit someone. Where could they be?"

"Don't be silly, Angus," Haggerty snapped. "When there's fun to be had, why would they hole up here? They're probably out at the compound, appearing as aliens in the crowd."

Angus gave his golden blond hair a shake. "Not with the Ruling Council on the warpath. We're all lying low right now."

"What a shame. It would be fun to hang with the guys." My stabbing pain made me hold my head in my hands. "Ooh! I can't think with this headache." That murmuring sound from the house wasn't helping, either. Now that she'd let me experience it, why couldn't Fiona turn it off? At least until this headache went away.

"Fiona, you've left her in pain?" The uncharacteristic sternness of an angry superior entered Angus's voice.

"Annabelle felt she should bear the consequences of her actions," Fiona said. "So she would think twice before becoming addicted to something like Soma Café again."

I knew it. She really could have cured it. And I really was addicted.

Angus blew out an angry huff. "Annie, you're going to fit right in with the Ruling Council when you're called home."

"Hopefully, it won't be soon." She held her ground against him, as she always did.

"Thanks to Myrddin for that!" he said with feeling, calling

on the name of the greatest trickster god of all. "We can't take any more of the righteous faction."

Angus stood before me. He placed cool fingertips on my aching forehead. The pain drifted away. My anxiety, too, I noticed, as the most wonderful sense of wellbeing spread through me. I wasn't sure whether he had cured it, or if I simply couldn't feel bad with Angus touching me. Getting over him was proving to be too tough. When, oh-when would that banishing spell start?

Suddenly energized, but breathless, I said, "I knew there couldn't be any such thing as aliens." Next they'd be telling me vampires existed. Get real.

Haggerty shook her head. "It's true that the sightings people talk about aren't real. That's just your playmates having fun." She glanced at Angus, who twisted his full lips with chagrin. "But there are beings on other worlds. Did you really think you were the only creatures on this entire plane of existence? How self-involved are you, Samantha?"

She knew me—pretty self-involved.

"One race came here long ago, and though they keep to themselves, their numbers have grown enormously," Annabelle said.

I snapped my fingers. "It's the Canadians, right? I mean, who's that polite, and what's up with that 'eh'?"

Haggerty threw her hands up. "How do you survive?"

She should know better than to try to insult me. "No, elephants. That trunk is too weird."

"It's not elephants," Haggerty said.

"Annabelle, don't tease her." Fiona sighed. "Coyotes, Samantha. The aliens Annabelle spoke about are coyotes."

"But…? Aren't they just some kind of dog?"

Fiona tilted her head. "Have you ever heard a dog that sounded like they do?"

Yeah, I'd heard their peculiar yipping in the distance last night, after the chatter of the squatters had died down. There was such an eerie quality to it.

"And that's it for aliens?" I asked with a squeak.

"Well, no. There's the Soma Café creatures," Fiona said.

"Soma Café? Say you don't mean it." I moaned.

Haggerty turned an I-told-you-so grin my way. "They came with the idea of enslaving Earthlings. They brought a substance from their world, to which Earth mortals proved to be highly addictive. They believed that and the fact that their coffee contains no caffeine would make everyone quite malleable."

Hah! I wasn't malleable. Addicted, sure, but not malleable. Now I understood how regular coffee gave me such a monster buzz. "You should do something about this, Haggerty. The FBI, I mean. They shouldn't be allowed to get away with this."

She rolled her eyes. "Don't worry. They'll have enough troubles without bringing the Bureau into it. Some venture capital group has initiated a hostile takeover of Soma Café. They won't be around much longer."

"And that's absolutely all the aliens presently on this rock?" I asked Haggerty.

With a trace of smug superiority in her voice, she said, "Every single one of them."

I believed her. From her unique position as a goddess and an FBI agent, she'd have to know, right?

I just wished I understood why Angus stared pointedly at Fiona. And why Fiona, who gathered the tea things instead of simply making them disappear, seemed determined to look away.

CHAPTER TWENTY-THREE

Gwydion, the Celtic god of enchantment and illusion, who'd posed for decades as the Roswell alien, surveyed his new accommodations. The militia had freed him from his mobile cell and transferred him to a bedroom within the compound. No windows, of course, and a locked door. But that had never mattered to him. Even in his powered-down state, he could leave at will. Child's play.

He sometimes made himself invisible and went to check on that installation deep in this compound where they kept the hostages. Not that he particularly cared how they fared, but others would, and he wanted the leverage of having taken care of them.

What fools they were, these mortals. How gullible, how capable they were of duping themselves. One of them had actually seen him in his natural state, when Gwydion had tried to save a little power by returning to his real form. Now it seemed they'd deliberately made the choice to forget how he really looked, when they discovered how he could look. *Why had he overestimated them?*

Unfortunately, maintaining his alien appearance now precluded him from laughing on the outside. He had modeled his guise on a space traveler from a 1940s movie, and that creature's mouth didn't lend itself to significant movement. Inside, of course, he quivered with laughter.

Was it any wonder he'd taken such pleasure from poking fun at mortals for decades? His mind reeled when he thought of how he might have handled this situation had he possessed his full powers. Damn the Ruling Council. If only the more righteous among his brethren weren't determined to become as responsible as they could be. Why should they? Why should any god feel entitled to sap the powers of another god? Well...unless, like Gwydion, that was the only way to survive.

At least the militia leaders were smart enough to outwit Handy Hanover. They let the soldier think they had a deal so he'd appear in their video. That he was identifiable as a legitimate soldier, one the press could discover had been assigned to the mysterious Area 51 military base, lent credence to the militia's claim. Once the militia leaders got what they needed from Handy, however,

MAGICAL ALIENATION

they locked him up, after dealing him a few good blows.

Gwydion heard footsteps snapping against the cement floor outside his room, and then the sound of the deadbolt being turned. A pair of men entered. Boys, really. Both wore the fatigues the militia favored. Those costumes must have been made for stouter men, however, because they ballooned around these slim ones and hung off their young shoulders.

One of the guards entered carrying a food tray. Like all gods, Gwydion didn't need to eat, but he enjoyed it, and he'd grown so accustomed to this century's provisions. They'd brought him a sandwich made from a thick slab of turkey between slices of homemade wheat bread, as well as a pile of potato chips and a canned soft drink. These survivalists' existence wasn't as ascetic as they wanted outsiders to believe, Gwydion observed with amusement.

The hands of the boy carrying the tray shook when he placed it on the bed beside Gwydion. While his eyes mostly remained downcast, he stole occasional glances at their captive. The other boy carried an automatic rifle, but he held it so indifferently, it appeared that he'd forgotten it rested between his hands. Though the armed boy's jaw hung open—whether in shock or because it never closed, Gwydion couldn't say—but awe glittered in the boy's gullible eyes. Gwydion could have turned that youngster's allegiance away from his militia masters in a heartbeat.

Just for fun, Gwydion directed his dark-glass alien eyes on them. And he pulled those eyes into the position he had discovered could convey anger. He hadn't been wrong about that expression. Those boys tripped over their own big-booted feet trying to get out of there as fast as possible.

Once he heard the sound of the deadbolt being thrown behind them, snickering sounds emerged from the alien's small, round mouth. Gwydion couldn't hold it in any longer. The irony of the situation was just too delicious. If only they knew the true nature of another of the inhabitants in their own compound.

CHAPTER TWENTY-FOUR

When my head hit the pillow that night, I drifted off, but not into my usual like-the-dead sleep. Agitated but exhausted, I vaguely noted when my spirit drifted up from my body, but I felt too drowsy to stop it.

Within moments, I found myself alone on a cloud. The cloud didn't feel anything like I expected, neither moist nor cottony, but even softer than the feather topper on Fiona's guestroom bed. While it had been night and kettle-black down where my body slept, the cloud was bathed in a warm, golden sunlight, the sky above me a brilliant indigo. Though I'd gone to bed in an oversized T-shirt, with my kimono draped across the foot of the bed, I found myself naked now, quite unselfconsciously so.

My skin tingled in some unidentified anticipation. Then Angus appeared at the edge of the cloud and slowly walked toward me, as proudly naked as I felt. I turned away. Without a word, he lifted my hair and planted a gentle kiss on the back of my neck. And so began the dance we'd engaged in countless times, but which always seemed new, and always exciting.

Angus left a trail of kisses from my breasts to my thighs, which ignited a mounting inferno within me. I felt absolutely beautiful, seeing myself as I must have appeared in his eyes, enchanting and ethereal. With our limbs entwined, we writhed with abandon under the glowing sun. Then I mounted my love god's magnificent sword and rode him like an untamed stallion.

Our voices mingled, screaming with delight. Cries of "Oh, yes!" filled the heavens. Our passions united, building each time to new heights. Until our fever finally materialized in physical form, exploding above us in a shower of tiny sparkles that rained down on us, which caused my skin to quiver with delight.

Contentment painted Angus's face, and the silver flecks in his eyes glowed brighter than ever. Feeling secure and protected, I curled up at his side. Time ceased to exist. A moment might have passed or a year, and I wouldn't have known. A soft sigh of satisfaction said it all.

Until…back in the physical realm, my body became more alert, more aware. With the echoes of "Oh, yes" still drifting among the clouds, "Oh, no" came to overshadow the sounds of pleasure.

I pulled away and knelt beside him. "Angus, what have we done? This…this…can't happen."

Confusion muscled the fulfillment from his handsome face. "But it's happened other times, Sammy. Why would you object now?"

"Like this?" I gestured to the cloud.

He nodded. "Astrally, sure. The only way we can be together, until you forgive me." His grin seemed to say that forgiveness would be granted eventually. "You see, my girl, I put a charm on you, allowing you to come to me like this when I called."

All the pleasure we'd found in each other only moments before vanished instantly within me. "Angus! Against my will? How could you?" Did a god's charm trump a mortal's spell? Was that why my banishing spell hadn't worked?

"I wouldn't! I'm not a cad."

Someone really should do something about his lingo. When was the last time anyone said *cad?*

"You've made the choice, Samantha. You have the power to refuse."

"Then why haven't I?"

Angus pressed his full lips together, holding back some thought. I glanced down at my body, suddenly aware of my nakedness. A flush of shame spread through me.

"Clothes. I need clothes."

"Samantha, it's not as if—"

"Clothes, Angus." The kimono I had brought with me, a red one with goofy-looking purple dragons, wrapped around me on its own. I tightened the sash. "This can never happen again. Don't issue any more invitations because…" I let that thought remain unfinished. "Send me away now."

This time I didn't drift back, I was just instantly in my corporal form, back in the bed. My eyes popped open, thoroughly awake. No wonder I hadn't felt sex-starved. It wasn't exactly like I was doing without it. I also understood why Haggerty hadn't seen my aura glowing, either. This—what Angus and I kept sharing—wasn't totally real, yet wasn't totally unreal, either.

I finally uttered within my own mind the thought I wasn't able to say to Angus. I couldn't have him issuing any more of these astral invitations—because I wasn't strong enough to refuse them.

I closed my eyes and tried to put behind me what had surely been the best night I'd known in a long time. How much sense did that make? If this was what Fiona meant by my fate, it sucked. Some surprise.

CHAPTER TWENTY-FIVE

My dismal mood survived the night. I awoke in too few hours, feeling like crap.

I'd never had much staying power—when the going gets tough, I was usually first out the door. But I had sensed from the start that if Angus and I were to have any kind of a future, I had to deal with him as an equal, not like one of the pushover mortals Haggerty said filled the mythology books. Even if our breakup hurt, I'd taken pride in my demand for fidelity. Now I was crushed to discover that I not only couldn't resist him, I was so wussy, I lied to myself about it.

I'd hoped to ease into the day. No such luck. Instead, I awoke to the sound of chatter. So much of it, I feared a herd of squirrels had invaded the house.

I shifted Mellencamp from where he'd slept on my kimono and threw it on. I cracked the door and peered out, in case the squirrels were poised to attack. Rather than rodents, I saw about a dozen tiny little men, who, despite their wrinkled faces and white beards, were the size of three-year-olds. They were all dressed in green suits and pointy hats, and they looked like us, apart from their Vulcan ears. Pixies?

The chatter was even louder without a closed door separating us. They all talked at once, though they spoke exclusively in chirps and whistles and clicks of their tongues. Even stranger than the sight of those little creatures was what they were doing—cleaning the house, at a frenetic pace.

Was it safe for me to leave my room? Would they be kind to a poor little fake psychic? Mellencamp wandered out from between my feet, greeting them with an indifferent, "Myrrh," which elicited an accelerated round of pops in response. Since they didn't appear armed, with anything more lethal than cans of Lemon Pledge anyway, I tiptoed into their midst. None of them paid the slightest attention to me. They just kept spritzing polish and whistling and clicking, as they flowed around me like a river streams around a rock.

Fiona picked that moment to breeze in from the kitchen. Before I felt ready to face her. Would she know what I did with Angus? She might have directed a momentary look of piercing scrutiny at me, making me wonder whether she sensed my secret, but it ended so quickly, I wasn't sure if I'd imagined it.

I tried to guide the scrutiny elsewhere. "Fiona…who are these…?" While the pixies hadn't acknowledged me, it seemed rude to ask about them while they were present. I cleared my throat. "Annabelle uses…a…you know…" I'd witnessed a small dark creature, clothed only in a loincloth, who cleaned Haggerty's house, yet the being had so weirded me out, I couldn't bring myself to speak of it.

"A brownie?" Fiona asked. "Yes, brownies are wonderful. So devoted. But I think a cleaning crew is more efficient, and lots more fun. Right, boys?"

Big grins spread across their tiny faces to reveal unexpectedly large teeth. The chattering and pops exploded.

"That's true, fellas," Fiona said with a laugh. "Thank Danu for pixies."

She heard their answer from those pops and whistles? I didn't want to know how.

"Samantha, the boys are baking us muffins for breakfast. Would you be a dear and go fetch the newspaper?"

The pixies finally turned their grins my way, chattering like a band of rogue squirrels in a nut plant. I escaped out the front door, with Mellencamp on my heels.

I didn't find it much more comfortable outside. Not with that crimson path and those red rock lions there. That was the trouble with being around Haggerty's family. I like to think of myself as freewheeling, not an anal-retentive bone in my lush body. Only they kept opening new worlds before me, worlds I never knew existed. After I discovered how little control any of us had, I realized how desperately I needed it.

Not during the fun times, not when we were making crop circles and icebergs. Only when the dark little corners of the universe beckoned me, and I knew I had no defense against what I'd find in them.

But I was stalling there on the doorstep, pondering pointless woo-woo issues, so I wouldn't have to step on that red path that could soften to quicksand in a flash.

I pressed my foot onto the path. No softening, no shifting. With a shrug, I trotted down it. Apart from a stone that pricked my bare toe, nothing bad happened.

By the time I reached where the folded newspaper lay at the end of the path, I decided that Haggerty had been having some fun with me when she told me that story about the rock people. With all the crystals I used in my job as a spiritual advisor, I knew rocks. I'd never sensed a person in any of them. I became so confident that the whole idea was a crock, that, despite the howls from Mellencamp, I leaned heavily on one of those rock lions, while I opened the paper.

And the lion moved! So help me. Its head twitched irritably. That stunned me too much to even budge. When the twitching didn't make me remove my arm, as it seemed to want, the lion threw its head back, tossing my arm aside. Then it opened its stone jaw and roared. I swear!

I jumped away. When I finally found the nerve to look at the statue again, it looked like a stationary stone lion once more. I glanced around the neighborhood for someone who might have seen what happened, and who could then assure me I wasn't crazy. But, for once, the street was empty.

I ran back to the house so fast, I couldn't remember my feet touching the path.

I zipped through the front door, holding it open long enough for Mellencamp to stroll in. The pixies were gathered now in Fiona's sunny yellow kitchen with its hickory cabinets, where they brewed coffee, squeezed oranges, and transferred pans of muffins to baskets lined with checkered linen napkins.

They turned bright smiles my way, before chirping at Fiona.

"The boys think you're related to one of us, too, Samantha," Fiona said. "Only none of us are sure who you might be descended from. Why else would the universe have brought you into our lives?"

Right. "Do the Celts have a devil?" I asked, taking a place at the pine table.

A twinkle floated into Fiona's blue-and-gold eyes. "Millions of them. A bit in all of us, and considerably more in some."

Too metaphysical for me at that hour. At any hour. I reached into the muffin basket and chose one with a sugary icing that Fiona described as a French toast muffin—it looked to-die-for. She also promised the elves would be making fresh bread and cheddar-ale soup for dinner. Enticing, too, but after what happened with the rock lion outside, I wondered if it was safe to eat anything the pixies made.

Before I could try a nibble from the muffin that smelled deliciously of syrup and cinnamon, I heard the front door slam. Only one person entered this house that way. Funny, I never saw her slam any other door. Was this the way she'd always entered her mother's house? Do we all become little kids again around our moms?

"Samantha? Samantha, where are you?" Haggerty called. She stepped into the kitchen doorway. "You're not dressed yet."

I wasn't fed, either, and I considered that more important.

"Come on, my girl," she said, more gaily than usual. "Let's get going. The Bureau is back in the game."

For that I should give up my breakfast? I grabbed another French toast muffin, as I allowed myself to be dragged away.

I dressed in record time, thanks to Haggerty's repeated poundings on the door. In honor of my first meeting with her, I wore my new Renaissance ball gown. I had worn my first one when Haggerty and I met, but that gown had bitten the dust in the course of that caper. This one was royal blue velvet, with a scoop neckline seemingly made for my ample cleavage. I wrapped a piece of orange organdy under my long hair and tied it into a huge bow on top of my head.

Haggerty lifted one of the bow ends. "Glad you didn't go to any fuss."

Hey, she wore those dorky suits so people would take her seriously as an FBI agent—this was spiritual advisor dressing.

The Bureau had provided her with a black Crown Victoria with a siren and rooftop bubble light. The siren helped Haggerty make her way through the swelling crowds, as we drove to Rand's inn. Along the way, she caught me up on things. The tour's promoter had been on the horn to the Bureau's higher ups, demanding confirmation that the Sex, Drugs & Rock 'n' Roll tour would proceed on schedule. The start was only ten days away now, and Rand was still being held here. If Rand worried about the tour being in jeopardy, he hid it well. For now, the FBI brass wouldn't budge on his house arrest. Haggerty also confirmed that although some military intelligence unit was still in charge of the operation, the FBI had been brought back to help with a sting they planned against the militia.

A sting? Now I understood why she wanted me along. If they were pulling a con, they'd need my expertise. I drew such a proud breath, my boobs nearly popped out the top of my dress.

A moment later, Haggerty said something to indicate that maybe she wasn't as taken with my skills as I thought. "When we get there, just follow my lead. Don't put your foot in it."

Me? Hah! What she knew about pulling scams wouldn't fill my gown's pockets—assuming they weren't already stuffed with muffins.

Rand's inn was as much a ghost town as it had been the first time I'd seen it. Some places were clearly better at keeping the squatters away than others. Haggerty brought the car to a halt in front of his suite.

She must have called ahead, because Rand opened the door before we knocked. He showed us to one of the seating areas in that huge room. The table there already contained some bottled fizzy water and dusty-looking water crackers.

For breakfast? Now that I'd sworn off Soma Café, I vowed to suck in as much caffeine as possible. Where was the coffee? The pastries? I felt doubly glad now that I'd made off with handfuls of macadamia nuts the last time I was there.

Haggerty perched on the edge of a sofa. "Mr. Riker, we're planning to take action against the militia, and we need your help."

With my shoulder pressed to hers, I could feel her anxiety.

"Sir, we'd like you to reschedule your benefit concert. Only this time, we want you to tell the public that you're hosting it to help, not Normal Frankly, but…the alien."

Not a line you hear every day.

Rand gave his head a thoughtful tilt. "Not a bad idea."

With that admission, Haggerty's tension level fell a notch. "You won't actually have to hold it."

"I might, though. I'll need to give every appearance of it being a genuine effort. You'll have to send me bandmates back. The press will catch on soon enough if I'm here and they're not. And you'll have to open the town to the public again. The people who buy tickets will expect that."

She met his suggestions with a tight nod. They were suggestions, though, not demands. Rand wasn't bargaining. With the time before the start of the tour dwindling fast, while the concert promoter had tried twisting the arm of every higher up in the entire Department of Justice, Rand seemed unconcerned.

"You don't think much of me, do you, Agent Haggerty?" He went on before she had a chance to answer. "Well, why should you, with the things I've done? When you're a star, people excuse everything. I'm trying to be a better person, just because it's right."

The word *right* came out sounding *raight* in his broad Aussie accent. Either way I wasn't buying it.

He offered her a wicked grin. "But people continue to make it easy for me to be bad."

Haggerty picked at an invisible spot on her skirt. "You'll probably find this hard to believe, but I know a little about that. There's satisfaction in overcoming the temptation to seize the easy way."

Rand didn't laugh at her, though he must have been cracking up inside. Imagine this stodgy Fibbie thinking she had any idea what it was like for a rock star. He should know that if he had laughed, she might have turned him into a toad, or an ugly, sexless guy, which would have been worse. Lucky for him, she'd been using her powers even less than usual.

"What do you say, Mr. Riker?"

"Happy to serve, luv."

Instead of seizing his agreement and running, she asked, "What if those fire letters return? How strong will your resolve be?"

"You're mocking me, aren't you? Why shouldn't you? Fire letters—crazy idea, what? I wonder if maybe I just had one of those flashbacks the anti-drug crowd always warns us about." He gave her an emphatic bow of his head. "I said I'm in, and I am. How should we proceed?"

"To begin with, we'll need to make use of Samantha."

Nice of her to tell me.

"We'd like you to acknowledge her as your personal psychic," Haggerty said. "You don't actually have to hire her back."

Nice of her to tell *him*.

Rand's dark head fell forward. "Yeah, I do." He raised his pitch eyes to me. "I treated you rotten, Samantha. I took it out on you because that Bureau bloke riled me. Can you forgive me?"

I nodded, tossing those bow loops over my eyes.

"Truth is, I've never taken you from the payroll. Me business man back in L.A. will have a check waiting for you when we return. Will you rejoin the team, Madame Samantha?"

MAGICAL ALIENATION

I gave the bow a shove. "I'll work for you, Rand, but I'd just as soon keep living where I am now. I don't want to field any more of your sloppy come-ons." I poured myself some of his crappy fizzy water.

Rand gave me a roguish grin. "I told you good behavior doesn't come easily to me. Sure thing, sleep wherever you want, but you'd be safe enough here. I'm actually trying to remain...celibate."

If I didn't have considerable impulse control—well, some—I'd have spewed his stupid water all over his face. I knew he was lying—there was no mistaking the nature of the laughter I'd overheard.

I got the feeling Rand had been toying with the idea of using another word in place of *celibate*. *Monogamous* maybe? Just as hard to believe. What could any one woman offer him that he couldn't get a thousand times over from others? Well, Fiona could give him unimaginable things, but who else could?

CHAPTER TWENTY-SIX
Haggerty

This was a nightmare of unimaginable proportions. Haggerty had been stripped of her powers now, until she was scarcely distinguishable from an ordinary mortal. Oh, she kept a bit of magical energy in reserve, but that was all. Perhaps that was all she would ever have, for the rest of her life.

She had to tell Fiona, she knew that. Yet she kept putting it off, hoping against hope that somehow this situation would reverse itself. She couldn't admit to her mother that she might have done this to herself.

She was being punished, though. The world had lost all its color. She and her kind experienced it with a greater intensity than mortals could imagine. And now that was gone.

A more serious consequence was that she was being forced to work blind, and at a time when she needed every resource she could muster. In every moment of this crisis, she was risking her life.

Even worse, she was risking Samantha's life by allowing Samantha to trust in her, even though she knew she couldn't save her friend as she should have been able to.

If anything happened to Samantha, how would she live with herself?

CHAPTER TWENTY-SEVEN
Samantha

While I stood before the gate to Normal Frankly's compound waiting to be admitted, with the press cameras in the distance rolling, my knees shook so badly, my heels wobbled like Jell-O in a storm. So much had happened the prior day, it had passed in a blur. Only now I found the details flashing before my eyes with startling clarity, like I was about to die. No exaggeration, I could seriously be living my final moments. Was it really worth doing *anything* to get on TV?

Within an hour of securing his agreement yesterday, Haggerty had Rand before the cameras, announcing his plans to reschedule the benefit concert, which would now serve the Roswell alien. Nothing short of surreal, I tell you. I figured the reporters would crack up when he voiced his intention, but everyone played it straight. Well, pretty straight.

"What expenses would you imagine this creature will have, Rand?" someone asked.

He'd need to build a spaceship, of course, since his got busted up when he landed. Were these people listening to themselves?

Rand went so fast into his scripted answer, I figured the questioner for a stooge. "He'll need a legal team, won't he? They've denied him due process all these years. And a place to live after he gets out."

Maybe a condo in Marina del Rey, in case he decided to star in a reality TV show.

"And something to live on," Rand went on.

Sure. If the TV gig fell through, there weren't many listings in the classifieds for space creatures. It all sounded so silly, I tuned it out. Until Rand came to the point of the whole exercise.

He looked straight into the camera. "Before we finish, I'd like to speak to the Arizona Friends of Freedom Militia. You know me—I'm no threat to you or your hostages. Won't you let me meet with him, the Roswell bloke? If you won't permit me enter your compound, please allow my psychic, Madame Samantha Brennan, to be my stand-in."

That was my cue to come to his side. I was told to offer the camera a goofy grin, but I would have done that anyway.

Not long after Rand's performance, Senator Campbell, speaking from his Sedona home, went before the cameras himself, denouncing Rand's offer, and especially, my role in it.

"You and I have areas of agreement in our politics," Kenny had said to the militia through the camera. "We all think government is too big." He cleared his throat. "I especially urge you not to meet with this…New Age person. Avoid the darkness of the occult."

That was Haggerty's attempt at reverse psychology. From the start she and François had hoped that the militia would regard me as less of a threat than Rand. And they thought that Kenny's disapproval would push them my way. Could those militia clowns be such confirmed dupes?

Turns out, they could. Even though the militia had succeeded in foiling the government, they were every bit as dumb as the Bureau hoped. Not long after Kenny's impassioned performance, the militia contacted the negotiator to say that I, not Rand, could enter the compound and meet the alien.

The Bureau really went to work at that point. Haggerty rushed me to their makeshift office, where I rehearsed their script.

Yet even when rehearsals went perfectly, François was never happy. He pursed his pale lips and said, "You sure you're up to this, Guinevere?"

"Don't worry about me…" I almost said, "Paleface." Finally, I substituted, "…G-Man."

Yet *I* worried. I feared I would blow it.

My spirits rose when Haggerty and I drove up to her mom's house, and I spotted a pair of ravens that were perched on the roof. They cried out when they saw us.

"Haggerty, look," I said. "It's Lugh and Taliesin." They, like Gwydion, were shape-shifter gods, and the raven form was one of their favorites.

Haggerty released a happy sigh. "Mom said she'd find them."

Despite her obvious relief, she bit her lip, scraping her mauve lipstick with her tooth. We both knew that what I had rehearsed with François was only part of the operation Haggerty planned. The rest would be the province of the beings that populated her secret world.

MAGICAL ALIENATION

Would they fall in line as easily?

I ran to the house, oblivious of the red rock lions. I assumed the ravens disappeared from the roof the instant I came through the door, since the guys were there to greet me.

"Sammy!" They smothered me in a group hug.

In their natural form, they're a funny looking pair. Taliesin is a stout, muscular god, with unruly brown hair and a wide, rubbery grin, who always wears yellow warm-up suits when he visits our world. Lugh, on the other hand, is as tall as a basketball player, but twice as thin, with a thick shock of bright red hair, who wears jeans, though they always hang over his perpetually bare feet. To say they're clueless would be putting it mildly, but I found that endearing. That was true for all the *Danaans*. They don't get our world, though they're convinced they do.

Once we separated, I saw that the boys hadn't come alone. Angus stood across the room, and I saw fury in that god's flashing blue-silver eyes. Was it because of the way our astral tryst had ended?

Fortunately, it wasn't directed at me. "Annie, what were you thinking with this plan of yours?" he'd asked Haggerty. "Samantha's mortal. You can't let her take this risk."

Haggerty's gaze avoided his. "She knows what she's doing, Angus."

That wasn't true. I never did. But I had made my choice.

"She's going to see Gwydion," Lugh had cried. "Let the girl have some fun. What's gotten into you, Angus?"

"He's in lo-ooo-ve," Taliesin teased, stretching the word out.

"It's too dangerous," Angus had insisted mulishly.

"It's not your business, Angus," I'd said. "Butt out."

Now, as I stood before the gate, scared witless, I wished I'd listened to him. Too late, though—the compound's fortified metal door was opening.

Two bruisers emerged carrying automatic rifles. Their wary eyes flickered over the area beyond the electric gate, which the government controlled. But, as agreed, there wasn't a Fed in sight.

When the electric gate slid open, I tried to walk through the narrow opening, but my skirt's crinolines made it tough to fit through. The guys each gripped one of my velvet-clad arms and lifted me off the ground, moving me through the metal door into the facility. The instant that door sealed shut behind us, they deposited me on a concrete floor, painted in rust-colored enamel.

No escape now.

The corridor was so dimly lit it took a moment for my eyes to adjust. It stretched out in both directions, taking bends at the points where it disappeared into the shadows. Its walls, poured from some high gauge metal, looked fortified beyond belief.

No-Neck met us there. Why hadn't he come out to escort me? Protecting his non-neck from the threats outside? Baldy joined him. Neither acknowledged knowing me. Despite the fullness of my dress, one of the guards gave me a very thorough frisking.

"This way," Baldy said in clipped tones. He led the way down the dimly lit corridor. No-Neck and the others followed us.

Automatic rifles, obviously controlled from some central command center, were mounted every ten feet or so, on those metal walls. The first time I saw one pivot on its own, I thought it was aiming at me, and I nearly collapsed. With those alone, not to mention their armed men, they could cover every part of that place.

Sounds echoed in the concrete and metal tube: Their heavy boot steps and the clickity-clack of my heels. The painted floor proved to be an unexpected benefit, which would make it easier to carry out my assignment.

"Whoops!" I cried, as I slipped to the floor.

Struggling ungainly to my feet, my hand slid along the side of my thigh, and then slapped against the darkish wall, seemingly for support.

We continued on. I really did have a hard time walking in heels on that floor. No faking required. I slipped again and had to hit the wall for support.

While lumbering back to my feet, I looked back down the hall. Where the dark corridor took a turn, a pulsing glow brightened that shadowy spot. A silhouette stood within that pearly radiance, someone with an elongated head and a stretched out torso. Normal Frankly. How had he produced that flickering light?

No-Neck yanked me to my feet. When I looked back, both the glow and the elongated figure had vanished. Had I imagined seeing him? Nobody else reacted at all.

After a few more pratfalls, one of the guys behind me asked Baldy, "Is she drunk?"

MAGICAL ALIENATION

"No, she's just dumb," he insisted.

Dumb like a fox. But I fell so often in that corridor, with its closed metal doors, that two of them finally took my arms and carried me the rest of the way. I hoped I'd taken enough spills.

They deposited me at a door with an armed guard standing outside of it, a younger guard than most of the men in the compound. His rigid stance spoke to how seriously he took his role, but his oversized Adam's apple bobbed so often, he looked like a high school kid who feared he wasn't gonna ace this alternative ROTC.

The kid stepped aside, and Baldy unlocked the door. Anxiety so overwhelmed me, I couldn't budge. Someone jabbed me with a rifle and shoved me into the room.

There, flopped on the bed—was the alien. A freakin' alien! No, wait. There was no such thing as an alien—coyotes and coffee barons, my ass. This was Gwydion, pal of my pals, just having fun. He looked so much like some bad movie space creature that it freaked me out.

I cleared my throat. "Are you being treated well?" I asked in a squeak.

"He don't talk," Baldy said. "Can't you see? He's being treated like a king."

Did that snotty remark reflect Baldy's resentment? I went into the script. "A great performer is working on your behalf to make your life better, however you choose to live it."

"Stupid broad," Baldy muttered. "Don't you get it? He doesn't know English."

But Gwydion turned his oversized alien head my way. Eyelids, previously unseen, sheeted down over his big, glassy eyes. Like he was blinking at me.

"Did you see that? Think he understands?" No-Neck's reedy voice rose octaves.

His fear made me more confident. "I want to shake his hand," I said, abandoning the contrived script, which would have built to that demand.

"Stay where you are," Baldy ordered

Before I could protest, Gwydion extended his alien hand to me.

"He *does* understand." That was from No-Neck again, shrieking now.

I grabbed the hand extended to me. His alien skin, which had intrigued me on the tube, felt like Neoprene. I held onto his four-fingered hand as if my life depended on it. Which it did, along with a whole lot of other lives.

Would this work? I was touching him, but nobody else was touching me. Haggerty and I had always used direct contact to pass visions, but she had more powerful gods in her camp now.

Instantly, I became so weak, it took all I had not to sink onto the bed. It was as if my life force had been sucked out.

An incredible range of emotions flowed through me: Fear…excitement…hope…anger. They were like breezes blowing through my weary body.

"Awright, that's enough," Baldy said, poking me with his rifle.

But I held onto Gwydion. His weird fingers tightened around mine. A little shock went through me, like a jolt of electricity. With that, my energy soared beyond normal.

He had sent me a signal, I felt sure. Or someone had.

What did it mean?

CHAPTER TWENTY-EIGHT

On my way from Gwydion's room to the exit, I tripped another couple of times.

"You sure she's not drunk?" one of my escorts asked again.

"She's just stupid for wearing those shoes," Baldly said sourly.

While I was neither, who says you can't be *both* drunk and stupid?

Once the compound gate closed behind me, relief made me so giddy, my body tingled. Yet I also regretted that my journey into the terrorist-whale's belly had ended. There's nothing like abject fear to make you feel alive. François was there to meet me at the gate. Though the weather was warm, he wore a long-sleeved knit shirt and had popped a Diamondbacks cap on his head. With his ultra-fair skin, tanning probably wasn't an option.

He brought me back to the mobile command post that had become the province of those MI folks. The rear door flew open, and I lumbered in, squeezing my puffy gown between those workstations. François, to my surprise, waited outside. Haggerty might believe the Bureau had been brought back into the game, but she and her paleface companion had been relegated to the grunt work.

A muscular man in his forties, with one eye that opened less than the other, giving him a permanent squint, met us there. That his choppy hair looked like he'd hacked it off himself, without a mirror, didn't add to his appeal.

The squinter never gave me his name. He just indicated for me to stand beside a young soldier, working with some kind of architectural computer program. He made me describe the layout of the part of the compound I'd seen, which the soldier translated into a floor plan. I knew they had blueprints from when the compound was built, but they probably wanted to see if the militia had made any changes since then. Too bad I'd seen so little of it.

"What about those disks?" Squinty asked. "Were you able to place any of them?"

"Nearly all," I assured him.

Knowing the militia would check to see whether I was

armed, the MI team never asked me to carry a weapon. Instead, they attached two rows of translucent disks along my thigh, which I was told to press to walls throughout the place. I didn't know what purpose those disks would serve, but they were why I was sent into that compound. The Feds thought I'd have a better chance of spreading around them than Rand. Go figure, but some people regard me as a flake.

"Any chance they'll spot the disks?" Squinty asked, squeezing that eye further shut.

I gave my head an emphatic toss, which sent my curly hair flying in such a wide radius, the guy before the computer had to duck. "Not a chance. They're strictly into ten-watt bulbs in there."

A few of the stony faces in that van gave each other pointed looks. They hid them quickly, yet not so fast that I missed them. Squinty glanced at me to see if I picked up on that collective glee, but I was better at hiding my feelings than he was.

The telling part of the whole debriefing was that nobody said anything about the alien. Not one word. The alien they still claimed had never landed here, whose spaceship had supposedly been a weather balloon. They didn't have to ask whether he really existed because they'd been holding him all these years. Sure, I knew the story about the Roswell crash wasn't true, but they didn't.

This military intelligence crew could give the militia crowd a real run for the gold metal event in the Simpleton Olympics.

When François drove me back to Fiona's house, the red rocks beckoned me so strongly, it was as if they called me by name. I'd resisted them so far. I mean, I was no hiker—look at the shoes you have to wear. But they kept luring me.

François asked me to describe what I'd seen in there. I told him about the metal walls and doors, as well as the mounted weapons.

"So it's as fortified as we feared," he said with a tense sigh.

"Is that why the Bureau hasn't stormed it?"

"That, and the lives of the hostages they're holding. The FBI doesn't need another Waco." While François acted distracted, he kept sneaking looks my way. Finally, he said, "Samantha?"

Whoa! No Guinevere?

He cleared his throat. "What about…the critter?"

The critter? I wondered if Gwydion took discounting as well as I did. "I'll tell you this, G-Man—it's not a Halloween costume." How was that for evasive maneuvering?

I told him he could drop me off at the Bureau office, and I'd hoof it to Fiona's. Instead, he made the turn into her street. Damn. I'd hoped some reporters would follow me there.

"Guinevere…" he began. "Not a word of what went on in there to anyone, and especially the media. Understand?"

Had he read my mind? Was everyone besides me psychic? It couldn't be that I was that transparent.

"I mean it. You flap your gums, and you'll wind up in jail."

He flashed me a flinty little smile. His eyeteeth were unusually long, I noticed; one more thing about him that put me off. Well, he wasn't *that* bad. With his full lips and the strong lines of his face, he was pretty cute, in a brooding loner-kinda way, if you could get past skin the color of kindergarten paste.

François warned me again about keeping my trap shut and drove away. As soon as he did, two ravens perched on the roof and greeted me. Once more, by the time I crashed through the door, Lugh and Taliesin waited inside. Haggerty and her mother stood behind them. Angus scowled at his pals from across the room.

"So? How did it go?" I demanded. "Were you able to establish a connection to Gwydion?"

It was Haggerty who suggested to Squinty that, if they could get someone disarming into that compound, they'd have a way of scattering those mysterious disks. And who could be less disarming than me? But Haggerty had always performed her job on two levels. Besides working as an ordinary agent, this time she also called on Fiona and their ancestors to form a psychic link with me, which they hoped they could use to reach Gwydion.

"We sure did." Taliesin laughed so hard, he looked like a banana blur. "You're an outstanding conduit, my girl."

I remembered the jolt I felt while holding onto Gwydion. Was that proof the link had been made? How long would that connection last?

"But he's quite depleted," Lugh said, shaking his wild red hair. "The Ruling Council has reduced his powers to their lowest levels. I don't know why they don't just yank him out of there, instead of humiliating him like this."

Haggerty piped up with, "Maybe the humiliation is meant to be a lesson."

They squabbled over the Council's right to strip any god's power. Lugh railed on about the case of that monster goddess that Haggerty had told me about, Rele-de, who was condemned to living life-after-life as a mortal, and how unfair that sentence was, as well as a few other cases. I yawned. The politics of my own realm didn't hold my interest for long, so why should I care about theirs? When I saw that, even though she had started it, Haggerty now quietly extricated herself from the fracas and slipped to the kitchen, I followed her.

Though I came in right behind her, she didn't appear to notice me. I watched as she took a glass from a cabinet, filled it with tap water, and then just stood there without taking a sip.

"So...I did okay?" I asked, giving her nudge. She'd never been that effusive with her praise. I had to squeeze it out of her.

"You were wonderful."

"And someone else...what? Stunk? Who else was involved?"

"Me," she said, with a sob catching in her throat. "I felt nothing. Nothing." She sniffed. "My powers are so depleted, Samantha, I'm scarcely more sensitive now than you are."

I always thought that was what she wanted. "Use it or lose it, babe."

I thought she'd deny it, but instead, she looked guilty.

"What have I done?" she whispered, so softly, I wasn't sure I heard it right.

Fiona stepped into the doorway. "Don't listen to Samantha, Annabelle. She doesn't know what she's talking about." She offered me a warm smile to soften the sting. "It's just...the harmonic convergence. Most of us find our powers strengthened, but a few find themselves depleted. You're just one of the unlucky ones."

Maybe that harmonica-thingie was all Fiona said it was. But she was also hiding something—I could spot her evasions now. What secrets were so important that she would lie to her precious daughter to keep them?

CHAPTER TWENTY-NINE

That night I couldn't get to sleep. I wasn't worried about Angus calling me. He might try his charm again, but not so soon after I chewed him out. The campers out in the yard had been noisy earlier, but that shouldn't have bothered me, either. My mom and I had crashed in so many places when I was a kid, that I could fall asleep along a parade route. Well, unless I'd just gobbled down a few chilidogs and maybe had a snootful of tequila, but that was true for everyone, right? I rationalized that my restlessness was the result of an exciting day. Yet as I tossed in bed, I'd swear those red rocks called out to me.

They cried out, not in some dreamy woo-woo voice with the mesmerizing echo effect they use in moody movies, but more like, "Samantha, get your big butt out here so we can talk." Okay, an exaggeration, yet that was how it felt. As if there was something important I would learn if I followed my instincts and went.

Last night, after the subject of that harmonica-thingie came up again, I'd questioned Fiona about it.

"So…this harmonica-thingie…"

Fiona turned me to face her. "Samantha, I really have to ask that you learn its name. I'm not sure we can take any more of your 'harmonica-thingies.' Repeat after me: harmonic convergence."

Hey, I wasn't an idiot. I'd learned how to say it. I just liked my own version better.

Fiona would have none of that. She covered my forehead with her hand, and she made me say it correctly. In an instant, I couldn't remember how I used to say it anymore.

"The harmonic convergence means that the planets are coming into their most favorable positions in ages," she said. "That will magnify the amplification properties of the vortices here by many times. And the lunar eclipse…"

Yeah, exactly how Haggerty had explained it. I still didn't get what that meant.

Fiona proceeded to explain with more patience than her daughter had ever shown me. "It causes feelings to be exaggerated, but sometimes it also brings about a great clarity of thought and a new focusing of energies."

Still trying to nail it down, I said, *"My* feelings, right? *My* feelings, *my* thoughts, *my* energies?"

"Not always. You might tap into the Great Collective Unconsciousness. Then you'd feel things you've never experienced before."

Great collective hooey, I thought at the time. Only here I was now, climbing out of bed at one-thirty in the morning because of something I didn't believe in.

Mellencamp tilted his head appealingly. Since I was getting into this feline communication, I knew he was asking to come.

"Not this time, boy," I said.

Fiona had tried coaxing me to hike with her, but I'd insisted I had nothing to wear. Not exactly true. Since I'd packed everything but my bathroom sink, somewhere in my mountain of luggage, I'd tossed in a pair of gray sweats and aged sneakers. I simply hadn't wanted to be seen in anything so ugly. Now, I found those things and put them on.

Fiona had shown me a vortex map, which she'd left in the kitchen. After padding quietly through the house, I studied it. With nothing else to go on, I decided to try Bell Rock, even though it was the farthest away, because the map described it as an easy hike and because I liked its name. I took the keys to her car from her purse, which she'd left in the living room, and crept from the house, to where she kept her ancient black Mercedes.

Sedona's magnificent daytime skies look like they're coated with crystal, the colors as pure as those in Fiona's paintings. But the nights, without the urban lights I was used to, were as strikingly dark as the days were bright. Black velvet skies that made the stars glow like diamonds. Despite Sedona's rugged beauty, though, I found the nighttime power of the place scary. Like maybe a Bogeyman lurked in the darkness.

The town had finally quieted down. I did see the glow from bonfires here and there. But most of the thousands of people packed into that space had settled in for the night. Since a curfew seemed to be the one edict that everyone obeyed, there were no cars on the roads. I expected to be stopped by a passing patrol somewhere along my route and figured I'd have to talk my way through. Amazingly, I didn't see any troops patrolling it now. It was like something had cleared the way for me.

Though it was farther than I thought, beyond a bunch of goofy roundabouts, I found the trailhead's parking area easily enough and climbed from the car. Given how many people had stuffed themselves into this little city, it seemed strange to find myself in a place that was truly empty. When I slammed the door, the sound echoed in the eerie stillness. Only after the echo died, did I set out.

The moon was more than three-quarters, and bright, so I found my way easily, although the trail climbed more than I was led to believe. My calves, tightened from years avoiding flat-heeled shoes, cried out in protest, but the hike really didn't tax me. Not physically at least. My nerves continued to cut through me like jagged glass, and the butterflies in my stomach swelled in number.

As I made my way along the trail, I challenged the vortex to make its presence known, but I didn't feel anything, apart from skepticism. When a jackrabbit hopped across the trail, I called out to it, derisively demanding to know if it was a magical being. Hah!

But then I heard the cries from a pack of coyotes that weren't far off. Aliens, right. Still, I stopped abruptly. The hairs on my arms didn't relax again until those cries drifted away.

I trudged on. The dusty crimson trail kept climbing, but I still found it pretty effortless to trod, even though Sedona was set at a higher altitude than I was used to. I wondered at my newfound strength. It couldn't possibly be because I was in shape. Nothing from the vortex, though.

Being there made me question my ambivalence toward the magic Haggerty's family practiced. I'd once seen Angus transform an ordinary apple into one made of gold. And forget about Lugh and Taliesin—after you've seen someone beach an iceberg in the tropics, you can't convince yourself it's all some elaborate video game.

But neither could I deny the dark forces within their numbers. I feared that part of them, and I hated being fearful—I'd always taken comfort in knowing I could handle whatever came my way. Now I knew how real that Bogeyman was, and that I was no match for him.

Yet I also envied them their gifts. I knew I wouldn't be as good a person as Haggerty if I could get away with the stuff her ancestors pulled. Some people didn't think I was all that good now, but I honestly believed that even if I wouldn't know a psychic vision from a Dorito chip, my work as a spiritual advisor performed a useful public service. Hey, if it weren't for me assuring my clients that their futures were safe, and that their loved ones were partying their hearts out on the Other Side, they'd feel as scared as I did right now. Was this any way to live?

I finally arrived at the rock. Bathed in the glow of the moon, it did look like a bell, wider across the bottom than at the top, with the lower rocks stretching out in gentle layers.

Still no vortex charge, though. Even if climbing wasn't my thing, I hoisted myself a small distance up the rock face. I didn't know where I was getting this vitality, but as long as I had it, I might as well use it. I climbed up to the next layer, and I began to circle the lower part of the bell. Still no amplification, no feeling at all. Zilch.

Then it hit me.

I felt it first as a tingling in my chest, which made my heart flutter. The sensation spread to the top of my head. I backed away from the place where I'd felt it, and the impressions within me lessened. Moved forward again, and the sensations sharpened once more. It got so I could pinpoint exactly where the energy was the strongest. I sat on a ledge that jutted out from that spot and drank the power in.

Fiona would insist it was my chakras that were reacting to the vortex power. I snorted in disbelief. To the New Age types, chakras are supposed to be revolving whorls of energy found in a vertical line from the top of the head through the torso. Sure, I threw the word around with my clients. But I'd taken biology in high school, and I distinctly remembered flipping through the textbook once before the exam. I never saw anything within the body that resembled a series of colored spheres, the way they're usually depicted in the woo-woo books. Yet now, I couldn't explain how I happened to feel the effect of the vortex right in the chakras' mythical centers.

It occurred to me belatedly that I'd felt a form of it all along, with my unaccustomed strength. Now I was soaking in the vortex's energy in its most intense form.

Maybe this was all a dream. Was I actually in bed at this moment, imagining all of it? I ran my hand across the rough surface of the rock I sat on. My finger caught on a jagged bit, and it pinched. That proved this was no dream.

MAGICAL ALIENATION

I also understood what Fiona had meant by the Great Collective Unconsciousness. Somewhere within me voices wailed. Despite the cheerfulness overtaking Sedona, I felt a deep sense of foreboding coming from those voices, like they knew something terrible would happen here before this ugly siege was over.

My own feelings were strangely at odds with it. I felt filled with hope, as if I'd been shot with a full clip from the automatic rifle of optimism. That sense of hopefulness felt so bright and good, it was like a drug I couldn't get enough of. I continued sitting there, sucking it in. I couldn't say how long I stayed there—I never wore a watch, and I lost all track of time. Long enough for the dark sky to grow paler. Only after I heard the coyotes again, did I rise to leave.

Still, I hesitated. I remembered something else Fiona had told me. She said if you ask the vortex a question, you'll often receive an answer.

What question mattered most to me? The fate of the world? The hostage siege? When that darkness that the voices within me had hinted at would overtake us? Where Fiona hid her chocolate? None of the above. I knew what I needed to know.

"Should I take Angus back?" I whispered into the darkness.

The answer came to me, with the same certainty I'd felt when I saw an orange organdy shawl in a shop window and knew it would do wonders for my complexion. The sense was that strong, I swear.

Too bad it was the one answer I didn't want.

With a sigh, I started back down the trail. Despite the brightness of the moon, I must have missed a turn somewhere, since I found myself on a trail I didn't recognize. I looked back at Bell Rock—sure enough, I saw it from a different angle now. Fortunately, my high energy level kept me moving at a good clip, even if I did take the scenic route this time. When I finally toddled into the trailhead parking area, it was from a different direction.

A few other cars were parked there now, including a dark Crown Victoria. I figured Haggerty's Bureau car couldn't have been the only Crown Vic in Sedona, but when I pressed my face to a side window, I saw her purse on the passenger seat.

So I wasn't the only one who needed answers tonight. I hoped she liked hers better than I had mine.

CHAPTER THIRTY
Haggerty

On the darkened path from the Bell Rock trailhead, Haggerty tripped on a Juniper root that stuck up through the dirt. When she fell, she skinned her hand on a rock. The scuff almost bled. Despite her flesh-and-blood condition, she couldn't ever remember cutting herself. Again, she wondered why she had ever sought this state.

She hadn't, though. She never wished for the downside of mortality. She'd created an idealized portrait of it, and she longed for that. But it was nothing like what she struggled with now.

When she pulled herself up, she discovered she'd also hurt her knee and had to limp back to the car. She couldn't say what had brought her out here tonight. She'd simply felt an overwhelming need to be here.

Despite the minor wounds she'd gotten, she began to feel the power of the vortex. Even without the approaching harmonic convergence, she respected the unique properties of this place. After she entered the trail from the parking lot, she'd spotted an ancient Juniper trunk that had fallen alongside the path. Time and weather had caused its bark to fall away, and beneath that skin, the tree itself had twisted into an impossible spiral, the result of decades of energy that shaped that tree. Yet the effect of this place wasn't enough to offset the fear that consumed her. Fear for herself, for her future, if she didn't find a way to reverse this awful curse.

Given her battered knee, she didn't make herself climb too high. Instead, she stood on Bell Rock's lowest level in the moonlight, facing the source of its awesome power, and asked it a question. Two questions, actually. She asked the vortex what had taken her power away and how she could get it back.

To Haggerty's distress, the vortex didn't provide any answers. Instead, all she heard was two names. Two ridiculous names—Gwydion and Samantha—who couldn't possibly have anything to do with her troubles.

No answers for Haggerty, it seemed. Despair threatened to drown her.

CHAPTER THIRTY-ONE
Samantha

When I opened my eyes the next morning, I couldn't believe how good I felt, even though I'd only had a few hours of sleep. I couldn't have felt more rested if I'd spent a week on a massage table at Rand's fancy inn. Nearly as good as I had the first time Angus and I did the wild thing. That vortex really was something. It could shoot me with its energy rays whenever it wanted.

Assuming I actually had been there. I did wonder again whether it had been some super-deluxe dream. Yet a little red mark still scarred one of my fingers, where I had caught it on that rock. I looked at my finger closer now. It wasn't just *one* mark, after all. There were two sore spots, separated by a white line. Like I'd been bitten. How could a jagged rock have created a mark like that? But it meant that last night really had happened.

It was pretty early when I made my way to the kitchen, yet Haggerty was already there and dressed in a pinstriped pantsuit. Neither of us gave any sign that we'd seen the other's car in that trailhead parking lot; perhaps she hadn't seen mine. Her face glowed with a bit more vigor than usual. The vortex, it seemed, had worked its magic on both of us. But she also gave her knee an absent rubbing.

She clutched a turquoise stoneware mug between her slender fingers. "I was just about to wake you, Samantha, but I thought I'd give it a few minutes more. You know what a peach you are when you don't get your beauty sleep." Gesturing with the mug, she said, "Coffee's made."

"Coffee? Who needs coffee?" I did a little pirouette that sent my dragon housecoat flaring out.

"Are you a shape-shifter?" Haggerty asked with mock severity. "What have you done with Samantha?"

We both laughed. Me, I giggled like it was the funniest joke I'd heard since grade school.

Haggerty returned to business an instant later. "If you don't want coffee, hurry up and get dressed, Samantha. Senator Campbell asked to meet you, and he has a busy day ahead of him."

"Me? Why's he wanna meet me?"

She shrugged, like it perplexed her, too. The idea of cozying up to some politician—at least one who wasn't likely to employ my services—bummed me enough to dim my good mood. I decided I needed coffee, after all, and filled the biggest mug I found in the cabinet.

A short while later, we were on our way. Haggerty made good use of her siren as her Bureau-issued car drove up 89A, through a couple of those nutty roundabouts, over the bridge that crossed the picturesque, tree-and-boulder studded Oak Creek and onto Route 179. I wondered whether we would pass Bell Rock, since that was the way I'd driven the night before. I longed to see it in daylight. Instead, we pulled into some gate-guarded community before we reached it.

The uniformed man in the guard shack made Haggerty show her ID. Once we were cleared for entry, she grumbled, "These guards make me show my ID every time I come through."

People had to be pretty officious to exceed Haggerty's standards.

The private road climbed swiftly into the soaring red-rock hills. No squatters there. On huge lots to either side sat enormous mansions. Many in that same pueblo style that I saw all over Sedona, only large enough to house entire tribes of Native peoples, while some homes were more ultramodern statements, with sheets of glass, and box piled on architectural box, and others were in a traditional Tudor style that fit that high desert landscape like my wardrobe jibed with everyone else's.

The Campbells' pueblo contained a sprawling main house, along with a couple of smaller buildings, one of which must have been the cottage Haggerty had been using. Unlike the usual tans and ambers, theirs was painted a sage green tone that blended beautifully with the gray-green shrubbery surrounding it. Unlike their neighbors' homes, however, ringing their property was a high wrought iron fence. A fence within a gate-guarded community? So distrusting. Had it been there before Normal Frankly tried to kill Kenny?

Haggerty asked for admittance through an intercom. A moment later, the electric sentry slid open. Her car climbed up a gray and rust driveway, made of Arizona flagstone, she told me as if she were a docent giving a tour, and parked before a carved double-door entry. Beside the door was a curved wall made from glass blocks.

After Haggerty rang the bell, a man appeared behind the blocks of wavy glass. Despite the distortion, I could tell it was the senator himself.

Kenny threw the door open. "Hey there, Annabelle." Behind his rimless glasses, his chocolate eyes crinkled attractively. To me he said, "You must be Samantha. I saw you at the courthouse with Rand Riker, didn't I? I'm Senator Campbell, but I insist you to call me Kenny, hear?"

The foyer gave way to a sunken great room, where a pair of leather sofas, in a soft butterscotch tone, framed a distressed pine coffee table. A plasma TV the size of Ireland covered a small part of one wall. Endless windows looked out on an infinity pool in a dusty blue, while craggy scarlet rocks rose up beyond it. Not far in the distance, Bell Rock called out to me.

Giving his glasses another one of those unconscious shoves, Kenny shouted down a corridor for someone to bring "grub."

Haggerty sat next to me, facing that wall of windows, while the senator took the sofa across from us. "So you're the famous Madame Samantha I've heard so much about." He quoted my name with his fingers.

For the first time he seemed to fully take me in. I could tell because his eyes widened to twice their normal size. I wore a court jester suit today, with puffy jacket sleeves and short pants in magenta and gold. Under the pants I wore bright purple tights. A bell dangled from the jester hat perched at a rakish angle on my curly blonde hair. I'd chosen high-heeled gold lamé pumps in lieu of jester shoes. Normally, I preferred dresses, but since I was visiting a politician, I thought the occasion called for some whimsy.

Kenny chuckled. "Annabelle said you were a character, and you sure are that."

Yeah, I'd bet that was how she described me.

A Latina maid, dressed in jeans and a T-shirt, came in pushing a cart. She spread out coffee, juice and fruit, along with a variety of pastries, on the coffee table. I'd seen hotel brunch spreads with less stuff.

"Kenny, the honeydew didn't look good at the market yesterday, so I bought cantaloupe. Hope that's okay," the woman said.

"You're the boss, Maria." He turned to me. "Maria does a

great job running our house here." Kenny curved and flicked his fingers before he said the word *great*. No question, he really didn't get the way most people used finger quotes, but he sure liked them.

I had to admit that Kenny Campbell was a charismatic guy. While he was probably the most conventional man I'd met in years, he genuinely seemed to like people and accept them for what they were. On the other hand, there was talk about him running for president, and a vote is a vote. But as I stuffed my face, and he entertained us with stories from Washington, while he seemed to take issue with the guys who sat across the aisle, there wasn't anything mean-spirited about the anecdotes he passed on.

What floored me was the relationship he shared with Haggerty. She seemed looser around him than she was with her own ancestors. She laughed like a little girl at his silly jokes, and her eyes glowed when she looked his way. As for Kenny, a tender vulnerability entered his gaze when he directed it at her. I wasn't sure about the nature of their relationship. It didn't feel romantic. Actually, it felt so unfamiliar to me, I didn't know how to categorize it.

I was still pushing pastries down my gullet when Maria came to clear the plates. Kenny's brow knitted. Time to get serious, huh? I knew I'd read that right when he began to question me about my journey into the compound the day before.

"Did you…you know…see Normal Frankly?"

I said I hadn't. Sure, there was that momentary sighting, but I discounted it now. Pulsing light? I thought he'd have asked about the alien, but Normal had tried to murder him. I could understand why Normal held Kenny's focus. I explained my earlier association with No-Neck and Baldy. Then I described everything, from the time I entered the place, until I arrived at Gwydion's door, including my sprinkling of those disks, even though I wasn't sure if Haggerty wanted him to know about them. He nodded thoughtfully on occasion.

He wasn't as accepting when I got around to talking about my encounter with the famed Roswell alien. "Aliens! How preposterous," Kenny said. He laughed so hard, his glasses almost fell off. For once he actually needed to adjust them. "That's just something the militia has faked to make our government officials look bad."

MAGICAL ALIENATION

I wasn't sure anyone had to *make* government officials look bad. They seemed to handle it fine on their own.

But Kenny wouldn't let it go when I repeated my remark to François from the day before about it not being a Halloween costume. He made me describe every aspect of the encounter. This time I left a lot out, especially my energy drain and the jolt I felt. Even with my edited version, Haggerty squirmed uncomfortably at my side. But Kenny seemed awfully curious about a creature he didn't believe in. Did he think Gwydion was gunning for him, too? Was friendly Kenny Campbell actually paranoid?

The front door opened, and Mrs. Campbell blew into the house. She wore the cashmere top that she'd had on at the courthouse, along with that same muslin thing around her neck that she folded to look like an oversized neck brace. Her short hair looked ruffled and windblown, and her skin reflected the ruddy glow it might get if she'd been out in nippy weather. But it wasn't cold outside.

"There you are, Kelly!" Kenny cried. He rushed up the steps to the foyer and tightly embraced his petite wife. "I was so worried when I got your message that you were staying down in Phoenix."

Mrs. Campbell gave her husband a laugh. "But, darling, my book club meeting ran long, and you know I hate to drive at night."

During the worst siege in this state's history, while she and Kenny were being heavily guarded, she drove a long distance alone to attend a book club meeting? Kelly must have been some reader.

She came down into the great room, where she introduced herself to me. Not a flicker of a reaction to my jester suit; Kenny might not have been a typical politician, but Kelly was a classic political wife.

"And Agent Haggerty, I see. Still making the world safe for democracy?"

Mee-ow. Haggerty emitted a little gasp.

Mrs. Campbell gave Haggerty's cheeks a maternal cupping with her hands. "Annabelle, dear, I'm only kidding. You're always welcome here. Even after your detail is over."

That sounded so sincere, I questioned my reaction to her earlier remark. Haggerty tended to take things too seriously, but I rarely did.

After Mrs. Campbell shouted to Maria for coffee, she sighed

deeply and slipped onto the sofa across from us. She began fussing with that muslin thing around her neck. She unclipped something from the side, which she held in her hand. Then she unwrapped the large amount of fabric she had folded under it. As it unfurled, I saw that it was another of those embroidered shawls, in the same colors as Fiona's. Since I'd tried on one just like that in Rand's suite, I knew those colors flattered me. Yet I couldn't see why she rolled hers up as she did and kept the metallic colored threads hidden.

Kelly deposited on the table the thing she'd removed from the side of the shawl. I stared at it in stunned disbelief. The object she had placed there—looked like the silver clasp I'd seen in Rand's suite. Yippy-skippy! Had Mrs. Campbell been the woman in bed with Rand the day I went to his suite? Was her scorn of him all an act? I gave her points for playing it well. Was there really was a meeting down in Phoenix last night, or had she made a return trip to Rand's bed?

I inched along the sofa in the hopes of catching a glimpse of the front of the clasp, where an "R" had been etched into the one in Rand's suite. But Maria arrived with another tray of coffee, and Kelly moved the clasp aside to allow room for the tray. Short of grabbing it, which she'd probably notice, there was no way I could tell.

When she happened to look my way, I directed my gaze to the window. I had a poker face, but that was too much to hide. For once the view didn't take hold of me. How could it possibly measure up against what I surmised?

But what was I thinking? Kelly Campbell and Rand Riker? What could that modern June Cleaver possibly have to offer Devil Boy to make him swear off other women?

CHAPTER THIRTY-TWO

From the comfort of his locked room, Gwydion noted that something was underway in the complex. His senses were finally alert enough to feel all the activity within the militia beehive. Even his meal delivery was late. Now back in his natural form, he clicked his tongue in wry amusement as he thought that he just might have to leave this place if the service didn't improve.

Everything had changed after the visit from that girl, Samantha. He had chosen wisely when he made her his facilitator, even if she hadn't induced her friend and Gwydion's descendant, Annabelle Haggerty, to work in his behalf. She hadn't even picked up on the fact that he wanted her to. His magical tricks really weren't what they used to be. What was even stranger was that Annabelle hadn't tapped into the commands he'd sent her, either. He really had been slipping in his powered-down state.

Still, it all worked out. Samantha had unknowingly set other things in motion, and they'd paid off for him. His powers had been restored to a strong level, and so far he had successfully hidden it from the Council. And Annabelle was still helping him, to the extent she could, whether she knew it or not. But she had even less magical energy to spare now than he had.

Gwydion was especially glad to have met Samantha, a woman he'd heard so much about. Angus had chosen well. If survival didn't require Gwydion's entire focus, he might have competed with Angus for the girl. When it came to women, it was every god for himself. And that body! In this age of stick-figured females, Samantha's presented a refreshing change. Gwydion could feel his loins stir just thinking about her.

Yet it wasn't merely her physical form that attracted him. She was such a spirited, independent thinker. Something less than a goddess, of course, but more than an ordinary mortal, he felt sure. When this was all over, Gwydion might have to show Samantha that while Angus was her first god, he didn't have to be her last.

A sound in the corridor brought his attention back to the present. The anxiety level he felt in this compound kept soaring. For now, he needed to keep his focus on his own survival. He might be the militia's greatest asset, but no god should ever trust any mortal with his future. And especially not mortals as unstable as these were. He quickly changed back into his alien form.

There would be time enough for frivolity later, when whatever these fools had planned was over.

CHAPTER THIRTY-THREE

Our return trip from the Campbell home proved to be more harrowing than the drive out, since Haggerty kept chuckling, and each time she did, she threatened to take out clusters of spectators along the road.

"You thought my mother and Devil Boy…" She broke into uncontrolled laughter.

The car's siren continued to wail. Shouting over it, I said, "Laugh if you want, but there was the business with the shawl. Okay, I know they've sold a million of them. But she *had* left the house, and the shawl colors were the same. Besides, it's not so crazy. She's a beautiful woman and he's…well, lots of women would kill for a shot at him. My mom would take out whole battalions."

Easing the car around a cluster of folks in alien costumes, she said, "Mine likes them more buttoned-down. I actually wish she had someone, but she seems to have given up. It's not easy for us, you know. You can't imagine how much goddesses threaten mortal men. That's not something you've had to deal with."

Like my love life was a roaring success. "You could always look among, you know, other creatures."

She glanced my way. "You mean paranormal beings?" She shrugged. "None of us can control who, or what, we're attracted to."

I sure couldn't. "Does that mean you're not into brooding albinos?"

Haggerty giggled. "Samantha, that's one thing I like about you—you can always make me laugh."

Why was that funny?

Her laughter kept building. "And now you think Kelly Campbell is the woman in Rand Riker's life. I can't imagine a more ludicrous coupling."

"She had that silver shawl clasp," I said mulishly.

"Which they've probably sold in numbers that rival the shawls," Haggerty insisted. "Southwestern silver jewelry has become so mainstream, they sell it in stores all over the country. Besides, why would either Kelly Campbell or Fiona Haggerty wear a clasp engraved with the letter 'R'?"

"Maybe that's how Rand brands his women."

Haggerty shook her head. "That clasp had to be his. Anyway, if Mrs. Campbell had someone like him going on the side, why would she find me so threatening?" Haggerty asked. "You have to admit I bother her."

Something about Haggerty pushed Kelly's nasty buttons, all right. Maybe the incredible bond Haggerty had formed with Kelly's husband. My highly tuned lust barometer told me sex wasn't at the root of whatever she and Kenny shared, but maybe Kelly's wasn't as sensitive. Still, if she had bagged herself a rock star, would she have cared about her dorky senator?

"Can't you tap into her or something?"

All Haggerty's merriment vanished. Her shoulders slumped as if something heavy weighed on them. "I told you, Samantha, I can't sense anything. My powers have been reduced to such a low level, I feel blind."

This time I didn't taunt her with any "I told you so" remarks. But I wondered if she unconsciously willed this into being. Why else would it have happened?

Some whackjob picked that moment to step in front of the car. "Hey, watch out for that Klingon. Can't you do something about clearing these people off the streets?" They were really pissing me off. How could I continue to look special with these jokers around?

"Help is on the way," Haggerty said.

For the screwballs, maybe. For the really insane world of romantic love, not a chance.

Within hours after she dropped me off at her mother's place, I understood what Haggerty had meant by "help is on the way." A battalion of infantry soldiers was dispatched to Sedona. Marshall Law had already been declared, but now they could begin enforcing it. People who didn't live in the area were sent away. Those who wouldn't go were arrested and transported to Phoenix in jail buses.

While that whittled down the number of celebrants in the streets, it didn't eliminate them. And the zoo continued to rage in other places. In New Mexico, the round-the-clock vindication party that began in Roswell, had radiated throughout the state. In cities across the country, rallies were held in defense of the alien, which more closely resembled some Other World Mardi Gras.

But not all the reactions were so positive. With all the chaos, militia groups sprang up everywhere, attracting folks who seemed to need more control than the universe was dispensing just now. Wherever rallies in support of the alien were held, counter demonstrators invariably denied his existence. And sometimes the clashes got ugly. Some guy in Dallas shot his neighbor for putting out his garbage can days before their trash pickup day because he regarded that as proof his neighbor was an alien.

It had all gone from silly to sinister in a heartbeat.

Kelly Campbell, who had merely stood by her man, began to speak out herself. Even if what she said sounded too high-toned to be of any practical use. "We need to shed light on the darkness that is this conflict. To be alert for the spark of communication in the areas where we are joined together." She called on the militia to "allow new peace-keepers to bring us together."

What was wrong with the old peacekeeper, me? Even though the image of me entering that compound had been beamed to news outlets throughout the world, nobody had asked me for an interview. A girl wears one or two crazy outfits, and she starts to get a reputation. If Haggerty weren't so powerless, I'd have wondered whether she erected a force field around me to keep the media away.

I wasn't surprised that, even though he'd allowed federal troops to be called out, the current holder of the Oval Office made no public statement. Gwydion's years of fun had represented a dirty little secret for every administration since 1947.

What did surprise me was that Kenny Campbell didn't exploit the situation for his own political gain. He made a few speeches, but even lamer ones than his wife.

"The breakdown of the family—that's what's at the root of all our troubles," he insisted to reporters. "When people don't have familial connection, they join gangs or militias. A parentless child, even after he grows up, has nowhere else to turn."

Like just being part of a family would solve everything. Look at my family. Look at Haggerty's. Yet he kept an awfully low profile for a guy making speeches, if that made any sense. He never even mentioned the presidency, which he was said to want badly. And unlike his wife, he gave all his interviews from his ultra-secure home. Why was this guy so afraid?

CHAPTER THIRTY-FOUR

I went to bed that night feeling bummed. Nothing in my life made sense anymore. Yeah, most people would swear it never did, but they'd be wrong. Believe me, I kept my eye on the brass ring. Now everything was fuzzy, and I wasn't sure where I was headed.

If Rand could be believed, I was getting paid; that was something I never took for granted. But why had he hired me at all if he thought the fire writing resulted from a bad trip?

It also soured my mood that I hadn't attracted any new clients. I still wondered whether Haggerty was keeping everyone away somehow. But what could I do about it? I risked my life to venture into that complex, and I hadn't gotten any mileage from it.

And the cherry on this sucky sundae? My love life, of course.

All the euphoria I'd drawn from the vortex the night before had abandoned me. Was this the Great Collective Funk I was feeling, or simply what my crappy life warranted?

Despite my mood, I fell into a deep sleep. Just as I was getting to the good part in a dream about Angus—one in which I was the goddess, and he the mortal—someone shook me awake.

"Samantha," Fiona whispered. "Samantha, dear, please wake up. Something dreadful is about to happen."

Even while groggy, that she'd used the future tense struck me at once. I struggled to sit up in bed. "If it hasn't happened yet, can we stop it?"

In the shadowy room, I saw her turn her head in the direction of the window. The moonlight streaming through the curtains cut tension crevices across Fiona's face. A moment later, I heard lots of cracking sounds in the distance. If it weren't for her cryptic warning, I might have considered them firecrackers, or a car relentlessly backfiring.

"Gunfire?" I asked. "At the compound?"

After nodding her sleep-tossed hair, she smoothed out the gauzy nightgown she wore, and sat on the edge of my bed. We waited for the popping to die out. Probably not more than ten minutes, but it felt like an eternity.

"It's over," Fiona said, with a sad sigh, once silence returned.

"Is anyone...?"

"Too many, I fear. I can't say for sure with the black cloud surrounding it all."

How did she mean that? Like a real cloud, or something else? I had a million questions, but before I could rattle them out, she held up a hand to silence me.

We went about getting dressed. I didn't even bother to throw on anything special, just some knit pants and a top. Fiona wore a colorful broomstick skirt and some sandals, and she wrapped a shawl around her shoulders. Not her pretty one, but a worn, woolen shawl, the kind designed to keep the chill away. We met again over coffee in the living room.

Once I got my bearings, I saw that she'd awakened me just before daylight. Even on the twenty-four hour cable news shows, there was little to report. The military had moved the press farther away from the compound and banned helicopters from flying too close. Now, though the media had reported the shooting at the compound, nobody knew what it involved.

From her intense concentration, I guessed Fiona was trying to discern something in her way. "Are you picking up anything else?" I asked.

With a frustrated scowl, she said, "It's all a muddle, as if someone were intentionally hiding it from me."

Who could do that?

For the longest time, as sirens wailed in the distance, her expression never changed. Then the confusion cleared from her face, and she sat up straighter.

"You got something?" I asked with a gasp. "What?"

With a sudden frown, she brought her attention back to me. Almost as if she'd forgotten I was there and wasn't entirely happy to rediscover it.

"Uh...no. I just remembered something I forgot to do yesterday. And really must...do...now."

She intended to perform that forgotten chore at dawn? Sure, she was the one with the psychic visions, while I was the fake, but once again, I had a strong sense that Fiona was such an incredible liar, her pants should have been a constant inferno.

She didn't waste a moment, as she bustled around the house, gathering her purse and car keys. "You'll be fine here on your own, won't you, Samantha?" she asked breathlessly on her way to the door.

"Do I have a choice?" I asked, but by then, I was alone there.

Not long after, when I was in the kitchen, searching for any French toast muffins the pixies might have left, I heard Haggerty's distinctive slamming of the front door. She came flying into the kitchen. A far cry from her usual pristine self, today her boxy jacket didn't sit squarely on her shoulders, and several clumps of auburn hair had pulled free of her neat bun. The sharpest change was in her eyes, which looked wild with emotions.

"They knew!" she shouted. "The militia knew what was coming."

Right, the popping sounds. "What did they know?"

With an angry sweep of her hand, she pushed those clumps of hair away from her eyes. "Those disks you scattered about the complex—they contained small amounts of explosives. The idea was to set them off a few at a time, but in rapid succession. So the militia would believe they were under attack by people already in the compound. Colonel Marcus thought it would distract them long enough to mount a real assault."

Colonel Marcus? Squinty? I remembered how covertly excited he became when I told him about the shadowy nature of the compound.

"But the militia knew about the disks, and they were waiting for the soldiers." Haggerty's voice kept rising in volume. "They killed them all. Then they threw the bodies out the door. They just tossed them." The outrage in her eyes ignited. "That's where they are still—between the door and the compound gate. Lying there, rotting in the sun."

"They didn't see those disks," I assured her again. "Not in that shadowy hallway. I'm sure of that."

"No, someone *told* them."

The emotion that rolled off her was so strong, I felt as if a wave had crashed into me. I tripped backwards, until I bumped into the counter.

"It wasn't me, I swear!" I shouted. "I risked my life scattering those stupid disks."

Haggerty's face instantly softened. "Samantha, I never suspected you. I would never have sent you in there if I didn't trust you."

"You trust me?" I said in a whisper. For the first time since last night, I felt a bit of euphoria return.

"Of course. Well, to the extent that anyone can, considering."

"Oh, sure." I wasn't offended—this was me we were talking about.

Spent now, she collapsed at the kitchen table. "No, it wasn't you who warned them."

I pulled a mug from a cabinet and poured her some coffee. "Rand. Had to be. He must have been in communication with them all this time."

Haggerty took an absent sip. "My thought, too, but we've monitored him. He hasn't made any calls from his room, and he hasn't left it. And we've shut down all the cell towers in this area for everything but official calls. If he's been communicating with them, it's by smoke signals."

We slipped into silence, until the sound of ravens on the roof caught our attention.

Haggerty eyes clouded over. "No," she said in a shocked whisper.

Yet if mortal communication had been cut off, what other kind was there? She leaped to her feet and ran out. I followed a moment later. When I reached the living room, Lugh and Taliesin were there.

"Quite a little dust-up they had at that compound that interests you so much, eh, Annie?" Taliesin said with a giggle.

"Please tell me you weren't responsible." Though she spoke in an intense whisper, I could hear how desperately she wanted to believe that.

The boys directed enigmatic smiles each other's way.

"What did you do?" Haggerty cried.

CHAPTER THIRTY-FIVE

"Tell me what you did," Haggerty shrieked at her recalcitrant ancestors.

Slouching on the couch in his yellow velour outfit, Taliesin looked like a giant banana. "Maybe we did something, and maybe we didn't," he said in a singsong fashion. "But you won't get anything from us if you're mean."

Not for the first time, it struck me as strange that this generation's gods and goddesses seemed more mature than their ancestors, who were centuries older.

Haggerty sputtered speechlessly, before finally finding her voice. "How could you? People *died* out there."

Lugh flexed his skinny shoulders. "So they cut this journey short and moved on to the next. You take everything too seriously, Annabelle."

Now *he* wore one of those embroidered shawls, in the same colors as Fiona's, wrapped across his shoulders like a cape. I thought about telling him that it wasn't a man's garment, but it wasn't as if it made him look any more ridiculous than usual.

Haggerty's fists clenched so tightly, the skin stretched across her knuckles looked as pale as François's. But one sad little tear trickled down her cheek.

"Lugh, stop teasing her," Taliesin said, swinging his sneaker. Mellencamp sat beside him and watched that twitching foot. "We didn't tell any of those soldiers anything, Annabelle. Not the real soldiers, and not the fakes."

I wished I could believe them, but they were both grand liars.

Haggerty angrily wiped the tear away with the back of her hand. "If you didn't, you told *someone* what was up, and that person conveyed it to the militia."

I wasn't sure whether she had some psychic insight there, or just made a mental leap. Either way, they didn't deny it. Who might they have passed the secret onto, if they hadn't tattled themselves?

"Either that, or there really is a rogue god behind this, one of ours. You two would have to know who."

Lugh pulled that maneuver we used to use when we were

kids and didn't want to talk. He locked his mouth with an imaginary key, which he then tossed away.

"You're everything I deplore about our people," Haggerty cried. "You with your crop circles, Gwydion with his sixty-year charade—why do you keep choosing things the people of this world fear?"

The boys shared a quick look. "Duh! That's what makes it fun." His head swiveled Taliesin's way. "Tali, have you heard this word, *Duh?* Isn't it groovy?"

The timing of pop culture tended to be lost on the gods. My merry friends were starting to piss me off.

"Why they're afraid I can't imagine. Coyotes never hurt anyone but cats." Without appearing to notice Mellencamp, Taliesin blew a sharp burst of air into the cat's face. Mellencamp cried in annoyance. "And those Soma Café fools—why they've run off with those bizarre three-pointed tails between their squat little legs." Taliesin cast his gaze to the side, something I'd often seen him do before setting up a joke. "That other creature, though—that's the one that should scare them."

Lugh broke into a round of high-pitched snickering.

With an angry toss of her head, Haggerty said, "There are no other alien creatures here. You're just making things up."

"That's rich, coming from you," Lugh said.

Haggerty frowned. "What does that mean?"

"Think about…oh, what should I call him? Daddy Dearest." Taliesin said. His chubby cheeks glowed with amusement.

"Daddy…?" Haggerty's brow wrinkled in confusion. "If you're talking about my father, you know I haven't seen him since I was a baby. I don't remember what he looks like. I don't even know his name—Mom changed my last name to hers after he left. But what could my departed parent possibly have to do with your games?"

Taliesin waved a sausage finger at her. "Oh, my girl, you've seen your daddy much more recently than that. As to what he has to do with the subject of our discussion…why, Annie, he's the point of it."

Haggerty closed her eyes. Lugh wrapped one of his long-fingered hands around her forearm.

After a moment, her eyes flew opened, and the blood drained from her face. "No. You can't mean it. You're not suggesting my father is—" A sob escaped from her throat. "That he's a—"

"What?" I shouted, not following.

Nobody answered me. Not Haggerty, who seemed so stunned, I feared I'd just learned what a *conniption* looked like, nor the boys, who shared silly, triumphant giggles.

Without a word, Haggerty grabbed the purse she'd dumped on the coffee table on the way in. She yanked a set of keys from it.

"Me too," I shouted. When she raced from the house, I ran to catch up with her.

Her car was parked in the street. Without giving a thought to the dangers that lurked in that red stone path, I dashed along it, right past the lions and jumped in the passenger side. I took control of the siren. Haggerty seemed so distracted, she neither noticed, nor cared.

With the security crackdown in force, there weren't many cars on the roads, and fewer people now. Those that were there would have been smart to clear out. Haggerty seemed so crazed, she would cheerfully have mowed them down if they slowed her progress. She made a screeching turn at the corner without looking in either direction.

I still didn't know who "Daddy Dearest" was. But once we careened onto Route 179, and she started taking all the roundabouts they have there on two wheels, a crazy idea popped into my head. No! Was that possible?

When Haggerty made the turn into the Campbells' complex, she hit the button to lower the window with enough force to stab through it. While cruising slowly past the guard shack, she shouted, "Open the gate!"

The guard, who always made her show her ID, accurately read her mood. He fell all over himself trying to activate the controls before she could crash through the arm that barred the road.

Haggerty's car roared through the private streets of the Campbells' pricey sanctuary. She screeched to a halt at their gated entrance. Instead of announcing her presence through the squawk box, she pulled an electronic keycard from the car's console and slipped it into a slot below the intercom.

"You've had a way into this place all along? Why did you announce yourself last time?" I asked.

"The Bureau decided we should protect their privacy unless we couldn't help it."

"And now you can't help it?" I asked.

"Now I don't care."

Parked off to the side of the home's big garage, next to a silver Lexus SUV, was Fiona's old Mercedes. Haggerty grabbed a second set of keys from her purse. After she found the keys, she hurled the handbag to the floor of the passenger side, beside my feet. We both climbed out, but she beat me to the door.

After unlocking it, she allowed me to precede her into the house. I walked into the foyer, staring down into that sprawling great room, empty now, where I'd enjoyed a great breakfast. Haggerty slammed the door so hard, the house shook.

Moments later, Kenny came rushing out from a corridor that led off to one side, hastily cinching a robe. He wasn't wearing his glasses now, obviously having taken them off along with his pants.

He stopped below the steps to the great room. He looked shocked to see us there, but as the seconds ticked by, the surprise seemed to give way to dread. His forehead crinkled with anxiety. "Annabelle and Samantha? What are you doing here?"

Haggerty snorted, but said nothing. Several times, during her restless shifting from foot-to-foot, she bumped into me. To my surprise, images tumbled into my mind. At first I didn't understand what I was seeing. Or how those pictures were coming to me. But Haggerty had transferred her visions to me in the past with contact—now, even in her powered-down state, we apparently still had that connection. Finally, I grasped that I was catching glimpses of whatever Lugh had sent her. What I saw confirmed my stunning suspicion. Every crazy bit of it.

Haggerty's mother tentatively crept out from that hall, wearing nothing now but a man's shirt. For once, her usual vitality seemed muted. "Annie, dear. This isn't what it looks like."

"Really, Mom? Because it looks like you're sleeping with a married man. Samantha, how does it look to you?"

Nope, she wasn't dragging me into it. I just came along to work the siren. This odd little family unit would have to settle things on its own.

"I mean it's not as damning as it might appear." Fiona drew a deep breath, which brought the shirt up dangerously high on her great thighs. "Annabelle, Senator Campbell is—"

"I know. Senator Family Values is the husband and father

who abandoned us."

"Noooo," Kenny moaned, combing shaky fingers through his messy hair. "The chickens have come home to roost. I always feared this day would come."

He didn't know what fear was yet.

"I've already heard who you are in my life," Haggerty spat at him. "But are you—That is, did—I mean, how—" She broke off in a frustrated sob.

I took a step closer and asked, "Senator, I think what Annabelle wants to know is this: Should we call you Kenny..." Though I kept my tone light, I couldn't resist pausing for a moment of drama. And then, what the hell, I used finger quotes when I asked, "Or E.T.?"

Senator Kenny Campbell collapsed on the floor.

CHAPTER THIRTY-SIX

When I went back to the house hours later, I found Fiona seated before the TV armoire, her focus intently engaged. Too bad the television was turned off.

Without looking my way, she rattled out some questions. "Annie back at work? Where have you been all this time?"

"We went for coffee."

When the circus was in town, it was almost impossible to get into any of the Sedona's many restaurants or coffee shops. Lines stretched down the block. Now, with movement so restricted, many places were closed. But we found a little café that was open not far from the Bureau's office.

We'd ordered coffees and took them to the table farthest away from the man working behind the counter. Even then, though the man showed no interest in us, Haggerty had hissed her anxious remarks to me in whispers. I didn't offer any advice, having absolutely no skills for this brave new world in which friends had alien fathers.

Fiona nodded absently. "Annabelle's still quite upset, I gather. Any particular part of it more objectionable than anything else?"

She was kidding right? Was any part *not* objectionable? "He is married, Fiona," I said, seizing on the most mundane aspect of the whole mess.

"Yes, darling, he is." Her full coral lips twitched with amusement. "To me."

I flopped next to her on the couch. "You mean you two were never divorced?"

"Someone would have told me, right?"

"That's how it works."

She shrugged. "There you have it then. Kenny and I are still married."

"No kidding? Senator Family Values is a bigamist." I snickered. I liked Kenny, but I enjoyed unearthing hypocrisy too much not to take some enjoyment from it.

"He's really not a bad man, Samantha. He's done lots of

good, some that people don't know anything about it. Do you realize how unusual it is for a politician not to scrape every speck of mileage from his good deeds?"

He was also one of those rare politicians who didn't sleep with bimbos, just his various wives. "He did some bad things, Fiona. Like leaving you and Annabelle." If Kelly had known about his marital status, she might have objected to his marrying her, too.

"Leaving us had to be the worst mistake he made in his life, but it was just a mistake."

With my own abandonment issues intertwining with theirs, I felt frustrated with her that she could still defend him. "He made that mistake again each day of all these years, whenever he decided not to step up and do the right thing."

Sighing, she nodded. She took my hand and led me toward the kitchen. Once we made it to the doorway, I saw that another tea service had already been placed on the table. The phrase, "as if by magic," took on special meaning in this household.

We sat at the table, and Fiona poured our tea from a pale blue china pot with steam rising from its spout.

"You should have told her, you know?" I said, peering at her across the rim of my teacup.

She nodded. "I thought it should come from him. He owed his daughter that much. And one day, when the opportunity arose…I decided to rattle the skeletons in his closet."

So she had engineered their association. Meeting Haggerty must have shook Kenny up. He had to know who she was. Given her name and that she looked so much like Fiona—she was obviously the daughter he'd walked away from. But I remembered the way he looked at her, the look I couldn't identify. It was that of a proud dad. I felt a pang of envy. However screwed up things were between them now, Haggerty had still experienced something I never would.

"So…Kenny…is he really—"

"E.T.?" Fiona asked, her eyes twinkling. "He…was."

She went on to tell a story that was practically a science fiction cliché. Boy comes from other world to explore the possibility of interstellar conquest. Boy meets girl, falls in love. Boy abandons home world in favor of a career in the Beltway. Well, there might have been an original wrinkle thrown in there, when you consider that the girl was a Celtic goddess.

"When we learned about each other, Kenny asked the *Danaans* to make him into one of us." She chuckled. "You can't imagine the ruckus *that* caused."

I noticed a plate of fresh-baked scones had appeared beside the teapot. As weird as I kept finding that stuff, I'd learned, when I ate the pixies' muffins, they tasted as good as the regular stuff. Better even. I smeared my scone with a big slab of honey butter, which I found in a little stoneware crock beside the plate, and bit in. Yum. These people did know something about heaven.

"I can't see why not," I said. "The Brits make people aristocrats. I hear if you got enough bucks, you can buy a lordship or whatever."

"Mortal status does not compare to deity, Samantha. When you truly become part of the family, you'll understand that."

How could I make Angus understand we were through if I couldn't convince his family?

"The *Danaans* did agree to make him an ordinary mortal Earthling, however. And that's what he is today, although he's a far more robust specimen than average. He hides how vigorous he really is."

I remembered noticing his glasses didn't have the corrective lenses that most people his age need. "What was he when Annabelle was conceived? Because she's a little worried about her DNA."

"Tell Annabelle that she is nothing more, and nothing less, than she has always believed herself to be," Fiona said airily.

"What exactly does that mean?"

Fiona scraped the lipstick off her lip the same way Haggerty did when she was anxious. "The timing of her conception is iffy." She sighed. "She's either a partial superior human…or…"

"Or…?"

"…something else. She does look like she's supposed to, but the *Danaans* could have engineered that." She shrugged. "It might be better if you avoided the subject of Annabelle's DNA."

I could avoid it, but how could she? I thought back to those images that our contact had sent tumbling into my mind, of that molten red liquid in a walking test tube that Kenny must have been at one time, no matter how he'd appeared. I tried to decide whether it made me feel better or worse that these perfect beings screwed their lives up worse than I did.

"What happened? You know, between you and Kenny?" I asked.

"He set out to be the best mortal Earthling he could be. To him that meant the most conventional."

"And a free spirited goddess didn't fit in that guy's plans, huh?" I asked. "His loss."

Fiona gave me a sad smile. We lapsed into silence, which I filled with scones. Once the refreshments were exhausted, I figured she might want to be alone, so I rose and wandered in the direction of the guestroom. But when a thought occurred to me, I rushed back to the kitchen.

"Fiona," I said. "What about Normal Frankly? How does that freak fit in?"

More sci-fi clichés spewed from her mouth. "He was sent from Kenny's world to eliminate him. Apparently, it's taken them this long to track him down. I can't imagine how they did, since the *Danaans* had surely covered his tracks."

While I clung to the belief that the whole business of aliens was a load of buffalo chips, I had to admit that if you bought into the scenario, this did fit. It explained why the other politicians Normal had targeted hadn't been in any real jeopardy. The FBI crime lab had determined that the vials he'd sent to the other politicians were a stronger grade of glass than the fragile one he'd sent to Kenny's office. It also explained the poisonous gas that nobody had ever seen before. And why Normal didn't seem quite...normal. And it explained the Campbells' fear. Well, Kenny's. He had to be keeping Kelly in the dark. Somehow I couldn't see the senator sharing his unusual history with his oh-so conventional not-quite wife.

I started snickering to myself.

Fiona said, with the kind of sternness I remembered my grade school teachers as using a lot, "Samantha, if you can find anything to laugh at in this situation, I wish you'd share it."

Through stifled giggles, I said, "The militia."

She laughed softly. "Yes, I see what you mean. They're parading the 'Roswell alien' around, when that's just Gwydion. While all this time, they've had a legitimate being from another world right in their midst."

"I've seen them up close, and I can't give 'em points for smarts."

MAGICAL ALIENATION

The thought of my time in the compound led me to remember those disks I'd placed about, and what had happened when the military set them off. My laughter died.

"Fiona, Kenny knew the military planned to attack the compound. He knew why I went in there, how I had placed those disks."

"What of it, Samantha?"

I hesitated, not wanting to spell out my suspicions any further. Fiona made the connection herself. I could see that when her eyes darkened.

"You think Kenny alerted the militia?" She snorted.

"Someone did."

"Rand Riker—you suggested that yourself, Samantha. He was always in their camp."

"The Bureau says he didn't." I ran my fingers through my wild hair, almost in desperation. I didn't want to be the one who said it, but someone had to. "Look, Fiona, what if Kenny had a way of contacting Normal Frankly? What if he made a deal to save himself at the expense of those soldiers?"

She gave me an emphatic turn of her head. "He wouldn't do that." She broke off, ceasing her efforts to defend him. Once again she bit her lip indecisively. Maybe she was remembering how the man she kept defending had abandoned them. How he preached certain values, while doing a piss-poor job of living them. She turned inconsolable eyes to me and asked, "Would he?"

Why ask me? She was the powerful being, the one so into fate. As it sometimes happened, unplanned words escaped from my mouth without passing through my brain. "Someone once said that character is destiny."

Whoa! What a scary thought.

From the shadow that passed through Fiona's vivid blue eyes, I'd say she found that pretty scary, too.

CHAPTER THIRTY-SEVEN

Once the excitement of the shootout between the militia and the military faded, Gwydion's world lapsed back into boredom. The power infused into him from his family, through Samantha, continued to strengthen. The approaching harmonic convergence must have been responsible, demonstrating how much the full effect would have to offer him, especially if he met it at just the right time, at the right vortex.

But it was still too early to take his leave from this place. From the whispers he'd heard from his various captors, he gathered the streets were tightly controlled now. He couldn't risk getting caught by some mortal official. Not when he was no more than days away from finally freeing himself.

Yet he could no longer endure idly waiting in his compound suite, either. After living for so long in a state of magical starvation, his new power vitality was akin to wealth. And he wanted to spend it.

The deadbolt rattled in the door, and the young men entered again, one carrying food, while the other guarded his companion. Gwydion felt their fear. For that matter, he sensed negative feelings surging throughout the complex. Having bested the military, they should have felt triumphant. But Gwydion suspected that many of them knew they had gone too far, that there was no way they could win now. Yet neither could they endure backing down. Worst of all, none could admit his private regret to any of the others.

The fear made them unstable, perfect fodder for one of his games. He concentrated deeply for a moment, thrilled to discover that his old powers were once again instantly at his command.

With no warning, the features of the shorter of his guards, the one with the food tray, twisted with ire. He flashed an incensed expression at the other boy. "What are you looking at?" he snapped, though the other guard hadn't gazed his way at all. "If you've got something to say to me, you say it, you lousy coward."

Gwydion hadn't bothered to seed a specific suspicion in that young man's mind. He merely suffused him with distrust.

He filled the other with hostility. "Hey, I don't take orders from you."

MAGICAL ALIENATION

Gwydion closed his fake alien eyes, to savor, with his other senses, the impressions wafting toward him. He heard the fierce noise of the guard's rifle being violently hurled to the floor. And then, the sound of flesh striking flesh. He felt the intensity of emotions mounting within those two fools, along with their irate words. He relished it all, as the emotional storm built higher and higher, until...yes, a crescendo. One had actually knocked the other out.

Making mischief—it was almost better than sex. He hadn't realized how much he missed it. Missed them both, actually, though sex would have to wait.

Now, what mischief could he perform next?

CHAPTER THIRTY-EIGHT
Haggerty

The whole house of cards that she had so carefully constructed over a lifetime flattened within her. All the denials she'd sold herself, all the lies she'd told everyone else. Gone.

Such as the fact that she walked the straight-and-narrow to make up for all the bad behavior her ancestors had displayed since the beginning of time. She'd not only made others believe that, she fervently believed it herself. Now she saw it wasn't true. It was all about *his* leaving. Deep inside she'd thought that if she became the best daughter possible, maybe her father would come back to them.

What a joke.

She'd made herself into a hypocrite for him, the ultimate hypocrite. The Family Values-imposter who had destroyed his family. The regular guy senator who wasn't even a real guy.

The worst part wasn't what Kenny did to her. It was the underlying sadness Fiona always carried beneath her surface merriment. Neither of them had ever been whole from the day he left.

First the loss of her powers, and now this.

Haggerty felt rudderless. If she wasn't what she always believed herself to be, then what was she? And what was this new stranger capable of doing?

CHAPTER THIRTY-NINE
Samantha

I awoke unceremoniously the next morning, to the sound of a voice calling in my head. Not a dream, mind you, and not *my* voice, either. It was Fiona's voice. In my mind.

"Wake up, Samantha," her voice cried. "They want you at the Bureau. Sounds serious."

Fiona's speech paused long enough for me to determine that: a) yes, I was awake, and not dreaming; and, b) no, I wasn't any crazier now than when I went to bed last night. She really was talking in my head.

Just as I thought that maybe I should reconsider that crazy part, her voice added insistently, "Now, dear girl!"

Like I was gonna fall back to sleep after that. I tumbled from the bed and padded through the house in search of the owner of the voice echoing between my ears. Not many schizos can do that. I found Fiona seated on a wrought iron chair on the small patio outside the dining room, soaking up some rays. Apparently, she had just relayed the summons she'd heard inside *her* head by monitoring her daughter, and was too comfortable there to actually move inside to pass it on.

"Before you go, Samantha... Do you see that owl on the fence?" With a nod of her head, Fiona indicated the block wall between her house and the one next door.

My gaze traveled the whole length of it. "Nope, no owls. A few lizards scurrying up and down, but no birds of prey."

"I was afraid of that," she said with obvious regret. "According to many belief systems, seeing owls is a bad omen, you know."

Seeing things that weren't there was worse.

Despite the unsettling nature of my abrupt awakening, not to mention our odd exchange about owls, once I got past them, I felt great. Humming with enthusiasm and optimism.

Fiona nodded knowingly when I shared my dynamite sense of wellbeing. "That's the harmonic convergence. It's not far off now, dear. The kind of power we used to feel right at the vortices radiates for miles around. They'll be even stronger in the days ahead."

"Some days it makes me feel awful, and other days it makes me feel great? What's up with that?" I demanded. I hated the roller coaster effect it was having on me.

She went on about its amplification properties, but I tuned her out. Not knowing how long it would last, despite having asked, I didn't care why I felt good, I simply wanted to savor it. I yearned to be back at the Bell Rock vortex, soaking up that psychic juice. There was something so intoxicating about its effect. I wanted more of it. I *craved* it.

Rather than risk hearing more strange voices, either inside or outside my brain, I threw myself together faster than usual, wearing an old favorite—a short silver lamé dress from the twenties. I feared it might have been too small for me now, because I'd put on a few pounds since I bought it. But I was proud to report that it wasn't one bit tighter than an ace bandage. I tied a scarf around my head, flapper style, and squeezed my chubby toes into a delightful pair of silver stiletto mules.

Since I wasn't about to walk in those shoes, I asked Fiona if I could borrow her car. I asked the regular way, of course—no brain transmissions, but merely by shouting over the murmuring house, which seemed louder than it used to be. Were our tensions adding to it?

At the Bureau office, I ran into François first. Fiona was right—this was serious. Anger flashed in his pale eyes like volcanic eruptions. With a taut tilt of his pasty face, he said in clipped tones, "We're in the conference room, Guinevere."

After risking my life in the militia wingnut factory, hadn't I earned the right to my own name?

Haggerty waited in their pink conference room. Dark circles ringed her eyes. When was the last time she'd slept?

"Riker's gone!" she blurted.

François pushed me into one of their mismatched chairs.

"Whattya mean *gone?*" I asked.

"What does it usually mean?" he exploded. "Your man left his hotel, despite our orders."

A discussion followed over how much "my man" Rand Riker

was. "Come on, G-Man, you know he had no use for me. He only kept me on the payroll because you guys asked him to. I wasn't exactly in on his private plans."

"So? You're psychic, aren't you? Can't you...you know...divine his whereabouts?" he demanded savagely.

I propped my elbows on the table and held up my head with my hands. That great sense of wellbeing I'd awakened with earlier had worn away fast, in what I suspected was Sedona's only vortex-free zone.

"François, surely you've noticed I'm a total fraud," I said.

Now Haggerty's eyes flashed angrily. Belatedly, I guessed I wasn't worth much as a psychic beard if I admitted to having no powers. What the hell, she wasn't sending me any visions. And, surely, my admission wouldn't shock him.

"Don't blame this on me," I said. "Why didn't you keep better tabs on him?"

With a sigh, he admitted, "Because we were a little busy, Fake-Psychic-Girl." Then, after a moment, "And because we didn't take him seriously."

After that armor-piercing admission, François's bluster calmed to a whisper. He began to question me without accusations. I really didn't know anything, however, and that must have been clear to him.

As much as he seemed to want to hold me there, I sensed Haggerty wanted me to leave. She kept trying to move me toward the door, continually reminding him that they always knew where to find me.

Finally, when he agreed to let me go, Haggerty said, "I'll drive her home, François."

"That's okay, I have—" I started to tell her that I'd brought her mother's Teutonic tank. But this time I saw the warning flash in her eyes in time to shut my trap. Okay, I got it now—she needed to talk to me alone. And she had to haul me there to do it? Fiona could just talk in my head. Sure, I hadn't liked that, either, but it was better than getting dragged somewhere for a chewing out.

"Wow! That'd be swell, Haggerty. How can I thank you?" When sarcasm is all I have, I use it like a club.

As soon as we hit the parking lot, she grabbed my wrist and started to drag me away from the door.

"Whoa, girl!" I said. "The shoes, remember?" I modeled my silly silver mules that were impossible to keep on if I moved at anything faster than a snail's crawl. With steam practically pumping from her ears, she slowed to my pace. All the way to Fiona's car, I watched with satisfaction as the muscles of her back bunched with irritation.

Finally, she collapsed against her mom's old boat. "It's worse than François knows," she admitted in a shaky voice. "A hotel employee described a pair of Riker's guests to me."

"So? That's helpful, right? What am I missing?" I leaned against the car beside her. "Wait. One of them must have been the woman. The one I heard laughing. You got a description of Rand's woman?"

"Forget the woman, Samantha. Even if she exists, she doesn't matter. While we still don't know when Riker made his escape, yesterday two men came to see him. One was described to me as a short heavyset man wearing a yellow workout suit, while the other was taller and barefoot, and the witness thought he might have been redheaded."

I shrugged. "That description fits lots of people. Hell, it would even fit Lugh and Taliesin."

A sob escaped from her. "It *was* Lugh and Taliesin. It had to be them."

"No," I insisted. "How would Rand know them? Or even know *of* them?" That there were Celtic deities among us wasn't exactly common knowledge. "Look, he's a major star. Do you think he'd welcome into his suite such goofy-looking strangers?"

After a helpless shake of her sleek auburn head, she pressed her forehead against the car's roof.

Once I thought about it, though, the implications floored me. "Angus said they'd visited someone here, right?"

She nodded without looking up.

"And you talked about a rogue god." I broke off in a sigh. "If you're right, you know what it means, don't you? Rand Riker has to be that rogue god."

She lifted her face. "Don't you think that, even in my depleted state, I would know if I were in the presence of another god?"

"Wouldn't a powerful god be able to hide it from you?"

MAGICAL ALIENATION

She'd already taught me about the ways magical beings conceal their identities from each other, how they erect mental barriers. I'd seen her keep out loads of beings, and once, I saw her accidentally let one in. That had nearly claimed both of our lives.

Haggerty shrugged grudgingly. "Wouldn't a rogue god have made better use of his powers than Devil Boy has?"

"Being a rock star's not too shabby."

"An *aging* rock star? Wouldn't Riker have given himself permanent youth, if he had that power?"

She had me there. I knew Rand found it troubling that his face now resembled a relief map. When Haggerty began muttering helplessly into the car's black paint, I stared again at the red rocks surrounding us. Even now, at this distance, I could feel their growing power, their lure.

"Haggerty, this harmonic convergence…" Damn, what had I once called it? I wished I could remember. "It's a once in a lifetime chance, right? That might not hold much appeal to a strong god, but what about a depleted one, like Gwydion? Or one defrocked of his status? Wouldn't it be a chance—maybe the *only* chance—to get back some of the energy that was taken away?"

Haggerty slowly raised her head.

"This goddess you told me about—Rele-de? The one you said was condemned to living life after life as a regular mortal?"

"What about her?" Haggerty asked in a harsh whisper.

"Just because she started out as a woman, was it ever decreed that she had to continue living those lives as one?"

CHAPTER FORTY

I left Haggerty to mull over my idea that the hyper-macho Rand Riker might have been the end result of a goddess-gone-bad, and I drove back to the house, where I planned to put the theory to Fiona.

Only the sight of a silver Lexus SUV in the driveway pushed that thought from my mind.

Unless those SUVs were breeding like fruit flies, that was Kenny's car. I'd pegged his and Fiona's little tryst as temporary insanity. But I found his being here now, where anyone could see him, significant. Was he leaving the little woman? Would Haggerty have a mom and dad together at last?

Inquiring minds needed to know. I left Fiona's car out in the street and shuffled up that perilous path toward the door as fast as my mules would allow.

Before I made it there, Kenny came rushing out, so fast, he plowed into me. I knew how wrong my speculations had been when I realized that wasn't joy twisting his face, but anguish.

"Sorry," he muttered and lowered his gaze. I wasn't sure whether he was apologizing for running into me, or for whatever had happened in the house. "Would you tell Annabelle that—" He broke off and gave his head a little shake.

With lips pinched tightly, he rushed off toward his SUV. The car jerked in reverse, before he abruptly shifted gears and peeled away. I watched till it was out of sight, before slowly dragging myself through the front door.

I found Fiona standing there, as still as a porcelain doll. I saw her aura again now, a blotchy gray sludge that slowly emanated from her body. I sensed she wasn't allowing me to see it as a gift now, she simply couldn't be bothered hiding it. She slowly turned my way, eyes glazed.

"He dumped you?" I demanded, aghast. "Again?"

"He's getting rather good at it," Fiona said with a dry laugh. "You have to give him credit, Samantha. This time he faced me, rather than merely stealing away."

Yeah, the man was a prince, all right. Anger mushroomed in me. "I don't have to give him anything. The first time he wasn't well known yet. Now, he's a high-profile figure—he knows if you wanted to, you could track him down. Telling you first was just damage control."

"I suppose you're right," she said softly. Right before my eyes, her face sagged. I felt like kicking myself for taking away her illusion.

I stared off across the room, trying to think of some way to revive her spirits. But that was when I realized we weren't precisely alone there, even if we didn't precisely have company, either.

A man stood silently. A see-through man, with a see-through bird on his shoulder.

"Uh, Fiona…"

"Forgive me, Samantha. Where are my manners? This is Alo, my spirit guide. He sensed what Kenny was about to do and came to see how I was handling it."

Really? How do see-through guys travel? He was a short, muscular man, in a plaid flannel shirt, with Native American features and bronzed, weathered skin. He wore a cloth headband over his forehead, and the sides of his hair were cut to his ears, a way I'd once seen described in a magazine article as an ancient Hopi style. I remembered Haggerty saying Fiona had been visiting a two-hundred-year-dead Hopi shaman.

My brain ricocheted away from that possibility, as I grasped for a stall question. "And the bird?"

"Hawk is *his* spirit guide."

It was crazy, but I felt the warmth of the man's greeting in my mind, though I hadn't seen his lips move. The hawk looked my way and tipped its head. And I could see clear through both of them to the wall behind them.

When See-through Man looked at Fiona, with a nod, she said, "Yes, Alo, you're right about that. It was a risk."

This one-sided conversation she was having seemed infinitely worse than hearing her talk in my head. Yet I couldn't look away from the faint, translucent colors of this man and his bird.

"I'll be fine, my friend, now that Samantha is here," Fiona added. "Thank you both for coming."

With that, the semi-transparent man and bird simply faded away.

"Alo has been there for me through so much. Have you ever

met a kinder man, Samantha?"

Maybe not, but I'd met some that were more alive. I couldn't stop looking at the spot where he had stood only a moment before. I *had* to get out of that room.

I took hold of her hands and dragged her toward the kitchen. "Come on, Fiona. Dump-days require food." So did seeing things that couldn't exist outside of bad drug trips.

Even as we came through the doorway, the customary tea service appeared on the table. "Uh-uh, tea won't cut it now."

The tea service disappeared. I went to the fridge, where I yanked open the freezer compartment. Apart from a bin of ice that had fossilized into some weird modern sculpture, the cold-cupboard was bare. "Sheesh, doesn't anyone in this family binge?"

"What is it you want, Samantha?" Fiona asked, taking a seat at the table.

"Ice cream. Häagen-Dazs or Ben & Jerry's is preferred, but anything will do in a pinch. Why don't you make us some Everything But...?"

"But what?"

"But...?" I began, puzzled. With understanding, I clarified before we went into some weird ice cream "Who's on first?" bit. "That's the name, Fiona."

Even with that confusion cleared up, she didn't comply. Fiona's red-rimmed eyes widened in disbelief. "I couldn't do that—it would be stealing."

Apparently, there was some code of ethics associated with conjured up food. Only stuff she already owned could be produced at will?

"Whaddya mean? You make casino winners all the time in Las Vegas." Haggerty had told me that. "Isn't that stealing?"

A flickering grin chased her sadness away. "I've lived in Vegas for a long time. The stories I could tell you! Believe me, that's fair game."

Honest people have always puzzled me, especially given how finely they split hairs. The nuances still weren't clear to me. Instead of arguing with her, though, I stood there silently, waiting her out.

"I suppose I could find some way to pay them," she said at last. Before another instant passed, a container of frozen ambrosia

MAGICAL ALIENATION

appeared on the table.

I hobbled over to the silverware drawer for a couple of teaspoons. After tearing off the top of the container, I stuck a spoon in it and passed it across to her.

Fiona's brow wrinkled skeptically. "You're sure this will help?"

This woman might be a goddess, but she wouldn't last a day in my world. "Trust me. When you get dumped as often as I do, you learn the drill."

She slowly freed the spoon and thoughtfully licked the ice cream that clung to it.

"Okay, Fiona—what did he say?"

"The same things he meant last time, but didn't bother to say. Blah, blah, blah, our lives aren't compatible. Blah, blah, blah, we don't fit." She shrugged. "Maybe he's right."

She passed the tub my way. I surprised myself by feeling too angry on her behalf to dig my spoon in. "What about fate? I thought…you know…that you two belonged together." Whoa! Was I admitting I believe in destiny?

Fiona gave her head an absent tilt. "Me too."

I finally took a massive scoop and stuffed it into my mouth. Instant brain-freeze, but it was worth it. "Tell me again how fate works." I passed the container back to her, even though she was still nursing her first little portion.

With a shred of impatience, Fiona said, "It's simple enough, Samantha. Our mother knows what's best for us. And periodically, she makes her wishes known. Of course, we're free to make other choices. But she will keep reminding us of the path we're meant to take."

"You mean, like some Mother-Goddess or the Mother-Universe? Because you sure better not be talking about my mom. She's so bad at running her own life, she really can't handle mine."

Fiona frowned. "You shouldn't say that, dear. Brie did her best by you. Some of the skills she passed on might be dubious, but you're strong and independent because of her."

A little shock went through me at the mention of my mother's name, Brie. Actually, her name was Berta, but she regarded that as so mundane, she changed it to Brie. Only later did she learn that most people don't spell the name like the cheese. But I had never shared that tidbit with Fiona. Why did the things she knew continue to shock me?

"I guess you're right," I admitted grudgingly, vowing to call my mother soon. Or buy some cheese. "What's the deal with Kenny? Is his destiny that he's meant to be with you, and he keeps resisting it? Or that he's not meant to be with you, and he's drawn to you in spite of it?"

"My guess? That Kenny is fated to be a better man than he is at present, and he's slowly working his way toward that."

With that evasion, she urgently directed all her attention to shoving her spoon back into the ice cream container. Instead of pulling it out again, however, she merely passed the whole thing to me. She rose to leave.

"Wait," I said. "Tell me one thing. With all your…you know, capabilities…how can your life be as messed up as mine?"

I thought that might anger her, or maybe she'd feed me some woo-woo bilge about her needing to learn from this journey, too. Instead, she pressed a gentle kiss on the top of my head and said, "If you find the answer to that question, dear Samantha, be sure you let me know."

CHAPTER FORTY-ONE

Collective tensions kept rising. By the next day, just two days before the harmonic convergence was supposed to peak, the whole town had reached the shattering point. Even worse, they lifted the travel barrier for Rand's alien benefit concert, now allowing limited movement within Sedona and the surrounding area, so people began flooding the place once more.

Fiona still seemed as lost as she had the day before, although she hid it with another visit from the pixie cleaning crew and her own frantic activity as she directed their chores. She did slow down long enough to warn me not to tell her daughter what Kenny did, and not to approach him. Of course, I don't follow orders well. Naturally, I tried Haggerty first thing.

She was too busy to talk with me, though, wrapped up as she was in a multi-state manhunt for Rand. For the entire band, actually. The Devil's Disciple's band bus had been found abandoned along the side of the Interstate. The crew and equipment truck were en route to Arizona. But the musicians were gone.

I knew I was right about Rand—he had to be the current rendition of the ancient rogue goddess, Rele-de. Even the initial was the same. When people use aliases, which they often do in my family, they usually keep the same letter. The concert that Haggerty had concocted, the one to aid "the alien," was still scheduled for tonight. Rand would return soon, I felt sure, to draw the power offered here. But it was anyone's guess whether he would show up for the concert, or if he'd blow off the entire tour. If he planned to chuck this life, why should he?

The shocking part was that Haggerty seemed to be taking my theory, that Rele-de had gone transgender in this go-round, seriously. So Haggerty worked furiously to find Rand, as François and the rest of the staff did, but for reasons of her own.

As if that wasn't enough to keep them busy, tensions had risen in the militia compound, too. Several series of shots had been fired within the facility. It wasn't clear whether they had killed the hostages, or if they were shooting at each other now. Squinty's limited negotiations with the militia had entirely broken down, with those in the compound now refusing all contact. Haggerty feared Gwydion was causing them to go loco somehow. Even more loco, that is. And with each shot fired, her tension over that siege rose. Yet she couldn't tell anyone. Well, anyone but me. I figured she considered that worse than nobody.

With all that she carried, I couldn't burden her with news of her father's latest defection. I could, however, cheerfully yank Kenny's miserable chain. I borrowed Fiona's car and went off to do battle with Kenny. During the drive, the red rocks pulsed with so much energy, I practically saw waves coming off them. The brilliant blue sky proved to be the perfect backdrop.

I talked my way past the officious guard who was always annoying Haggerty. But I'd forgotten about the gate surrounding the Campbell home. Decisions, decisions: Should I alert Kenny through the intercom, giving him the chance to turn me away, or just shed my dignity and scale the fence? While I hated physical exertion, dignity was never a priority with me. I hiked up the antique ivory nightgown I wore now and hurled myself over. I didn't even take the time to adjust the nightgown. I just rushed to the door and rapped heavily. After a moment, Kenny answered.

His face twisted with dismay. "Samantha, what—" Bowing gracelessly to the inevitable, he stepped aside to let me enter.

The plasma TV showed some soccer match in progress, but the sound was muted. I stood with my back to it.

Maria, the maid, walked by, carrying a large suitcase. Greeting me with a, "Hey, Samantha," she kept going toward the bedroom.

I waited until she was out of earshot before saying to Kenny, "Leaving, huh?"

He gave me a tight nod. "Kelly left this morning. She should be at our house in Phoenix by now. We'll leave for D.C. tomorrow morning."

He frowned when his gaze drifted to a cordless phone on one of the couches. I guessed she hadn't answered his call. Maybe the little woman had learned about Kenny's encounter with the first Mrs. Campbell. The *only* Mrs. Campbell.

"The police and the FBI don't think there's any reason why we have to remain here," he said.

Were we really going to pretend *that* was why he was going?

There was a bottle of something that looked like hand lotion on the coffee table, only when I looked closer, I saw it had a prescriptive label. I picked it up.

"That's Kelly's pore-opening lotion. She keeps bottles everywhere, uses it constantly. She can't stand for her pores not to be open."

I now knew more about her hygiene than I ever wanted to know.

He went on with, "A pharmacist makes it for her. It's the same chemical they use in those stop-smoking patches, to facilitate the spread of the ingredients through the skin."

"Kenny, can the science lecture. Let's get back to the fact that you're leaving."

He cleared his throat. "I have to get back to work. The Senate is in session, and there are votes—"

I planted my butt on one of his sofas. "Yeah, yeah—duty calls. That's the only reason why a man would bug out suddenly, even if he'd unceremoniously dumped his wife. For the second time."

Kenny pushed his glasses up on his nose and threw an anxious glance toward the hall where Maria had disappeared. "Don't start, Samantha. This is between Fiona and me."

He picked up the TV remote from the coffee table between us, and un-muted the TV. The sound of urgency filled my ears even before I looked at the screen. The network had broken into the game with a news update. Filling the screen was an image of the militia compound, from the vantage point of a helicopter hovering as close as the government would allow. A reporter in the copter reported more shots having been fired.

The TV seemed to rivet Kenny's attention. I might have bought his intense focus, if I didn't know how much he wanted to avoid me. As soon as he absently placed the remote back on the table, I snatched it up and muted the TV again. Like it or not, Kenny was going to hear what I came to say.

"Listen, Mr. Family Values, you don't get to act like an absolute louse without hearing about it."

When I placed the remote back on the wide table, I spotted that silver clasp that Kelly had used with her shawl. This time I grabbed it and saw that it was indeed engraved with the letter, "R." I snapped the catch open. There was another engraving inside: "Desert

Sands Realty," it read. I asked Kenny about it.

"Janice, the real estate gal who arranged our purchase of this house, gives those out to clients for promotion. Kelly and some of the ladies on my staff got them."

So Haggerty was right—there really was no shortage of those silver pieces. My fingertip traced the "R" etched on it. For *Realty?* If the broker wanted it engraved, wouldn't she have used her company's initials? Or the client's? I tried to remember everything I could about the piece I'd seen in Rand's suite. Could it really have been this one? "Mrs. Campbell didn't make any changes to this piece?" I asked.

Kenny shrugged. "I don't know. What changes would she have made?" For emphasis, he finger-quoted "made."

I was just grasping.

"Surely you can see why I can't leave my wife," Kenny said, leaning closer and speaking in a confidential tone.

I decided not to remind the bigamist that it wasn't his wife he was staying with.

"Kelly has done so much for me. No wife could be any more supportive of her husband's career."

Did love enter into that relationship?

"Why she even changed the most fundamental thing about herself, the root of a person's identity, so that in case we were blessed, we would all have—"

What? Kelly had a sex-change operation? What else was that fundamental? I finally lost it. "Kenny, you *were* blessed. Annabelle is your daughter. And she deserves better from you."

He gave those glasses a pointless shove. "My leaving is better for Annabelle. This has all been too unsettling for her." He cleared his throat. "That's why I told her superiors that while I want to keep my security detail until this business with Normal Frankly is settled, I don't want Annabelle on it any longer."

"You really are full of buffalo chips," I said in a hushed whisper. And Fiona believed this guy was working his way toward being a better man. Lucky for him he'd started with the bar really low.

"Not to worry. I made it clear my request had nothing to do with her job performance."

"Warmed over, day-old buffalo chips." Did he honestly

believe the Bureau would take his feeble praise of her seriously after he had her dismissed? He'd rather destroy his daughter's career than face her scorn.

"E.T., is everyone from your world such a weenie?" I asked.

Kenny blanched and stared over my shoulder.

"Can't even look me in the eye, you wimp?"

"Hush, Samantha," Kenny said, still staring.

I realized it was the silent TV screen that had caught his eye. I whirled around. Projected there now in crisp colors across the wide screen was—Rand Riker. Naked, apart from the scarlet paint that covered his entire body, with his cape unfurled in the breeze behind him, Rand stood atop a giant RV rolling into the edge of town, judging by the scenery I saw behind him, with his clenched fists raised over his head in victory.

"Golly, that's a sight," Kenny said.

"A sight" didn't begin to cover it. Rand had returned in all his glory. Dark threatening clouds had come to cover the brilliant blue sky I'd remarked on earlier, a perfect milieu for Devil Boy's triumphant return. Was there any doubt he had divine connections?

CHAPTER FORTY-TWO

The storm threat worsened. Thunder shook the earth so furiously, it sent boulders toppling from the red rock spires onto the streets. The shaking reminded me of some of the temblors I'd felt back home in California. Easily a 5.0 on the Richter Scale. Not enough to bring down buildings, but more than enough to toss drinking glasses out of cabinets. Plenty big enough to shatter nerves. Bolts of lightning had set fire to small stretches of brush, though the fire department put them out fast enough. The rain had not yet begun to fall, but I'd never seen such a violent build-up. I thought for sure they'd cancel the concert, which was to be held in an outdoor arena. But Rand insisted that the concert would go on, rain or shine. Given what I saw, "shine" wasn't an option.

Back at the house, despite the blustery weather, Fiona continued to sit on that little patio, lifting her face to the angry clouds as she once had in the sun. I hovered inside, trying not to intrude on the post-dump process, but staying close in case she needed me.

I changed into my Adriana layered chiffon dress, which I hadn't worn since I'd flown to Arizona. That felt like a lifetime ago, instead of a week and a half.

While watching over Fiona, I heard the front door quietly close behind me. To my surprise, our visitor was Haggerty. I'd gotten so used to her slamming the door, I'd forgotten she could enter a room like everyone else. More dressed down than usual, she wore jeans and a navy T-shirt with "FBI" printed on the back in yellow lettering.

Clouds even darker than those in the sky filled her troubled eyes. She burst out with, "Samantha, I need..." But her voice trailed off when she saw her mother seated outside in the stormy weather. "Is my mom okay? She knows, doesn't she?"

Knew what? I'd often wondered since whether, if I'd told her the truth about Fiona and Kenny, things would have turned out any differently. But I made a judgment call, and we all know how bad my judgment is. I decided that Haggerty was in no shape to hear about Kenny's defection.

"Okay? Are you kidding? She's great," I said, really laying it on. "Didn't you know how much she loves storms?"

"If you say so." Haggerty still looked doubtful, but she accepted it, proving to me that it was what she wanted to hear. "Samantha, I need you to come with me. I want you along when we talk to Riker." She turned and headed back to the door, without waiting for my response, but after a few steps, she twisted back toward Fiona. "How could she possibly enjoy *this* storm, knowing what it means?"

Huh? It was a storm. A bad one, for sure, but what meaning could there be in the weather?

At the Sedona Cultural Park, an outdoor amphitheater on the fringe of Sedona, where the Devil's Disciple's benefit concert would be held, Haggerty turned off a paved road into one of a series of unpaved parking lots. I couldn't imagine where she thought she would park. Those lots were a sea of cars that stretched all the way to the horizon. But a cop waved her into a roped off area I hadn't seen at first, which was designated, according to a hand-lettered sign, for officials.

The stage was placed in a deep cavern between two hillsides. It was a huge affair, covered on the top by three wide semi-circular strips of wood that rose over it, and which lent it such an otherworldly quality, it gave me chills. The expansive outdoor seating rose up on the opposite hillside and wrapped around the stage in a big crescent, cramming in more people than I'd ever seen gathered together anywhere, except for the area outside the militia compound. When the object of the benefit concert had been Normal Frankly, they couldn't give the tickets away, but Rand's shifting the concert's recipient to the alien made it a sellout. The roar of the excited crowd rose to deafening levels, but it still failed to drown out the sound of the storm.

The concert was sure to be this decade's Woodstock, a show everyone would claim to have seen, even if they hadn't. I mean, Woodstock, as crazy as it had been, according to my grandma, wasn't about raising bucks for a freakin' alien.

After I stepped from Haggerty's car, a flash of lightning struck the ground not two yards from my feet, catching a dried clump of weeds on fire. I shrieked and leaped back toward the Crown Vic, grabbing the door handle, but she had already locked it.

Pursing her lips as if to whistle, Haggerty blew out softly in the direction of the flare, as if she intended to put it out with her breath. Nothing happened, nothing at all. She looked stricken when she wasn't able to perform even that minor a magical task. She ran to the fire and angrily stomped it out with her shoe. Absolute devastation flickered across her features before she donned the mask again, but she never quite hid the resigned frustration in her eyes.

The thunder continued to roll menacingly. I gave the clouds a guarded look. "I'd rather wait here in the car. Can't you bring Rand to me?"

"Suck it up, will you, Samantha. No matter what he's dealing with, Angus is always going to watch out for you."

Angus? What did Angus have to do with this storm?

She started walking down a winding gravel path, studded here and there with dim outdoor lighting. After a moment, I followed along. But the downward slope was too steep for my stilettos, making me slow to a crawl. According to Haggerty, we were meeting Rand in the huge RV, on whose roof he'd ridden into town, which was now parked near the rear of the stage. There were several small buildings on either side of the big stage, some of which must have held dressing rooms, but apparently, Rand was using the RV in that capacity.

François stomped his feet in annoyance while waiting for us outside the RV. Haggerty joined him, and they both cooled their heels, as I continued navigating that path. Did whoever designed that place think about how the really well dressed—like me—would manage that descent?

We eventually climbed into the RV, and found Rand seated before a theatrical mirror, applying white and crimson greasepaint in the shape of hellish flames that rose up on his face. The cape he'd worn while riding into town hung from a hook behind the door. Rand's body was still painted red, and the tint was all he wore. Whoever painted Little Rand—which flapped around freely and, as you might have guessed, wasn't *little* except in name—hadn't missed a spot. To think I'd suspected both Fiona and Kelly Campbell of having enjoyed that honor. What a joke.

François plunged in on the questioning, demanding to know why Rand left town.

MAGICAL ALIENATION

Rand fired back now with, "Don't know what you're complaining about, mate. I didn't break any laws. You'd lifted the travel ban by then."

"Riker, you were under house arrest."

"Till you sent the sheila to ask for my help," Rand said, with a nod in Haggerty's direction. "Then all bets were off."

François continued pounding at him, but his questioning sounded lame even to me. Yes, Rand had left, but he'd returned, and it was to put on the concert they'd asked him to do. After a little more posturing, François wound down.

Rand glanced at us in the mirror. "Agent Haggerty, how come you and Madame Samantha always seem to be together?" Even made-up, there was no mistaking his smirk. Was he just needling, or did he understand the exact nature of my relationship with her?

François frowned. "I've been wondering that, too, Annabelle. What exactly does Guinevere bring to these proceedings?"

Guinevere again? How long had it been since I wore my medieval gown?

Haggerty paused uncertainly. Then she squared her shoulders and said with exaggerated dignity. "Agent Gerard, we can't always pick our friends."

Boy, did that make me feel special. To my surprise, since it didn't answer anything, François merely nodded. With a flick of his finger, he indicated that we should go.

When I brushed against Haggerty on the way to the door, I could feel her tension. François had only been taking his frustration out on Rand, but I knew Haggerty desperately wanted to know what connection Rand shared with her ancestors.

Maybe I could get the answers she longed for. Outside the dressing room, I drew close to François and tugged at his sleeve. "François, can I talk to Rand alone for a minute?"

"Is there something you can't say in front of us, Fake-Psychic-Girl?"

Was there ever. "It's personal stuff. I still haven't been paid."

He inclined his head. "Sure thing. Go get him."

I didn't even glance at Haggerty when I headed back to the RV. I entered without knocking. I spotted a chair at a dining table, and I placed it next to where Rand sat before the mirror. Initially, he didn't react to what he might have considered crowding.

Then he asked, "Something on your mind, Madame Samantha?"

Where to begin? "Rand, we both know there are people in this world, who…aren't like you and me. Beings with amazing powers."

Thunder clapped overhead with all the strength of a twenty-foot wave crashing against the shore.

Rand raised his eyes to the ceiling. "Too right. With weather like this, how can we doubt the existence of the gods?"

So we were going to be more direct. But again with the weather? What was everyone talking about?

I was about to go on, but I forgot how Rand liked his monologues. "We both have a patron among them," he went on conversationally. "The difference is, yours isn't worth spit, while mine will rule the universe someday and give me everything I want."

He was right about Haggerty being a dud as far as goddesses went. Look at how easily she could be stripped of power. But who was Rand's protector? I'd felt so certain Rand himself was a god, powerless or not.

In case he was not, I decided to share the wisdom of my experience with him. "Better watch it, Rand. The gods have a way of discarding the likes of us."

"Speak for yourself. My patron will always want me at…*his*…side."

His? He ended with a twisting of his thick lips. Taunting me. Just as he had once before when he said he was celibate. Was he lying now, or intentionally leading me astray? Or was Rand Riker actually the plaything of a god? A male god?

CHAPTER FORTY-THREE

Rand's admission made my head reel worse than it always did after a couple of tequila shooters in an iced mocha. Brain-freeze and instant drunk—what could be more potent? Absolutely nothing, I would have said, until I sat down to dish the dirt of the universe with my boy, Rand.

I stumbled out of the dressing room, only to find Haggerty waiting there for me. During my time with Rand, she'd picked up an automatic rifle from somewhere.

"Anything good?" she asked absently, stealing a look at the turbulent sky before staring out over the crowd.

I snorted. "You're not going to believe it."

"Tell me later. I'm on security detail here."

"Wait. You mean we're not leaving? What am I gonna do here?"

She shrugged. "Watch the concert? Lots of people have paid plenty for it."

Lots of people were probably less disenchanted with Rand than me.

Unlike the sloping path that wound down to the stage from where we'd parked, they had built stairs where the outdoor seating rose up the opposite hillside. Haggerty made her way up those steps, with me trailing behind. I continued to follow her when she traced a path along the top of the seating, from where she surveyed the crowd.

She must have heard me muttering to myself. Speaking now over her shoulder, she said, "Sorry, Samantha, I don't have time to take you back to the house."

I couldn't see why not. There were loads of cops here, all as heavily armed as she was. You couldn't walk two feet in any direction without tripping over someone carrying an automatic rifle. But I did need to tell her what I'd heard, even if I could barely digest it myself. I still couldn't decide whether Rand had lied, or shared something real and personal with another Celtic deity groupie.

There were gay gods, of course. Everything about them was reflected in our own diversity. But for Rand Riker to start pitching for the other team at this stage of his life strained my credulity. Still, why would he need to lead me astray? Did he think I could guess his patron's identity? He obviously overestimated my intelligence. Then again, he might be willing to do anything for whatever goodies his protector had promised him. Or maybe he knew he would return to near-goddess status once more, and had a god waiting in the wings for him.

Either way, who was his mysterious supporter? Haggerty insisted Lugh and Taliesin had visited him, but I'd never sensed even a hint of sexuality from either of them. They were like full-sized six-year-olds. It was even possible that his protector really was a female, that he'd lied because the role of consort wasn't a comfortable fit for him.

The possibilities made my brain throb.

The temperature must have dropped twenty degrees. Loads of people in the crowd donned the sweaters they were smart enough to bring. Shivering in my flimsy dress, I said, "Feels like Greenland out here."

"There's a wool blanket in the emergency kit in my trunk." Haggerty pulled a set of keys from her pocket and held them out to me.

That was the kind of person she was—someone who kept an emergency kit in even a loaner car, when she had the powers to get herself out of any jam. Well, she'd had powers at one time. Me, I'd rather trust intuition and the kindness of strangers, willing or not.

When I hesitated about taking the car keys, she said, "Samantha, do you want that blanket?"

"You mean, cover my dress?" I fluffed out the organdy layers.

She rolled her eyes. "Suit yourself." She walked off.

People don't realize the price I pay to be a really special-looking celebrity psychic. In my flimsy dress, with goose pimples the size of Cocker Spaniels on my arms, I trudged along behind her.

The crowd's excitement was as electric as the storm. Of course, it helped that most of those people were higher than the dark clouds overhead. People openly shared drugs and bottles of booze; the air reeked of weed. Haggerty was right about Devil's Disciple fans—a good part of the band's success could be attributed to the fact that their audience remained perpetually stoned.

I stood next to Haggerty, the layers of my dress flapping so fiercely in the gale force wind, I expected to start spinning like a top.

"Blanket?" Haggerty asked, while continuing to monitor the storm.

Man, did I want it. But... "Dress," I said.

She shrugged, as if to say, *It's your funeral.*

Great, now we were talking in shorthand. That didn't bode well for my ever ending this relationship. Rand was right—as a divine patron, she sucked. If she couldn't make it balmy out there, at the very least, she should have produced a driver to take me home.

"To think that I should have to be here in *this* storm," she muttered, "and still feel so powerless."

I didn't understand the strange references she kept making. Finally, I broke down and asked, "What's with all the weather references?"

"Can't you tell that this isn't an ordinary storm?" Haggerty asked.

She stared up into the clouds, which looked darker than ever. The thunder still rocked the earth, and as twilight overtook daylight, the lightning lit it as brightly as the sun. Yet the rain failed to fall.

Despair twisted Haggerty's face. "This is a war of the gods," she went on to say. "The tensions on the Ruling Council have broken out in battle. Surely you can see how extraordinary it is. When have you heard thunder like this, seen lightning that ignites the earth, and yet there's no rain?"

I should have told her she was nuts. War of the gods? Where did she get this stuff? Yet what came out of my mouth instead surprised even me.

"What about Angus" I asked anxiously.

Haggerty smiled tolerantly. "If I know Angus, while he's drawn to the side of the rebels, he's there in the middle trying to mediate tensions."

That fit. I didn't want him back or anything—I didn't. But neither could I bear for anything to happen to him.

"This must be awful for you," I said.

Her eyes widened in surprise, as if she didn't expect empathy from me. Hey, I had feelings. The mask fell away from her face, and I saw unimaginable grief there.

To distract her, I spat out the shocking news that Rand had shared with me.

She stared at me as if to assess whether I was pulling her leg. Apparently deciding the joke wasn't mine, she pursed her lips as she considered it.

"I don't buy it," she said at last. "How about you?"

I shrugged. "As good as I am at people reading, they fool me all the time."

Haggerty bit her lip, clearly trying to avoid saying something insulting. I wanted a new patron.

"So you think it's true?" she asked.

"I didn't say that. There are a just couple of sure things I've discovered about Rand: He's always playing some kind of game, and he holds more pieces of the puzzle than you think he does."

Rand must have heard his cue. As soon as I finished my remark, Devil Boy, in all his wild glory, stepped from the RV. He took center stage, strapping his guitar across his scarlet torso. His bandmates took their places there as well. I remembered that the empty band bus had been found by the side of the road, yet here they were now. Had the other musicians been inside the RV that Rand rode into town on? While also made-up, strangely enough, the other guys wore clothes. The audience positively roared for all of them. The special effects on the stage were awesome. What looked like real flames rose up around their feet.

The bad boys of rock went into song. Finally, something to drown out the sounds of the storm. The audience loved it, reveling in the sixties' counter-culture lyrics. I scarcely noticed Rand's nudity now. It was so over-the-top, and the old boy had stripped too many times. The audience was still entranced by his antics, though. Everyone there grew intoxicated on Rand's rebellion. More intoxicated.

The temperature kept dropping. The Cocker Spaniels on my arms grew to the size of Doberman Pinschers. I was at the point of relenting on that blanket. Who was I trying to impress?

Suddenly, with no warning, Angus appeared at my side. That banishing spell was clearly never going to work. He sounded a trifle breathless, as we mortals might if we'd just run into a room. "Sammy-girl, don't leave me for him. I can't stand it. You know it's always been you, only you…really."

It was that "…really" that meant it wasn't *actually* just me. We'd argued it too many times to go into it now. I wanted to scream at him, *You're a god—why can't you see he means nothing to me?* If love blinded him to it, I couldn't admit it, even now.

A look of concentration came over his face.

"No," I said. "Don't turn him into a frog. Angus, read the fairy tales—it's been done."

His face brightened, as it always did when he thought I understood him in a way no one else did. "I won't, Sammy. I've been studying the music of this period. Remember how I helped Annabelle when we first met? That gave me an idea of something even better I could do to him."

When had he helped Haggerty? Well, I did remember once during our first caper, when she wanted him out of the way, she asked him to... Oh, no!

In a heartbeat, before I could stop him, Angus carried out his threat. Suddenly, the flames disappeared. The other band members were stripped of their instruments. Rand was no longer painted red and no longer naked. Instead, he wore tight black pants and a blue satin shirt, unbuttoned to his waist. Gold chains draped over coarse gray chest hairs. His long black hair had also vanished in favor of a more conventional short cut, with a forelock drooping over his forehead. And he no longer held a guitar, but sat before a piano.

In contrast to all of that, the most shocking transformation was his music itself.

"Fee-ee-lings," he moaned, as his long fingers tripped over the keys.

"Angus!" I shouted. "You turned Rand Riker into a...a...lounge singer."

Angus beamed proudly. Sadly, the audience had also reached the same conclusion. No one seemed as shocked as I was by the inexplicable transformation, but like I said, they were all pretty high. Still, they knew that wasn't the music they had paid big bills to hear.

The jeers started almost immediately. Followed by people storming the stage. I looked to Angus, silently pleading with him to fix what he had broken. But just then a bolt of lightning struck the earth near where he stood.

"Dagna, protect us," he whispered.

I knew that was the father god of the Celts, the god of magic and wisdom.

"Samantha, my people need me. Stay safe, my girl." After

that, he vanished.

     Stay safe? So much for Haggerty's belief that Angus would watch over me. He had left me there with thousands of people who thought that it was not the events of the last week, or even this storm, but the change in Rand Riker's music, which truly signaled the end of the world.

CHAPTER FORTY-FOUR

Almost time. Gwydion was really going to pull this off. He was actually on the verge of succeeding in stocking up on enough power to elude the Ruling Council. For as long as it took for the trickster gods to oust the others anyway. At first, when his captors planned to move him to a more secure facility, it had seemed like such a foolhardy chance to direct them here instead. And then, to fall prey to these fools—that could have gone horribly wrong. How wonderful it was to know he hadn't lost his touch. To take a wild chance and have it pay off—well, that was just a god's right.

The strength of the coming harmonic convergence had grown to awesome levels. He knew its power could be painful to mortals, but in his body, it felt like the most delicious of wines. He breathed deeply now to drink in more of it.

The only question was whether he should make his way out of the complex now, or wait. He could leave with ease. He wouldn't even have to make himself invisible to do it. His game of stripping these militia fools of what little sense they had and making them turn on each other had worked beyond his most outrageous dreams. Those that were left were so oblivious they wouldn't notice him now if he kicked them in their naughty bits on his way out.

Yet it might behoove him to wait. The god-mail demand that he'd sent out for aid had been received this time. He could feel that. Despite the distraction of the war of the gods, his kind would know where the power would be the greatest. It wouldn't do to be careless about that. He'd need all he could get. He just hoped his plan for containing it would work. But why was he worried? Having come along so well, his fate wasn't going to turn around now.

Still, he was bored here with so few diversions. No females at all—what kind of world did these militia dupes inhabit? There wasn't any more fun to be had at their expense, either.

He remembered he hadn't checked on the welfare of the hostages lately, and he supposed he could use up a little time with that. But no—he refused to do it! He'd watched out for them enough, it was time they took care of themselves. Besides, what could happen to them now, with the militia so disabled?

No god should ever have to baby-sit a mortal—unless it was that delicious mortal, Samantha. He'd take care of her anytime. The rest of them could rot for all he cared. How could that possibly hurt him?

CHAPTER FORTY-FIVE

The Bureau staff, along with some infantry troops, had helped the local police process the rioters they'd arrested at the concert. Starting with the other members of the band, who attacked Rand after his unexpected metamorphosis. The really bizarre part was that they all acted as if Rand had changed to spite them all. No one seemed to regard his transformation as the inexplicable act that it was. Worse still, once again there was nobody free to drive me anywhere, so I was stuck at the cop-shop till the wee hours of the morning. When I'm up at that hour, I expect the party to be more fun.

After the video of Rand's incomprehensible alteration hit the Internet, the promoter cancelled the Sex, Drugs & Rock 'n' Roll tour. The police escorted Rand back to his inn, where he was being guarded.

The storm—or battle, if you believed that—kept raging. By the time we dragged ourselves to Fiona's house at four o'clock in the morning, my nerves were raw from the noise and the electric charge in the air. But I also felt so exhausted, I knew it wouldn't keep me awake. Haggerty must have been just as tired. She curled up on the living room sofa, rather than return to the Campbells' guesthouse. Obviously, nobody had bothered to tell her she was *personae non grata* around those parts now.

The next thing I knew, it was late morning and Haggerty was shaking me awake. "Samantha, wake up. What are you doing in bed at this hour?"

Had it really been so long since she'd seen it that she didn't know what sleep looked like? I dragged myself from bed and wrapped myself in my red dragon robe. We went to the living room.

The storm sounded as fierce as ever. The horrific claps of thunder shook the house. I started to turn on the TV—anything to dampen the sound of those shattering rolls of thunder.

"Don't bother," Haggerty warned. "You'll just have to endure the speculation from all the talking heads on this unprecedented worldwide storm."

Worldwide? The storm covered the whole freakin' globe? The god-war theory was starting to sound less crazy.

"Where's my mom?" she asked. "I need her help."

How should I know? Fiona might talk in my head, but I didn't keep tabs on hers. Still, I offered to help Haggerty look.

There was something odd about the house now, but I couldn't put my finger on what it was. We tried the kitchen first. Fiona had left tea service for us there, with tea so warm, steam rose out of the pot's spout, along with fresh biscuits that filled the room with their just-from-the-oven scent. I would have found that picturesque breakfast a comforting sight, if the pink-flowered envelope, propped against the teapot, hadn't given me an uneasy feeling.

Haggerty must have sensed it, too. She hesitated before reaching for the envelope. It was only then that I realized what was different about the house—it was silent now. The murmuring of emotions and energy had been turned off.

Haggerty finally grasped the envelope. But she didn't open it, she just clutched it in her hand. "She's gone. Mom's gone. Along with Mellencamp."

I wasn't any more psychic than a pickle, and even I guessed that.

Eventually, she opened the envelope and began to read from the handwritten letter. "Darling daughter," Haggerty read aloud. "I'm sorry, my dearest. I know my leaving now comes at the worst possible time for you, but I couldn't stay here any longer. Samantha will explain why."

I didn't have to. Haggerty's eyes rose above the sheet of paper and met mine. "Kenny, right? He did it again?"

I nodded. I didn't have the heart to tell her that Kenny hadn't merely ditched her mother, but, in asking for Haggerty to be removed from his case, he had dumped her, too. She'd probably find her things piled out on the Campbells' curb, awaiting garbage day.

She lowered her gaze to the pink-flowered stationary. Apparently, she couldn't stand to read any more and thrust the letter at me.

"Gwydion has been robbing your power, Annie," I read aloud. "I didn't want to add to your worries by telling you. I had hoped that after we increased his vigor, he would stop siphoning yours. Such a greedy boy."

Fiona sure saw the best in everyone. That fake alien was just a pig.

"I hope you're feeling a surge of your own strength now—I've done everything I can to sever his borrowing of yours. If you're not, I can't explain it—perhaps it really is the effect of the harmonic convergence, but I must tell you, darling, I just made that up. It really shouldn't work that way. However you're feeling, your own powers are too unstable to rely on now. You need Gwydion, Annabelle," the letter read. "With me gone, and the war in *Tir na N'og* growing worse, he's the only one you can turn to. And I sense that tonight, when the harmonic convergence is at its peak, something awful will happen. You'll need support from someone. Don't let your feelings toward him stop you from accepting the help he can provide."

Haggerty's poker face abandoned her now. She looked stunned by her mother's suggestion.

I went back to reading. "By the way, darling, I've maintained the force-field around Samantha to keep the media and others away from her, as you asked. But you're going to have to remove it at some point. The poor girl deserves some exposure for all the chances she takes for you."

I glared at her. "I knew it!"

Haggerty didn't even have the decency to look guilty when she shrugged. "I didn't have the time to keep tabs on you." She gestured toward the letter. "Keep reading."

I would keep reading, I decided, but at some point, Former-Goddess-Girl and I were gonna rumble over this.

My gaze dropped to Fiona's closing remarks. "I hope you girls will stay in the house there in Sedona for as long as you wish. Or come back whenever you want. That place will be good for both of you."

That I could continue crashing there was the first good news I'd heard in a long time. And considering that I wasn't going to get any press mileage out of this whole fiasco, I needed a place to land.

Haggerty looked considerably less thrilled by the idea. Or maybe it was what I'd already read that had soured her. She grabbed the sheet of stationery from my hands and tore it into little pieces, which she flung to the floor.

"How could she do this? How could she leave me, when I need her so badly? If something so horrific is about to happen, how can I deal with it alone?"

"There's Gwydion—"

"Turning to Gwydion is not an option," Haggerty insisted. "How could I trust him?" Without another word, she walked out of the room. A moment later, I heard the door close with enough force to rival the storm.

She returned a couple of hours later. The tortured expression she'd worn when she left was gone now, replaced by the resolute strength I was used to seeing from her.

"I've been given permission to try something tonight, and I'll get some support from the Bureau and the Military Intelligence unit," she announced.

Whatever she planned must still have been a long shot. Squinty wouldn't have agreed to help if he had any other options.

Then she added, "Of course, you and I know I'll be doing things in ways they can't imagine."

Yes! We were back in the goddess-realm. Finally.

"Samantha, we'll have some walking to do. If you have anything more appropriate to wear, you should put it on."

Her tone made it sound so ominous. I went to the guestroom to change. While I stood before the closet, trying to decide if I had anything less dorky than the sweats I'd worn that night at Bell Rock, Haggerty wandered into my room and sat on the bed. Bad sign—it wasn't like her to need company.

Unfortunately, if we were going to walk, it looked like it would have to be the sweats and tennies for me. I started to pull off my dress. But Haggerty suddenly appeared at my side, clutching a handful of half-burned sheets of paper.

"What are these?" she asked with a confused frown.

Ooh, crap! Those were the letters she'd written to their cousin Lucinda, which I'd used in my banishing spell.

"These are my letters. I wrote them when I was young. But why are they burned? Was this the way Lucinda had them?"

Lucinda—sure, I'd blame her. Only somehow I didn't. Before I knew it, I spilled the story of the spell I'd performed to try to keep Angus away.

To my surprise, she actually beamed at me with approval. "A spell? You performed a spell?"

"Yeah, one that didn't work. Angus still isn't getting it."

She stared at the letters. "How could he? You'd only banish him if you used *his* letters. What were you thinking, Samantha?"

I told her again what I did, this time in more detail. How because I didn't have a copy of Angus's signature or a lock of his hair, I used her letters, which mentioned him.

A strange look stole over her face, like one of dawning comprehension. "Tell me what you said during this spell. Exactly."

This time I recited the language I'd used. After repeating the whole thing, I finished up with, "I said, 'I name thee Angus's power,' And then, for good measure, I added, 'I name thee Annabelle's power,' since they were your letters."

She choked. "Don't you see what you did? You shut down my powers. Completely. Gwydion may have drained my magical energies, but you banished them entirely."

"No way."

She laughed. "Way, my girl." Approval spread across her face once more. "To think our Samantha actually performed an effective spell." Anger came to replace it. "And you directed it at me. Me!" Then astonishment. "But it worked." She gave her head a disbelieving shake.

She should know how I felt.

Haggerty jumped to her feet. "Okay, Samantha, show me the supplies you bought. I know a little about mortal spells. Now you're going to perform another one to reverse the first."

While I reached to the closet shelf for the box of kits, I muttered, "I actually performed a spell that worked."

Haggerty threw her arm over my shoulder in a show of uncharacteristic warmth, while the expression she wore looked anything but friendly. "Before this day is over, you better have performed a second, or you're going to be doing spells from the grave."

No pressure, though.

Under Haggerty's able direction, I performed another spell. I insisted that she should do it—after all, what were the odds that lightning would strike twice for me? But she maintained that the spell-maker needed to do the reversal. Within a short time of our completing it,

Haggerty said she felt the first stirrings of power. I guess we'd know for sure when she had to call on her skills for whatever she had planned for tonight. More pressure.

I eventually donned my cruddy walking clothes. I couldn't find Haggerty after I finished changing. I looked for her in the kitchen and on the patio. Finally, I eased open the door to her mother's bedroom. It was a girly room, with a white canopy bed and dusky-rose carpet, which still retained the slight scent of the wildflower cologne Fiona sometimes wore. Along one wall was an altar, like the one I'd seen in Haggerty's house, where I knew she prayed to her ancestors.

I spied her now before her mother's altar. Haggerty held an ornate dagger above her head, which she drew in a circle. I crept away and left her to perform her ritual alone, though, if she was right about the war of the gods, nobody in her homeland was listening.

She emerged a short time later. The signs of strain weren't entirely erased from her face, but as always after her rituals, she looked more refreshed. With a jerk of her head, she indicated for me to come with her.

We went to her car and began driving. Shortly after we turned onto 179, I casually glanced out as I typically did when we drove over the bridge that crossed Oak Creek. But something really caught my attention there. Instead of the creek that typically rippled gently well below the road, I saw a raging body of water that had exploded its banks and whose tumultuous current now flashed white water, as it easily carried about giant boulders and heavy tree trunks.

"Uh...the creek has risen," I said, astounded. "Without rain, it's overrunning its banks. Could it flood tonight?"

Haggerty snorted. "Are you kidding? It could *boil*."

Boiling creeks? Ooh! We were talking real wrath-of-the-gods-time now. I shivered and thought I should bail from here, and quickly. But if this storm truly covered the whole world, where would I go?

As we drove, at first I thought we were going to Kenny's house, where Haggerty was likely to get a nasty shock when she found out how unwelcome she was there. But she drove past the entrance to his complex.

"Have you changed your mind about asking for Gwydion's help?" I asked. I couldn't explain it, but I wanted to see that strange alien-god again. Who else might protect me from boiling creeks?

Her full lips tightened into a taut line. "I have no choice but to appeal to him. Even with my powers growing, I can't risk relying on them."

I didn't feel too guilty. Nor too proud. I'd performed two spells, and they both worked! That the object of the first one came out totally wrong just gave it my own personal style.

"I'll help him to tap into the harmonic convergence in exchange," Haggerty said. "I have no doubts that he's thought about how to do it on his own—that has to be why he directed his caravan here—but I can make it easier for him. I can help him get out of that place. Ease is sure to appeal to someone like Gwydion."

"You hate it, huh? Having to work with him."

"He's everything I despise about my ancestors." She stopped and shut her eyes. "Everything I did despise, that is." She shook her head. "Doesn't matter. Gwydion will get what's coming to him someday."

Right. I tried not to snort too loudly. Justice is just a myth that people like Haggerty cling to. In my life Justice had never hit anything but foul balls.

"Haggerty, lemme ask you something. This harmonic convergence—I get that it conveys great power, but how does someone like Gwydion get to *keep* that power?"

When Haggerty glanced my way, she showed her surprise with one raised brow. "Good question, Samantha. The combination of the harmonic convergence and the lunar eclipse bequeaths great power to everyone exposed to it in those moments. But the power flows through us. To harness it, it's necessary to find a way to store that power, and then use it to generate more." She shorted derisively. "I'm sure Gwydion has thought of a way."

Haggerty pulled into the Bell Rock parking area. The effect of the harmonic convergence on the Bell Rock vortex was awesome. Its power had grown by many times—I could feel it all the way from the parking lot. Still, the force it was putting out didn't make me feel as great as it had that night. The energy from the vortex had become such a physical entity, the pressure of the waves emanating from it made me feel like I was in a sausage machine. It hurt to be that near, and Haggerty insisted that we walk even closer.

At first I also thought I was seeing things. Tiny sparks of

light appeared here and there in the distance, yet vanished in a flash. Fireflies? I knew some places had them, though I'd never seen one myself. Besides, weren't they only visible at night? Despite the dark clouds, it was still daylight. When I asked Haggerty about it, she said the energy streaming from the vortex was so intense, it was breaking out in small explosions.

"You'll see even more of it later, I promise you," she said. "It's one of my favorite parts of a harmonic convergence."

Not mine, I felt sure. Those sparks reminded me of the night when Angus and I had made love on a cloud and our climax became a shower of sparkles. I didn't want to remember any part of that night.

The emotional effect of the vortex staggered me, too. Waves of feelings—not my own—kept crashing through me. I wanted to laugh hysterically and sob with eternal devastation all at once, and I was powerless to control any of it. Like PMS on steroids. Adding in the relentless noise from the growing storm, I wanted to go back to Fiona's house and bury my head beneath a pillow.

At some point in our hike, I couldn't take it anymore. No matter what Haggerty said. I turned and began walking back to the car.

To my surprise, she didn't fight me. "You're right, we've experienced enough here. But try to remember how this feels."

Like I could forget anything that had happened to me since I arrived in this crazy town.

We returned to the car and drove to the Cathedral Rock vortex, not far away. Similar reaction. Then it was back to the car once more, and we went to West Sedona, the section of town where Fiona's house was located, and onto another vortex along the road to Sedona's small airport, the Airport Mesa vortex. And lastly, to someplace called Boynton Canyon. As horrific as all the vortex energies had been, my reaction at Boynton Canyon felt even stronger. Once again, I stopped on the trail when I'd endured all I intended to. But I stood still and looked at the red rocks ahead, and the curious shapes they took.

Haggerty came up beside me. "They're called Kachina Man and Kachina Woman."

I could see how the red rock formations had been carved over time into something resembling human figures, with the female-shaped one carrying her baby on her back. So many of those minute energy sparks ignited around them, it resembled a swarm, yet it made me feel like they were in love. I longed to visit them up close, but I couldn't bear to draw any nearer.

"Which vortex was the strongest?" Haggerty asked.

"This one, Boynton Canyon. No contest," I said. "They were all rough to endure, physically and emotionally. But here, where that rock man and woman live, the power is the strongest."

Haggerty nodded thoughtfully. "I think so, too. Okay, it's decided."

What was? I waited, but she said nothing more. Screw it. If she wouldn't tell me, I wouldn't ask. "Can we leave now?" I asked instead, with an unexpected sob.

Back at the house, she began placing calls from the kitchen phone. She telephoned some Wiccans she knew in California and asked them to create a quickie phone tree among their Arizona friends. She celebrated rituals with a coven back home that worshipped her. Apparently, now, she was getting them to spread rumors for her. What kind, I couldn't say. My mind drifted off, as it always did when she went into witch-talk, since I never understood half of what they talked about.

She also called Rand at his hotel, where he was still being protected against the threat of violence from irate fans that wanted his ass.

After identifying herself, she said, "Mr. Riker, I wanted you to know you're no longer under suspicion by the Bureau, and you're free to leave town."

What was she doing? I felt certain that Rand was the defrocked goddess, Rele-de. Besides, with the police guarding him, he was safer here than anywhere else.

With an amused twitch of her lips, Haggerty punched the button for the speakerphone.

Rand's mumbling voice filled the kitchen. "Thank you very much, darlin'."

"Great," I said when she disconnected. "Not only has he lost his Aussie accent, he's channeling Elvis now. What did Angus do?"

"Still think he's a threat?" Haggerty asked.

I didn't know what to think.

All amusement vanished from Haggerty's beleaguered

features at that point. She took a deep breath and squared her shoulders, before dialing another number. After a moment, she said, "Maria, put Kenny on the phone."

Did that mean Kenny had stayed in Sedona, after telling me he intended to leave? I remembered the way his gaze had gone to the phone when he mentioned Kelly. Was she AWOL again, at another "book club" meeting? I never thought those words could sound so dirty.

Maria must have argued with Haggerty, because she added, "I don't care what he's doing. Unless he wants his secrets broadcast to the world, he'll talk to me now. Tell him that."

From the smug satisfaction that stole over her face, I guessed she convinced Maria to pass on the message.

After a moment, someone obviously had come on the line. In a voice so cold it could have flash frozen a side of beef, Haggerty told her listener that she required his services that night, insisting she'd explain why later. After another moment of silence, she snapped, "Senator, this isn't negotiable." It must have been settled at that point, because she hung up shortly, that superior smile still teasing her lips.

"Okay, what the hell is going on?" I shouted. I hated that I'd broken before she did, but I had to know. Curiosity rules my life.

Haggerty's smile grew stronger. "Soon, Samantha. I'll tell you everything soon. I have one more bit of help to solicit."

She walked out the front door. I rushed to the window to watch her. I expected her to go to the car. Instead, she walked down the path and stopped at the end, with the red rock lions.

She looked at the lions. Then her lips began to move. At one point she dipped her head in a deep bow. Finally, she rested each of her hands on the head of a lion. And she continued speaking.

She was talking to rocks! Did they ever talk back?

CHAPTER FORTY-SIX

Haggerty left after her chat with the rock lions. Some time later, Kenny's silver SUV careened into the driveway. Despite the tinted windows, I could see that Haggerty occupied the passenger seat.

Their body language, when they made their way to the front door, could not have been clearer had captions been flashing in neon. Haggerty kept her shoulders stiff, with her arms locked at her sides, as if she feared she might brush against Kenny. A paper grocery bag hung from her fingers.

While Haggerty controlled her movements, Kenny's were anything but. The body beneath his form-fitting navy knitwear moved with jerky, springy steps. I couldn't tell whether he had come so unstrung by whatever she'd asked him to do that he could no longer restrain his muscles, or if he was just trying too hard to please her.

They burst through the door. Haggerty paused long enough to survey my getup. I still wore the gray sweats, but I'd stuffed my hair under a black cap that just appeared on my bed. Her powers were obviously back if she could send me boring hats. Her scrutiny ended with a nod of approval, which was more than she ever gave my nice things. Her taste never failed to amaze me.

When she drew closer, I saw the grocery sack contained dark clothing. She must have picked up some of her stuff at Kenny's guesthouse. She said she needed a minute to change and carried the bag to Fiona's bedroom.

That left Kenny and me alone. Awkward silences never bother me. I stood by the French doors, glaring at the treacherous bastard, while he twitched more than a drop of fat in a hot pan.

I knew he'd crack before I did. With a thoughtful frown, he twisted his head this way and that. "Hey, there's no sound in the house now. Before…uh…it sounded something like choral singing." When I didn't respond, he jumped in with, "Those were the echoes of emotions, the residual energy and feelings of the people who've lived in this house, you know. I wonder why we can't hear them anymore."

I love it when people give me setups. "The last emotion added was so sorrowful, no one could endure it. We had to shut the whole thing down."

Kenny choked, so violently, he ran to the kitchen.

Haggerty emerged from Fiona's room an instant later wearing charcoal clothing. She'd also tied a dark scarf over her bright auburn hair. Though her loose-fitting top draped over her pants, I could see where her semi-automatic's holster was hooked onto her waistband. Her pockets also bulged with objects I couldn't identify.

"Where is…the senator?" she asked.

"With any luck, drowning in a glass of water."

We weren't that lucky. He emerged from the kitchen, wiping his mouth with the back of his hand.

"There you are," Haggerty said in a crisp, formal tone. Though she addressed us both, she looked pointedly at me. "Does everyone know what's expected of them?"

"I don't," I said. "You haven't told me anything."

"You'll know soon enough, Samantha."

So she didn't actually mean me, yet she kept looking my way. Finally, with clear reluctance, she twisted her neck toward Kenny.

"I understand perfectly, Annabelle," Kenny said. "Don't worry, I'd never let you down."

That obvious untruth hung in the air between them. Haggerty looked so stricken, she had to rush to the door to hide it. Kenny followed along behind her, bouncing with that same jerky stride. There was an air of satisfaction about him now, self-congratulations maybe over how well he was pulling this off. What a clueless boob.

Haggerty had already commandeered the SUV's backseat by the time I followed Kenny outside, leaving me no choice but to climb in next to him.

Night was beginning to fall. I wouldn't have thought it possible, but the magnitude of the war-of-the-gods storm was intensifying. Now those claps of thunder no longer just shattered nerves, they were taking a horrific toll. Trees had toppled everywhere, in some cases crashing into the roofs of houses. Many boulders that had fallen from rock formations crashed through windshields, leaving stunned and bloody victims. The sirens of emergency vehicles streaking around town rivaled the sounds produced overhead. The air smelled of smoke from the fires the violent lightning strikes kept starting. And the concentration of those strange energy sparks, which floated everywhere now, had become so thick, they caused the skin of my face to burn.

The power of the vortexes had also grown to an overwhelming degree. Even within the protection of the car, my body felt as if invisible lashes kept striking it.

Despite the treacherous conditions, people filled the streets again, often carrying candles. The collective agitation level had reached the breaking point. The troops patrolling the town had quadrupled tonight, but the force wafting out from the vortexes hobbled some of them. We kept seeing people, occasionally even guys in uniform, curled up in the fetal position, or sobbing wildly, or laughing with total abandon. My own emotions were being jerked in so many different ways, it was like I was living in a giant washing machine that kept thrashing me about. It took all I had, but I didn't give in to those emotional extremes. Who'd have thought that I'd become the controlled one?

As we approached the Airport Mesa vortex, the streets became nearly impassable. Kenny had to drive his SUV onto the sidewalk. Haggerty and I got out, leaving him in the car.

Despite the huge crowd, I actually ran into someone I knew there. Princess Holly O'Neill, the flight attendant from Rand's chartered jet. She wore an Indian sari tonight and had her short blonde hair done in stubby little cornrows. Her dumb-ox boyfriend was still in tow.

Holly's gaze fell on my drab duds with obvious disapproval. With a slightly superior laugh, she said, "Samantha, are we exchanging wardrobes? *You* used to be the flamboyant one."

I still was! Hey, this was a fashion emergency—couldn't she tell? Still, I'd never felt so embarrassed.

"Can you stay here tonight?" Holly shouted over the noise. "Something awesome is supposed to happen here."

The number of candle-holders crowding the area, and the huge contingent of troops, told me that most people believed the Airport Mesa vortex was where the power would rise to the strongest levels that night.

I turned to Haggerty to confirm what we'd determined

earlier, that the Boynton Canyon vortex would be more powerful.

With the barest trace of a smile, Haggerty drew close and whispered, "Shush, Samantha. Nobody can know."

So that was the rumor her Wiccan friends had spread, that this was where the energy would be the greatest when the harmonic convergence peaked, so that more people would cluster here.

I told Holly that we couldn't stay, as I watched Haggerty return to the car, which Kenny had kept idling. I was about to follow her, but fear for Holly and her boyfriend struck me. I knew Haggerty didn't want me to reveal anything we'd learned, but Holly was the closest thing I had to a friend here.

I grabbed her hand and squeezed it hard. Where to begin…? "Don't go near the creek, okay? Promise me you won't go near the creek tonight." That wasn't enough of a warning, but it was better than nothing.

Holly's happy smile wavered. She didn't know whether to believe me. I'd always thought that nobody would take me seriously as a spiritual advisor if I didn't dress the part, and now I had proof.

I escaped from Holly as soon as I extracted the promise from her, before I could reveal any other secrets or apologize for my awful sweats.

Back in the car, we drove to the militia compound. That area was being heavily guarded tonight, and the public kept well away. To my surprise, we didn't pass through the government's gate. Haggerty directed Kenny to park near a cluster of giant boulders in the deserted public area.

When we finally moved through the gate, a soldier told Haggerty that Colonel Marcus was expecting her. We trod the distance to the command truck, where Marcus, or as I continued to think of him, Colonel Squinty, waited for us with François. With all the little firefly-lights breaking over the compound, it looked less like a militia stronghold now and more like some deluded Disneyland.

Squinty narrowed that one eye at Kenny. "Senator, I would never have agreed to this pointless exercise if I weren't out of options."

I piped in with, "You might not be out of options if you let the Bureau do its thing, instead of hogging the show."

François turned away, but not before I caught sight of a stifled smile spreading across his pale lips. Call me a racist, but if it weren't for his pasty color, I could almost get to like the guy. Haggerty's eyes flashed me another one of those *shut up* warnings, but it had to be said.

Unfortunately, it didn't have to be heard. Squinty acted like I never said a thing. "This goes down the way I fear, you're on your own, Senator Campbell. Odds are Special Agent Haggerty won't be able to pull off her part of the operation. You still in?"

Haggerty busied herself applying a wireless radio to her neckline and didn't rise to his challenge. From somewhere within the compound, a shot was fired. Kenny's Adam's apple trembled within his skinny neck. Nobody else reacted much. There had been so many shots fired within the compound in recent days, they didn't surprise anyone anymore. Anyone but Kenny, that is. Finally, he nodded his agreement.

With that settled, Haggerty told me we were leaving. While Kenny remained behind, she and I, along with François, went out through the gate.

Normal Frankly's compound was constructed around a huge rock wall. But the compound didn't encompass the whole extended wall. It began before Normal's property and continued after it.

Haggerty led us to where the wall curved away from the government's truck. As the ground rose along the rock, I fell further behind. Not because the climb taxed me—I still had amazing stamina. But the butterflies that Angus banished from my stomach had returned and were rising up my gullet, threatening to choke me. Panic was starting to immobilize me. Fiona had warned us something awful would happen tonight. I even remembered my own insight during our flight there. I'd sensed that I would regret it if I ever stepped onto that red dirt, and I had sure been right about that.

"So what's the deal here, Haggerty?" I asked.

"It's very simple." She said that too fast, which always meant she wasn't telling the exact truth. She wasn't the world's best liar. Well, of course not—I was. "Senator Campbell is going to create a scene at the gate, which should distract the militia, so we can slip in unnoticed."

My heart stopped. "We're going in?" I'd made it out of that zoo once, but would I be that lucky again? "How? Isn't the fence electrified? We can't climb over it without getting fried."

Haggerty's lips twitched with amusement. "We're not going

over the fence…exactly."

By then, we'd followed the rock wall to where it ended in several huge boulders tumbled together, beside where we'd parked Kenny's SUV.

Haggerty and François squared off against each other there. I sensed there was something odd going on here. Edginess made Haggerty fidget, while he looked vulnerable, though he attempted to hide it.

Before I could figure out why, he asked, "You said you needed something from me, Annabelle. What exactly?"

"If there's any way you can move these boulders, I'd be deeply appreciative."

"Haggerty, are you nuts?" I said. Those boulders were all four or five feet in diameter. I'd never seen such massive rocks. "That would be like moving a house."

To my surprise, François didn't laugh. Instead, he asked quite seriously, "What do I get if I can?"

Haggerty hesitated. "You get to see how Samantha and I are going into the compound."

It was that unexpected, our way in? "How does Colonel Squinty *think* we're getting in?" I asked, my voice rising in panic.

"There are crevices in this rock," François explained. "We've always known that. We just haven't been able to determine whether someone could access the compound interior through them."

"Can we?" I asked with a squeak.

"Not a chance," Haggerty said. "François?"

He shrugged. He stepped over to the farthest boulder, leaned against it and pushed. And it moved. It moved! A man—and a small one at that—pushed aside a rock nearly as tall as he was. First, one rock, then another. It wasn't that he wasn't straining—he was. He grunted and reddened enough to make his face look downright attractive. But he was moving boulders bigger than Volkswagens.

At the end, he leaned against one of the rocks he'd shifted, breathing heavily. I stood there, my jaw hanging slack. Haggerty had also reddened, even though she hadn't lifted a finger. She pulled me close to her, and when we bumped, she transferred her feelings. Then I understood—she wasn't happy about having to hold up her part of the bargain, having to reveal how we would gain access to the place.

So they were playing "Show me yours, I'll show you mine."

MAGICAL ALIENATION

Why hadn't she simply moved those boulders herself with her renewed powers, the ones I'd released with my reverse spell? Perhaps she was afraid to trust them. But I sensed she was about to reveal to François that she wasn't precisely an ordinary person, something few people knew. How could she stop him from sharing that information with others?

She drew me up to the rock wall, which was exposed now that the boulders had been shoved aside. "Samantha," she said. "Stand close to the rock-face and press your hands flat against it, as if you were doing a push-up."

Like I had ever done a push-up. But I mimicked her stance, pressing my palms against the jagged surface of the rock. Then something started sucking me into the rock. I swear! I tried to pull back, but the suction grew stronger. Right about the time my arms had disappeared into the stone right up to my elbows, I let out a yelp, and began to cry for help. To my surprise, I cried for Angus.

CHAPTER FORTY-SEVEN

Despite my determination to resist, I was pulled completely into the rock, crying all the way. Rounds of "Help me, Angus," alternated with, "Haggerty, I can't breathe!"

Sounds echoed strangely in there, like I was under water. Our movements were also dramatically slowed, to a slug's pace.

Haggerty took hold of my forearms and gave me a slow-mo shake. "Samantha, you *are* breathing!"

When I glanced down, sure enough, I could see my own chest rising and falling.

She offered me a contrite grimace. "Maybe I should have warned you, but I thought it might scare you off. They've altered things in here so we can breathe."

They?

My eyes adjusted to the murky interior of the rock wall. We weren't alone in there. Surrounding us were beings, of a sort. They looked like stick figures drawn in broken and jagged lines. Smudged across stick-figure skeletons were shadowy areas, a little muddier than the interior of the rock itself. Were those smudges their bodies? Thousands of them filled that space, all squished together. And they all seemed to be staring at us.

With her face set in grim lines, Haggerty huddled against the interior wall of the rock. "Don't wander about, Samantha. It's not safe."

Wander? Where would I wander? "Why isn't it safe?" I asked in a slow whisper.

"I told you—most of them hate us topsiders. They're more likely to do us harm, or side with our villains, just to create havoc for us."

And I was stuck in a mountain with thousands of them! I remembered that night at Bell Rock, when I thought I pricked my finger on the rock's rough surface. Had one of these beings bitten me? Even though they didn't exactly have faces, I knew they were glaring at us.

With a scream on the tip of my tongue, I searched for something to distract me. "So...François—crazy strong, huh? Are all albinos that brawny?" A muted chuckle echoed toward me. "No, don't tell me I make you laugh, Haggerty. What's going on?"

"You really don't know? You must be the last person on earth who still believes in albinos. That's just a politically correct fiction we agree to accept."

"Albinos don't exist? Come on. I see them everywhere. More and more all the time, actually."

"Samantha, François is a vampire. All albinos are."

The rock slowed my hands when I attempted to wrap them around my neck.

"Don't be silly, Samantha—they've been vegans for generations."

"Shut the front door! No blood?"

"Tomato juice is as strong as they go today. They've evolved, in every way possible."

"Wait. How can a vampire work in the daytime? Isn't the sun supposed to turn them into crispy critters?"

"Honestly, how can someone so unobservant present herself as a psychic? Recent scientific advances have made it possible, of course. Who do you think buys all that SPF 3000 sunscreen the drugstores carry these days? Not you mortals, with that healthy melanoma glow you all crave."

I'd actually seen sunscreen smeared on François, though I thought it was hand lotion.

"A vampire." How many times had I rubbed shoulders with them and not known it? "Is all the other vampire lore true?"

She shrugged. "They are said to be strong, and you saw how he moved those boulders."

"Yeah." At least I understood why she was willing to reveal herself to him. They had a stalemate going. "Are they all as tight-assed as François?"

Haggerty sighed. "When they gave up the blood, they did lose their *joie de vivre*."

I desperately yearned to return to the time when I didn't know mythical creatures existed. About as much as I yearned to be out of that rock. I was starting to think I was the only one who was actually normal. Scary thought.

I stared again at those rock skeletons pressed together. Two of those beings separated themselves from the others and floated toward us. One reached out to me with its stick-arm.

I shrieked and tried to pull back, but it was as if I was stuck in a vat of maple syrup that had gotten really stiff.

"Samantha, it's okay. They're the lions from the path at Mom's house. Remember what I told you—they're rock royals. They've made it possible for us to be in here."

So far I didn't see any reason to be grateful to them.

We made our way through the viscous interior of the rock. Who knew that something so hard on the outside could feel gooey on the inside? There was also a hum that rose up from the ground below us, causing it to tremble, making our footing unstable. The lions, in their rock-skeleton form, led us through. Some of the creatures filling the mountain's core moved aside for us, but others refused to. I felt myself pinched and poked. It took all I had to keep those butterflies in check.

Eventually, we came to a part of the interior that shimmered like a wave. One lion-stick-guy motioned for us to put our hands there, as we had on the surface of the rock outside. How odd that they didn't talk in here. While in lion-mode, one distinctly roared at me. Unless I imagined it. Maybe I was imagining all of this. You'd think if I was gonna start hallucinating, I'd see myself on a beach in Hawaii, or living in one of those mansions in Kenny's 'hood as Sedona's most famous celebrity psychic, instead of moving through a mountain with a bunch of angry stick-figures.

The lion guy gestured once more, with greater urgency. The underground tremor grew stronger. Before I could follow through, one of those stick figures rushed at us with its jagged arm extended. No question, he wanted to hurt us. Does every culture contain terrorists? Haggerty saw it peripherally, before I did. She turned remarkably fast for that place and held up a hand to stop him. Within that viscous interior, I could see waves of energy emanating from her palm. The power in her gesture caused the stick-rebel to freeze. It occurred to me that her vision was as good as Kenny's. Maybe someday she should explore whatever superior human traits he might have bequeathed to her, in addition to the powers her mother had given her.

Now, though, we had to get out of there. I placed my hands

against the jelly-like surface. I found myself pushed out. Moments later, we were no longer within the rock's interior, but in a cavern that had been cut into rock, breathing regular air.

Instantly so relieved, it was as if my tummy butterflies had an orgasm, all at once. That great, I swear. I struggled to return to regular breathing.

"What is this place?" I whispered.

"It's part of the militia's compound."

One dim light bulb hung from the top of the cavern, but it threw out little light. Haggerty pulled a small flashlight from her pocket and directed the beam around it. Roughly in a circle, the cave extended maybe fifteen feet across. Not only did it contain a cache of guns, it also held boxes of canned goods.

"If I've calculated right, we should be able to access the heart of it from here." She directed the flashlight toward a dark opening I hadn't noticed on the far side. "There's the tunnel," she said softly. "Let's go."

With the flashlight beam leading the way, we crept down a narrow tunnel with a dusty smell. After about thirty feet of inching along, we came to a door. Haggerty handed me the flashlight, while she took some small tools from her pocket. Still avoiding her powers, except when foiling stick-terrorists.

"You didn't see this," she whispered, as she began to pick the lock.

Did she really think I'd care? Honest people never failed to crack me up.

After putting her tools away, Haggerty said, "Now we need to find Gwydion and the hostages."

She probably figured I could help with that. But I hadn't come in through a rock wall last time. Haggerty motioned for me to dim the flashlight and took out her nine millimeter, and we crept through the door.

Those shadowy halls looked more like a graveyard now. The bodies of the dead, many in those stupid militia uniforms, were scattered everywhere. The living militia guys weren't any more threatening than the dead. They didn't seem to notice we were there. They staggered among the bodies, disoriented, often moaning so loudly, they drowned out the sounds of the war-of-the-gods storm we could still hear. Most of the wall-mounted weapons had been yanked out, and those that were left never pivoted in our direction.

I was so struck by the sight of a kid stumbling along, with blood dripping down the side of his face, that I failed to notice I was about to trip over a body, until Haggerty stopped me. The body was No-Neck's. I let out a squeak and sagged against the wall.

"Pull it together, Samantha. We need to save those hostages."

If Colonel Squinty had any idea how much conditions had deteriorated in here, he could have blown through the front door and rescued them himself. But despite the shots being fired, he didn't know. It really was up to us to save those people. I straightened up and stepped over the body. Concluding our wanderings in the Land of the Living Dead, I picked up my pace and led Haggerty to Gwydion's room.

She started to pull out her lock picks, but I figured the zombies probably weren't being careful with locks anymore. Sure enough, the doorknob opened in my hand.

The surprises kept coming. Gwydion no longer appeared in his funny little alien personae. Instead, leaning against the edge of the mattress was the most perfect boy I'd ever seen. He seemed to be around seventeen or so. And he was so hunky, he made me rethink whatever hang-up I might have about cradle robbing. His blousy antique shirt, like the ones pirates once wore, and the way his rich sable hair turned in soft ringlets, reminded me of the covers of the historical romance novels I read whenever a guy dumps me. His eyes were pure emerald. And his full mouth made Rand's thick lips look coarse and crude. When he offered us a wicked smile, his flawless teeth sparkled like sun on fresh snow. The kid was hot, and he not only knew it, he'd known it for centuries.

While his emerald eyes glinted suggestively when his gaze took a swipe over my body, he greeted his descendant first. "You're Annabelle, Fiona's child."

Haggerty skipped the chitchat. "What did you do to them? The militia members?"

"Nothing they didn't deserve," Gwydion answered with brusque indifference. He obviously didn't appreciate being challenged by junior goddesses. "You should applaud my gesture. I thought you were so devoted to justice." With a flicker of his startling eyes, he dismissed her and zeroed in on me. He took a step closer. When he suddenly clasped my hand, an electric shock went through me, and a heat wave moved in south of the equator. "So we meet again, dear Samantha. Angus was a fool, but he's not the only god, you know."

From somewhere in the distance, I heard persistent shouting. Maybe that was the diversion at the gate Kenny was supposed to stage.

Haggerty looked at her watch. "Gwydion, arrange your love-life later. We have hostages to save."

Gwydion didn't budge. "You've taken your time about it. Anything could have happened to them by now."

"It wasn't as if my powers were operating at full strength."

His disinterested shrug seemed to say that she should get over that. He sure didn't accept any responsibility for it. The emerald gaze bore into her. "You know what I want."

Her head inclined in a nod. "The harmonic convergence. I'll lead you to the most powerful spot, but I need something from you as well."

He gave his soft ringlets a toss. "You need my help in saving the hostages, and perhaps, confronting someone beyond your capabilities."

A decisive sweep of his arm made his billowy shirt cling attractively to the firm body beneath it. I had to keep reminding myself he wasn't really a kid, so what I was thinking wasn't really icky. Gwydion gallantly offered Haggerty a bow of acceptance. Why did I have to be born in this century?

We left the room, with Gwydion leading the way. He strode through the dim halls, sending out echoes of the decisive snap his old-fashioned boots made against the shiny concrete floors. He led us through a metal tunnel between buildings within the complex, and finally to another fortified structure.

Three padlocks secured this facility, which Haggerty quickly opened with her picks.

As soon as we entered, people crowded us, begging for help. Judging by all the hollowed out eyes and drawn skin I saw, they were in bad shape. Some I remembered, such as the aging female judge and a cute bailiff, from the court case in Phoenix, which now felt like a lifetime ago; others were strangers, some in army uniforms.

With all of them shouting at once, it was hard to distinguish any particular words. Eventually, we came to understand that they hadn't had anything to eat or drink in over a day.

Haggerty turned to her ancestor. "We can't free them like this. They won't follow orders, and they're likely to get themselves killed. It's still dangerous in there."

"You want too much, young Annabelle. Are you really asking me to use my strength to stun them into submission, when I have so little left?"

"Do I need to remind you that whatever magical strength you have is partially mine," she snapped. "I said I'd do everything I could to see your powers are restored, so you can put yourself beyond the reach of the Council."

"With a little luck, the Ruling Council will be no more."

Haggerty tightened her lips. I guessed they'd agreed to disagree on that point.

Gwydion acquiesced, though. With a flash of concentration, he rendered the hostages into glassy-eyed robots. We led them through the compound.

Back in that chamber of horrors, I had the scare of my life when one militia guy came to a stop before us and lifted his gun. Was this it? Would my life end in a zoo full of crazy fake soldiers? To my eternal shock, when he fired, I didn't end up with any extra holes in me. The bullet went into another militia goon passing beside me. I nearly collapsed with relief.

I'd had enough! I wanted to flee out the front and hand the hostages over to Squinty. Instead, Haggerty said we had to plunge once more into that creepy rock-domain.

We returned to the cavern and ushered the hostages into the rock by placing them so the rock-lions could pull them through. Then we crossed the barrier ourselves. The welcome there was just as hostile as before, though no one charged us this time. The tremor beneath the earth felt stronger now, making it harder to move when the lions led us from one side of their domain to the other. At the end, they pushed us back into the outside world, right where Haggerty and I had started our journey.

François was gone now, but Kenny waited there for us. "You did it," he said with a huge sigh. "My little scene didn't attract any attention from them. I was so afraid for you."

"Yeah, they're a little past noticing much," I said.

Kenny looked at his daughter. "Annabelle, please take me

MAGICAL ALIENATION

with you. I didn't accomplish anything here, and I want to help."

After a brief hesitation, she agreed with a wordless nod.

The storm kept worsening. The lightning strikes were multiplying. Off in the distance, I saw brushfires gaining ground. The air smelled of scorched brush. I wondered if the creek had risen any higher and if it did boil.

Gwydion made the hostages lie down, and he put them to sleep. "They'll be safe enough here for now. When they wake up, they'll remember an entirely different version of their escape. They'll all be heroes."

"Wait," I said. "They need food and water. Can't we grab Colonel Squinty and his boys?" I still didn't understand why we hadn't just gone out the door and handed the hostages over.

Gwydion and Haggerty shared a look. "This Squinty chap, he might hold us up."

"He would," Haggerty said. "We can't involve him, Samantha."

"But the hostages—"

"I'll radio François once we're clear, but we're not going back that way," she said. "We're headed..." She pointed *up* the mountain.

First push-ups and now this? "Ah, Haggerty, no. I don't climb hills." Okay, I did once, but she never had to know that. "Can't we just take the Lexus?" Those seats were so butt-friendly.

In the brightness of the full moon, I saw a glint of mischief in her eyes. "Tonight a different form of transportation awaits us."

Something told me I wasn't going to like this mysterious transportation any more than I liked climbing hills.

CHAPTER FORTY-EIGHT

Thunder shook the rock wall so furiously, I feared the centuries-old cliff would collapse.

I still balked at the idea of climbing up that mountain. Haggerty went into her usual speech about how the future of the universe depended on me. Right. If I had a dollar for every time the fate of the universe rested on me, I wouldn't need to give phony readings to rock stars to survive.

"Fear not, dear girl," Gwydion said with a wicked grin. "I'll give you a boost." He cupped his fingers together.

I put my shoe into Gwydion's hands, wishing I'd worn my sexy silver mules instead of those ratty sneakers.

While I never paid much attention in science classes, I know how gravity works—what goes up eventually comes down. So that I didn't immediately fall back to the ground, I grasped at a jagged ledge jutting from the craggy rock, and groped with my foot for a toehold. To my surprise, the bit of rock my fingers had clutched disappeared—one instant it stuck out; the next that part of the rock wall had flattened. I grabbed another outcropping, and…same thing. I shrieked for help.

Haggerty positioned herself alongside me. "I know, Samantha. The rock people are playing games."

She shouldn't have enlisted the help of the rock-royals if they were so at odds with their citizens. She might end up responsible for toppling the rock-monarchy.

She took my left hand and held me up as I struggled to find places I could grab onto. She and Gwydion had to call on some of their precious magical powers to make it up the wall. Kenny just scampered up like a monkey. No question, she should explore some of the strange and wonderful genes he might have passed on.

While Haggerty pulled herself over the top, she advised me to hang onto a branch of a bush growing there, until she could help me over. I grasped the branch, figuring the ordeal was over. You'd think I'd learn.

With only a hiss of static as a warning, something struck my back with a sudden blistering pain. I felt chopped in half, as thoroughly as a butcher's cleaver chops through a chicken breast. The difference was my cleaver had been held first in a flame. The searing heat burned clear through me, cauterizing my insides. I couldn't speak. I couldn't breathe. Though I heard Haggerty's scream, and Kenny's remark that I'd been struck by lightning, I couldn't react. The only positive in the unbearable situation was that the pain caused my hand to tighten around the branch, preventing me from dropping to the ground. Everything else was sheer agony.

Haggerty and Gwydion lifted me onto the ground at the top of the wall. She yanked off my wool cap and touched my hair. It crackled under her touch. A peculiar whooshing sound filled my ears, like the sound a breeze makes flowing through leaves.

I gradually caught my breath. Still, I couldn't produce anything but a helpless huffing noise. Words remained beyond me. I vaguely knew that time was passing, especially when Gwydion took to impatiently stomping the ground in his heavy boots. Yet Haggerty stayed at my side.

Eventually, they revised their plans. "I'll radio for help," Haggerty said. "Senator, you'll have to stay with Samantha until the rescue workers arrive."

Considering its intensity at the moment of the lightning strike, the pain and heat had lessened now. I still heard that hushed murmur in my ears, and I buzzed inside as if I'd consumed gallons of caffeine. Mostly, though, I just felt loopy, and as if I didn't exactly occupy my own body anymore.

Suddenly, an irresistible impulse to move came over me. With great effort, I made myself roll a few feet away on the ground. As soon as I stopped, another bolt of lightning struck the ground where I had been just an instant before.

While Kenny yammered on about my luck, Haggerty rushed back to me. "I can't leave her," she insisted with a sob.

"Young Annabelle, you gave me your word—"

I couldn't say how much time had passed. Despite the wildfires, the sky had grown blacker. The deafening roar of thunder threatened to blow the Earth apart, while bold white flashes put on a dazzling light show against the intensely dark sky.

I finally found my voice, which had become unnaturally raspy. "Nobody has to stay. Not even me."

Not only didn't that sound like my voice, it didn't even

sound like something I should say. Shouldn't I have demanded a helicopter ride to the hospital, and a week's stay in some classy spa? Having ridden the harrowing ups and downs of the harmonic convergence, I should have wanted to be rid of it. But somehow I felt as if we were inexorably linked. I knew I had to be there when it peaked. My hair stuck out in every direction—all the conditioner on the planet probably wouldn't tame it—yet my stamina had begun returning.

From somewhere within the whoosh filling my ears, a soft voice said, "Watch for movement."

"Movement? Who said that?" I asked.

They all just stared at me. Whatever. It couldn't have been important.

Though Haggerty looked doubtful about my recovery, she said, "If we're all really going, it has to be now."

Only...how? As we stared into the distance, it was clear that even after all this time, Haggerty's "alternative form of transportation," hadn't appeared.

"She isn't here," Haggerty whispered, disappointment evident in her voice. "I thought for sure..."

So that was what she'd prayed for earlier at Fiona's altar. She'd begged one of her ancestors for help. Given the fury of the growing storm, I wasn't surprised that her request had gone unanswered.

Before I finished that thought, however, a vision drifted through the smoke. It was that of a beautifully ethereal woman sitting bareback on a milky-white mare. While naked, the woman's long, platinum hair covered her body and fell below her feet, mingling with the horse's snowy mane.

"Bow your head, Samantha," Haggerty said. "You're in the presence of the goddess Epona."

Haggerty's inconsistencies, with respect to her ancestors, were hard to follow. I'd been in the presence of the *Danaans* loads of times—in the sack with one—yet I never bowed before them. To make her happy, I did it now, but I inched up my gaze to see what was so special about this Epona-chick.

This goddess actually awed me. Just as she had morphed moments earlier from a ghostly translucent image to a solid, substantial one, she transformed again. She went from being a woman *on* a horse, to becoming an even larger horse herself. Two other mares, also snowy white, joined her. The Epona mare threw back her head and cried out in a voice that was half horse and half human. It was so eerie, goose pimples formed on my arms, despite the heat I carried inside.

Gwydion sidled up to Haggerty. He gave his sable curls a shake. "We've three mounts here, but four riders. You should have planned better, young Annabelle."

Even though I didn't like the way he kept sticking it to her, I had to suppress a giggle. It struck me funny that this guy who looked like a hot high school kid—kinda Eighteenth Century 90210—kept calling her "young Annabelle."

"Samantha and I can ride together," she said in clipped tones. Her forehead wrinkled with concern when she looked at me. "You're sure you're up to this, Samantha?"

"Wouldn't miss it," I said in my new whiskey voice.

"If the sweet lass rides with anyone, it'll be me," Gwydion said.

He hurled himself up on one of the secondary horses. He galloped to my side, reached down and yanked me off my feet, as if I weighed no more than...well, Haggerty. I found myself sitting behind him on that mount, holding on to his washboard abs.

No more gods, I kept repeating to myself in my loopy internal voice, while wondering how just one more could hurt.

Haggerty climbed onto the main mare, the goddess Epona, while Kenny mounted the third horse. Together we took off across the barren open countryside, with only the infrequent moonlight to guide us.

I don't often look ahead, but I did during that ride. Haggerty's plans rested on so little: The whim of a goddess; Gwydion, who took more pleasure in needling than helping her; Kenny, who had never come through for anyone; and me, an electrocuted flake. If a confrontation with a rogue god awaited us, or someone determined to be a rogue goddess once more, would we four be any match?

A frightening sense of foreboding clutched my heart, and while I told myself it was just the result of the lightning strike, I wondered which, if any of us, would make it through this night.

CHAPTER FORTY-NINE

We took an overland route, galloping hard to make up for lost time. Apart from those hairy javalinas they have there, which look something like wild pigs, we never saw another soul. In the distance, coyotes yipped their strange cries from the mountaintops, while the wildfires consumed trees and brush in every direction.

Where was Rand right now? Granted, Angus had altered his musical skills, but had he also made Rand into Super Buffoon? Was he at a vortex tonight, waiting to be transformed into a goddess again? Or had some patron god cleared the way for him elsewhere? All the gods seemed pretty distracted by their own struggles now. Surely, only the strength of Haggerty's devotion made Epona appear.

The good thing about distracting thoughts is that they actually distract. While I remained lost in agonizing possibilities, we arrived at our destination, Boynton Canyon. Unlike the Airport Mesa vortex, this trail was empty.

Haggerty slowed her goddess horse and motioned for the others to do the same. After Kenny and Gwydion slipped off their mounts, Gwydion helped me to the ground. The Epona mare pawed at the earth. Haggerty nodded in response, as if she understood the sentiment being conveyed.

We set out on foot along a dusty trail. It grew harder with every step. The power that wafted out from the vortex pummeled my organs until I wanted to whimper in pain. But tonight, turning away wasn't an option.

The sounds above reached a fever pitch, with huge bolts of light being hurled in every direction. Was this like the last burst of fireworks in the Fourth of July show? When they sent everything up? Could the war have finally reached a climax?

We all stared momentarily up at the sky, before trudging on. I stumbled at times, still disoriented, still buzzing, but I made it there only slightly later than the rest of them.

We gathered together at the base of the rock. Despite the harsh glow of a moon peering out through a small break in the clouds, the shadows of Kachina Man and Kachina Woman loomed menacingly above us. We braved their threatening stance and climbed up to those figures and now stood between them.

"You're sure, Annabelle?" Gwydion asked. "This is the place?"

"At this moment, there's no stronger spot on earth," she whispered.

To my stunned surprise, Gwydion started growing in size. Sucking in the essence of that place through his mouth made his girth swell to an enormous size. His pirate shirt and pants swelled with him, making him look less like a cute young guy and more like Balloon God. Then, as a look of intense concentration stole over his face, he compressed all that power inside of him and returned to his normal size. Only to start again.

Through the heavy clouds, a sleeve of darkness began to slide over the moon. The lunar eclipse, when the harmonic convergence would reach its strongest point, was beginning.

Between the whispering in my ears, and Gwydion's noise, I couldn't hear anything at that deserted vortex. Apparently, Haggerty's hearing was sharper than mine. "Who's there?" she demanded, looking at where the stone figures blended with the pitch night sky. "Make yourself seen."

In the pale light given off by the sliver of moon, Rand stepped into the open.

So I was right about him! Strangely enough, now that he was there, I couldn't believe it. The Rand of old—sure, him I could see as that conniving, but I couldn't believe it of this guy, who still sported the superficial expression, with which Angus seemed to have branded him.

Haggerty acted just as surprised as I was, and even more shaken. "You can't be here. Not you." She quickly collected herself and spat with certainty, "You're too late. Gwydion's claimed the power."

Maybe not all of it, though. Gwydion continued to swell and compress, swell and compress. If he feared Rand's presence, it didn't break his stride.

In the scant light, as the moon inched toward total darkness, I saw Rand's forehead crinkle uncertainly. He spoke over his shoulder into the shadows, "Relly? Relly, what now?"

Relly? Who the hell...?

From within the darkness, a bitter voice spat, "Fool!" Kelly

Campbell stepped into the clearing between the two rock figures.

My blood iced over. As Kelly Campbell she'd been a creepy enough chick. Tonight, she was a wild card.

Kenny sputtered, "Kelly, what—"

"Not Kelly," she snapped venomously, hitting the "K" extra hard.

"Honey, I know it used to be Relly, but—" Kenny started to say.

Kenny had said she changed something fundamental about herself. Her *name*. Yet she had engraved an "R" on the shawl clasp. For Relly, not Realty, as I had stupidly imagined. It mattered so much to Kenny that his name and his wife's, as well as all their future offspring, would share his initial. What a dork.

The estranged Mrs. Campbell corrected him. "Not Relly. It's Rele-de."

Of course. *She* was the defrocked goddess, forced to live life-after-life as an ordinary mortal. She'd probably found life with Kenny extra ordinary. If fear hadn't frozen me to the spot, I'd have kicked myself.

Kenny couldn't meet Haggerty's gaze. He must have talked to his wife after he agreed to help Haggerty. And he told Rele-de where he would be tonight. Just as he'd once told her about the disks I'd scattered in the militia compound. He probably hadn't explained everything—this was all part of his secret life that his conventional wife wouldn't have known anything about. Yet he must have given her enough of a clue that she was able to figure it out. Kenny had betrayed his daughter again. With so much at stake, he couldn't keep his lip buckled.

It all made sense. Lugh and Taliesin, who believed that Rele-de had gotten a raw deal, had been working with her to oppose the Ruling Council. They used Rand, her lover, as their go-between.

Rand's lies and distortions fell into place. I even understood why he helped Normal Frankly, with whom Rele-de must have conspired to kill her former-alien husband. And why Rand had hired me, to hook Haggerty into it, the child of her husband's first wife, whom she obviously hated. I even understood why he lied to me in his dressing room before the concert. I was right then—macho, randy Rand couldn't be seen as some woman's plaything, even if the woman had once been a goddess.

How did Rele-de feel about him? Did she care that Angus had turned her bad boy into a lapdog?

"You're too late," Haggerty said again, this time to Rele-de.

"Doesn't that depend on what I'm after?" Rele-de's thin lips twisted enigmatically.

There was a luster about her tonight, even in the dim light. I remembered Gwydion's energy spike when the other gods sent him power through me. Had someone—perhaps Lugh or Taliesin—pumped up her magical energy? She was dressed strangely tonight. She wore that shawl again. Instead of twisting it around her throat, as she had at other times, she draped the triangular fabric over her shoulders and tied the ends to her wrists. Her arms were crossed over her chest.

Despite Rand and Rele-de's appearances, Gwydion continued sucking the power in and compressing it. And though the moon had now been reduced to the barest sliver, Rele-de seemed unconcerned, like she was biding her time. She had a mission here, and it didn't bode well for us.

Thunder still clapped above us, but fainter now. Was the war finally winding down? Even so...we weren't out of the woods. As if Rele-de wasn't enough of a reckless threat, the rock below us had begun humming, the same hum we'd felt crossing the interior of that rock-domain.

While I'd figured most things out, and Haggerty also looked clear on them, Kenny seemed lost. "I don't understand any of what's happening here," he moaned.

"It's easy, Kenny," I blurted with nervous energy. "You married, not one, but two goddesses."

His face twisted with confusion, while his not-quite-legal wife laughed.

Strange, but that voice I'd heard earlier, the one that warned me about movement—it was Rele-de's. How could I have heard her when she wasn't there on that ridge with us? I glanced at her shoes, which were even stranger than the odd way she wore her shawl. They looked something like boating deck shoes, with rubber soles designed to grip surfaces, only the soles stretched way out beyond the tops of the shoes, making them look like deck pontoons.

"Since I'm still an ordinary mortal, I must use ordinary means to fight my battles," Rele-de said.

The hum below us grew into a rumble. I'm a Californian born and bred—having experienced earthquakes since before I could walk, I knew how they felt just an instant before the shock. While I couldn't explain how I'd heard her warning, I grasped what movement she'd meant. I sat fast, positioning myself between a rock and a bush. Before I could warn anyone else, a temblor hit, shaking the rock with a hard snap. Gwydion only barely held his footing, and Haggerty stumbled. The rock-people must have produced that earthquake—Haggerty had said they loved helping our villains.

Rele-de pulled out a gun she'd hidden within her shawl. "Kenny, tonight your brat is going home."

No!

She aimed the gun at Haggerty. "I hope you've prayed to Danu, my dear, because your life on this plane ends now."

I longed to help her, but I felt too terrified to move.

Another quake struck, knocking Haggerty down. In that moment, Rele-de, whose shoes gave her good footing, fired at Haggerty. Kenny, that nimble monkey, leaped in front of his daughter and took the bullet. He fell before Haggerty, bleeding.

Haggerty screamed, as she clutched her father's wounded body, sobbing.

Rele-de clicked her tongue. "Not what I planned, but you know, I think I like this outcome even better."

She cast a glance at Gwydion. He had now sucked in even more of the power, and it made him gargantuan in size. Rele-de gave a signal to Rand, who also wore those geeky deck shoes. Rand bent so his head was at waist-level, and he charged Gwydion. The force of Rand's head pounding into Gwydion sent the power he had collected whishing out of him. It came with all the might of a gale wind.

When that force came at her, Rele-de opened the shawl. The power coming from Gwydion glided into her. I remembered too late about her pore-opening cream. When she'd captured it all, she closed the shawl around her. Its metallic threads kept the power within it.

Gwydion collapsed in a heap, spent and empty. A moment later, he looked to the sky. "Noooo," he moaned in answer to a call that he alone heard. Then he simply disappeared. I guessed the Ruling Council had finally brought him home for his punishment.

Rele-de had undergone a transformation, too. Her pale skin took on a greater glow than she'd shown earlier, like the luminescence I'd seen on Fiona, and gold glints formed in her eyes, which reflected the last of the moonlight. She probably still wasn't quite a goddess, but neither was she a mere mortal anymore.

In the midst of all that chaos, Angus suddenly appeared between Rele-de and me. I gasped at the sight of him. His right arm dangled unnaturally at his side, as if it were broken, while cuts all over his body bled freely. He seemed weak, too, like Haggerty after she'd performed some great magical feat. I'd never seen one of the *Danaans* in such bad shape. I wouldn't have thought they could sustain such abuse. But a god-on-god war changed all the rules.

"Sammy, the war is over," he said. "I'm yours, my girl. Yours alone, for eternity."

A causeless sense of grief flooded me, as if something even worse had already happened than Kenny being shot. The feeling so confused me, it robbed me of the chance to take some action, or warn Angus. Instead, I sat there, scared and bewildered.

Another sharp shake knocked Angus to his knees, though he continued speaking. "I'll forsake all other females for you, my Sammy, I prom…"

I didn't understand why his voice trailed off, until I looked at Rele-de. She, with her new power, seized the advantage over Angus. She clamped her hand over his shoulder, stilling him completely.

He slumped against the surface of the rock. Then, before my eyes, he hardened into stone, until he became one with the rock.

"Angus, no!" I cried. Now heedless of danger, I crawled to him, touched him, kissed him. But she had truly turned him to stone. My love was indistinguishable from the stone surface below us.

The darkness closed in completely. I couldn't see a thing. I heard some scuffling, but Haggerty's sobbing, and mine, covered the sounds. When the light finally began to glimmer again, Rele-de was gone. But she had left Rand behind.

"Where's Relly?" Rand demanded. "What about my eternal youth?"

Nobody paid any attention to him. As Haggerty tried to stop the flow of her father's blood, and I screamed into the night, pounding in frustration against the rock my lover had become—it occurred to me that none of us got what we wanted that night. Except for Rele-de. And even she had left her now-useless lover behind.

CHAPTER FIFTY
Haggerty

Haggerty yanked the scarf off her head and pressed it to Kenny's wound. While she struggled to stop the flowing blood, one astonishing thought kept racing through her mind: He had jumped into the line of fire for her. He took a bullet for her and saved her life, allowing her to remain on this plane that she loved so well. Kenny had. Her…father. Tears spilled down Haggerty's cheeks onto the man bleeding in her arms.

"Don't you die, Kenny Campbell," she said. "Don't you die."

"Trying…not…to," he said with effort. In the scant moonlight, just beginning to return, he found the strength to give her some semblance of a grin.

She took his hand and squeezed it, for the first time. The first time in memory anyway, and with every ounce of the great store of energy she now felt within her, as she willed him to live, hoping it wouldn't be the last time she got to clasp her father's hand.

She remembered how adrift she'd felt when she realized her value system was mostly a reaction to his abandonment. Even if she were no closer to knowing how she should live her life, she didn't feel as lost anymore. Now she knew that, with a little luck, she might get to make those choices with the help of the man who had given her life, twice.

An explosion erupted somewhere not far away, sending a huge fiery ball into the sky. Normal Frankly's compound—her internal goddess-GPS was back in force, so she could identify the site of that explosion with certainty. But it was beyond her to wonder what happened. All her energy now had to go to Kenny.

Don't die, Kenny. Don't you dare die on me. Would her will, and his own, be enough to save him?

CHAPTER FIFTY-ONE
Samantha

The tough decisions started instantly. Though it wrenched my heart to leave Angus, I knew there was nothing I could do for him right now. Kenny had a chance, and Haggerty needed my help.

In a night of ongoing surprises, we experienced one more, when Epona and the other mares appeared beside us on the top of that rock. Epona threw her head back and issued another one of those eerie cries. Together Haggerty and I draped Kenny's unconscious body over the goddess mare's back, then we each mounted another horse.

How would we go down that steep slope? The sharp descent was covered in slippery little stones that had made it tough enough to climb *up*. And I had never in my life ridden a horse alone, unless you count the pony rides at Griffith Park in Los Angeles, when my mom dated a guy who worked there. I couldn't see how we'd get down without breaking loads of legs.

The shocks kept coming. Epona and the other mares unfurled unexpected wings. Then we simply flew above the grade, drifting gently down to the ground.

"Wait!" Rand called from the top of the rock.

I'd forgotten that he was still there.

"What's to become of me?" he called.

"You're on your own, dude," I shouted.

"I demand you return and help me down, Samantha! Do you hear me? I'm your employer, and I insist on it."

Had he really become so moronic that he didn't know how to climb down that rock? As we galloped away, I hoped someone came along to lend a hand because I hated the idea of leaving him there with Angus. But he wasn't getting any help from me.

Sedona doesn't have a hospital, just a small ER that operates as a satellite of the hospital in nearby Cottonwood. I couldn't believe what I saw when we arrived there. It was a war zone. The emergency room had spilled out into the parking lot, where loads of volunteers treated hundreds of wounded people.

Some victims had been smudged by fire, while others looked scalded; perhaps Oak Creek really had reached a boil tonight. Hell, it might have rained toads and locusts when I was too busy saving the world from annihilation to notice. There were soldiers, a few in bad shape. I realized now that it must have been Normal's compound that exploded, injuring some of them. There were also people with makeshift splints and crutches, who must have stumbled when the eclipse went dark, and others with black eyes and cuts, who clearly got into fights. Across the parking lot, I saw François tending to the wounded.

In the midst of all that, while I pulled Kenny from Epona, Haggerty shouted, "We have a dying man here. We need some help."

When everyone ignored her, I added in my loud, raspy voice, "Senator with a gunshot wound."

Apparently, senators with bullet holes trump everything else. A pair of nurses produced a gurney and whisked him inside, with Haggerty following close behind. Within a moment, Epona and the other mares just disappeared.

François found me where I waited out there. He took in my wilder-than-usual hair, and maybe the loopier-than-usual look in my eyes, but said nothing.

"The compound blew?" I asked.

He nodded. "Normal Frankly's lab, anyway, just when Colonel Marcus's men had stormed the facility." François hesitated. "Frankly's missing, believed dead, along with...the critter."

The critter. I could have told him about Gwydion, but I figured he still wasn't on our need-to-know list. But Normal Frankly? He'd probably gone back to his world. Would they send someone else for Kenny? If he survived tonight, would Kenny always have to worry?

François said, "Samantha, when I saw you and Annabelle sucked into that rock... Do I want to know how you did that?"

"About as much as I want to know how you moved those boulders, G-Man." François grew paler than usual and went back to tending the wounded.

From within the buzz in my ears, I heard someone say, "I won't kid you, Agent Haggerty. He'll be lucky if he makes it to the OR."

I whirled around to see who said that, but nobody stood beside me. Besides, it sounded like something a doctor would have told Haggerty. How could I have heard it out here?

Haggerty appeared at the ER door and waved for me to join her. Having stabilized Kenny, they loaded him and us into a helicopter for the flight to the hospital.

I remembered another helicopter ride we'd taken not long before, one that I'd found so full of fun and hope. The fun had all evaporated now—for me, when I lost Angus. The only hope left was that Haggerty's father would make it through the ten-minute flight.

CHAPTER FIFTY-TWO

Chaos continued to rage all over town, but Haggerty and I only heard about it through infrequent calls from François and rumors whispered by the hospital nurses and staff.

The FBI made finding Normal Frankly its highest priority and put François in charge of the search. I hated the idea of he and his team wasting their time, but not wanting to end up in a loony bin, I kept to myself my theory that Normal had turned back into a walking test tube and returned to his home world.

Colonel Squinty stayed on to carry out a secret mission. Rounding up their missing alien would be my guess. *That* manhunt I was happy to see continue. I giggled every time I thought of Squinty peeking behind bushes for a creature that supposedly never existed. I was starting to appreciate the fun in Gwydion's charade after all.

Against all odds, Kenny survived the flight, but he'd lost a lot of blood. With blood bank supplies low after the post-concert rioting claimed so much, they asked everyone to donate. Haggerty hesitated, fearful the lab would catch onto her relationship with Kenny. I thought she should worry more that they'd notice a goddess and some molten liquid had produced her, but it turned out her blood looked like everyone else's. Since she and Kenny shared the same type, it went right into her father.

Haggerty insisted I be examined, too. I had to kick up a fuss to avoid being checked into the hospital so they could watch for lightning strike side effects. Instead, a doctor told me what to expect, but with all that noise in my ears, I didn't really pay attention.

Through a long, scary night, Haggerty and I sat side-by-side in a small waiting area outside an operating room. She kept trying to reach Fiona psychically, but wherever Fiona had gone into hiding after leaving Sedona, she apparently didn't choose to receive the signal. I got the feeling that we wouldn't see Fiona back here anytime soon.

We talked only in fits and starts, punctuated by long silences. At one point, I told her about the voices I'd heard, and the sensations I'd had about things that hadn't yet happened.

Haggerty threw back her head and laughed. "Congrats,

Samantha. Lightning strikes do strange things. You're not only a little psychic now, but also telepathic."

"But it's useless," I stammered. "I don't know whose voices I'm hearing, or how to make sense of the impulses I feel."

"Welcome to my world."

I didn't know whether to cheer or cry. I finally decided to pretend she hadn't said it.

By morning Kenny's surgeons declared him to be a medical marvel and were cautiously optimistic that he would make it. No question—the *Danaans* had made some super genes there.

A frazzled François came by later that day to check on Kenny and probably to see why his second-in-command had deserted him.

He led me some distance away for a private chat. "I know Annabelle's dedicated to her job, but this vigil for the senator seems excessive, especially when there's so much to do back in Sedona."

"You can't make her leave, François. Don't ask me to explain—you'd never believe it."

"Much as this surprises me to say it, Fake-Psychic-Girl, I think I'd accept most anything you told me. If she believes in you, so do I." He looked Haggerty's way, and for a moment, his professional mask fell away to reveal an expression of intense longing for her.

Whoa! I did not see that coming. So much for my being psychic. I wondered if Haggerty knew how he felt about her.

With a brisk nod that attempted to cover his reaction, he said, "Tell her to stay as long as she needs to. I'll cover for her with the brass."

I could almost get to like that pasty albino. But a vampire? Get real.

While Kenny's health slowly inched back, his career went into the Stratosphere. The official story given to the media was that he had been shot leading the charge into the compound, causing his approval rating to soar. When the press learned that his wife was missing, presumed dead at the militia's hands, his popularity went off the charts.

Kenny was regarded as a shoe-in for the presidency. A former-alien Family Values candidate, who was actually a bigamist who'd abandoned his wife and child, whose second-fake wife was now a powerful rogue near-goddess out to wreak vengeance on the world, in all likelihood. Politics—you gotta love it.

But Kenny surprised everyone. He gave up his Senate seat and withdrew from the political arena, explaining to reporters that he had personal issues to deal with. People speculated that he'd be searching for Kelly, but we knew better. Maybe Fiona's prediction about him was right after all, though I figured he'd missed the boat with her.

Haggerty took a leave of absence, and she nursed Kenny when he came back to his Sedona home. She never said how things went for them, but for once, she wasn't hard to read. At first she rode a roller coaster of emotions, from stormy to giddy and onto sad. Eventually, though, she seemed more at peace, and even looser, a word I would never have used to describe her.

Me, I spent every day with Angus. I even bought hiking boots, if you can believe it, to make my trek easier. At first light, I went there every day, and I stayed until darkness fell. I called out to every god I'd ever met to save him. I tried conning them, and when that didn't work, I gave them a really sharp talking to, but Angus remained frozen in stone.

The war had decimated the homeland of the Celtic gods, Haggerty told me, and they needed to rebuild their society. They were taking things in the order they considered most important. Gwydion received the god-equivalent of jail time, while Lugh and Taliesin got some form of community service, though they weren't permitted to serve it here on Earth.

Though their highest priority was apprehending Rele-de, she remained at large. Haggerty's theory was that, after drawing all that power from Gwydion, when Angus appeared, given his battered state, she was strong enough to also suck all his strength. That made her Queen Bee of the universe. You gotta admit, she played it so well. Rele-de wasn't someone to underestimate.

When Kenny was deemed well enough to be on his own, Haggerty finally returned to work. And Sedona returned to normal, for Sedona anyway.

One day, weeks after that awful night, when I came home from my daily visit with Angus, Haggerty waited there for me.

"I have good news and bad news. Which do you want first?" she asked.

I'd always hated that question. I only ever wanted good

news.

Naturally, she insisted on giving me both. At least I got the good news first. "We closed up the office here today, but the Bureau wants me to stay on temporarily in Flagstaff."

"Hot damn! We get to stay here," I said. "What's the bad news?"

"Even though Flagstaff is only about an hour's drive from here, they want us based there."

"What's this us-business, Kimosabe? I'm through with the Bureau. Every time I hook up with the FBI, I nearly get killed." Besides, Angus was here.

"They've promised you'll be paid twice over."

She had my attention now.

"There's a job there that François wants you to take. You'll get paid for that, and naturally, you'll also get some FBI consultant pay."

"What's the job?" I asked mulishly.

She shrugged. "He said you'd never believe what you'll have to do."

Did that mean *I'd* never believe it, or *he* wouldn't? Big difference. Sure, I was broke. If it hadn't been for Fiona's charity, I wouldn't have survived this long. Rand was never going to pay me. The other guys in band had sued him for staggering sums because he had wrecked their operation.

And, of course, Angus was here. My heart contracted just thinking about him.

"Leaving is really for the best, Samantha. You can't keep going to see Angus. How long do you think it's going to take before someone notices a woman in silly gowns, hiking to the same spot every day?"

I wanted to look my best for Angus. Even in Sedona, it seemed, that might attract attention.

"Besides, if anyone looks too closely, they'll notice the surface of the rock has changed shape. It's best not to draw attention to it. The *Danaans* will restore Angus when they can."

"You really don't know what kind of job he wants me to take?" I asked.

She shook her head no. "François did say if you take it, you might be responsible for bringing the war on terror to an end."

That wouldn't be too shabby. Since I could get some mileage from it, I allowed myself to be persuaded.

We set out for Flagstaff in Fiona's Mercedes the next morning. I insisted on driving, so I could keep an eye on the rearview mirror, to stay as close to Angus as possible, even if the mountain my love had joined wasn't visible from the road that rose up through the canyon that connects Sedona to the North Country.

I sensed Haggerty agreed to my driving because that allowed her to stay more alert. Wherever we went, her eyes were always moving. Always watching for Rele-de.

"Where do you think she is now?" I asked.

"Long gone from here, but our paths will cross again. I'm sure of that," Haggerty said with anxious regret.

To distract her, I started bitching again about getting stiffed by Rand.

"I wouldn't write off your fee just yet, Samantha."

"Come on, Haggerty. If he settles with the guys in the band for even a fraction of what they're asking, he'll be as busted as me."

With a grin, Haggerty said, "I guess you haven't heard the latest. Rand Riker has just signed a contract to appear in Holiday Inn lounges from coast-to-coast."

We laughed so long and hard over the idea of rock's former bad boy wailing away in motel bars, that by the time I stopped snickering, I'd caught my first glimpse of pine trees rising up along Flagstaff's alpine hillsides, and I began to itch for whatever adventure awaited us there.

AUTHOR'S NOTES AND ACKNOWLEDGMENTS

Special thanks go to all the readers who embraced Samantha and Annabelle in their first adventure, and especially those who made *High Crimes on the Magical Plane* a Lefty Award nominee.

Thanks also to all the fabulous bookstores, especially the indies, and great libraries that hosted me for the many signings and talks I did, and especially the booksellers who hand-sold my books to their customers. I know you have a choice of which authors to devote your resources to, and I'm grateful for your support, and that you allowed me to give presentations in your wonderful facilities.

Holly O'Neill West, one of my former students, bid at the Los Angeles Left Coast Crime to have a character named after her. Holly O'Neill, the character, makes frequent appearances in this book, *Magical Alienation*. Holly, the person, I hope you like what I did with your name.

Gratitude goes to Susan Budavari and Suzanne Flaig of Red Coyote Press for giving Samantha and Annabelle a wonderful home. Thanks for your editorial guidance—your insights helped to make *Magical Alienation* a better book.

I've taken liberties with Sedona geography. The rock wall I described does exist, though it's not nearly as close to the highway as I placed it, and, naturally, in real life, there is no militia installation built into it. The Sedona Cultural Park has been closed for ages, and will probably eventually fall to the developer's axe. But I thought it be such a perfect venue for the concert, that I brought it out of retirement for this book. I used as much of the actual landscape as possible, though all the buildings and homes I depicted are a product of my imagination. I did once see a garden in another part of town that reminded me of Fiona's, and I liked to think that it was placed there by magic.

This book is dedicated to Pam Clark of MassageMatters of Sedona, and her beloved dog Star, who moved onto the next journey. Both bright lights and generous souls.

And as always, boundless thanks to my great husband, Joe, for his unwavering belief in me and for hand-selling loads of my books at our bookstore, The Well Red Coyote.

ABOUT THE AUTHOR

The first novel in Kris Neri's Magical series, *High Crimes on the Magical Plane*, was a Lefty Award nominee for Best Humorous Mystery. She also writes the Tracy Eaton mysteries, which have garnered Agatha, Anthony, Macavity and Lefty Award nominations. She has published some sixty-plus short stories and is a two-time Derringer Award winner and a two-time Pushcart Prize nominee for her short fiction. Also a bookseller, Kris and her husband own The Well Red Coyote bookstore in Sedona, Arizona. She blogs with the Femmes Fatales: http://femmesfatales.typepad.com/my_weblog. And Kris welcomes readers to her website: www.krisneri.com.

HIGH CRIMES ON THE MAGICAL PLANE
Book One of the Samantha Brennan and Annabelle Haggerty Magical Series

2010 LEFTY AWARD NOMINEE for Best Humorous Mystery

Praise for *High Crimes on the Magical Plane*

"You'll enjoy the unlikely twists and turns...and both characters are delightful."
　　　　–Charlaine Harris, NYT Bestselling author of the Sookie Stackhouse/True Blood series

"More fun than an overstuffed clown car! Kris Neri turns the paranormal on its head with a phony psychic, Celtic goddess, a missing movie star, oh yeah...and clowns!"
　　　　–Casey Daniels, author of *Dead Man Talking*

"...delicious; a funny, pell-mell romp of an adventure rife with psychics, FBI agents and clowns."
　　　　–Diana Gabaldon, NYT Bestselling author of the Outlander series

"Mystery and magic!! Plus a little romance!! What more can one want? HIGH CRIMES ON THE MAGICAL PLANE not only delivers that and more, but is a fresh, new take on the paranormal!"
　　　　–Shirley Damsgaard, author of *The Witch's Grave*